ROGER ZELAZNY

is
"ONE OF SF'S BRIGHTEST LIGHTS."*

His **AMBER** novels
are
"DARING AND MAGNIFICENT.
THIS IS WHAT SF IS FOR!"**

The newest in the series,
BLOOD OF AMBER,
is
"SIMPLY GREAT!"***

---

  * *Library Journal*
 ** *Magazine of Fantasy and Science Fiction*
*** *Other Realms*

ROGER ZELAZNY

BLOOD OF AMBER

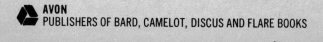
AVON
PUBLISHERS OF BARD, CAMELOT, DISCUS AND FLARE BOOKS

AVON BOOKS
A division of
The Hearst Corporation
105 Madison Avenue
New York, New York 10016

The Arbor House edition contains the following Library of Congress Cataloging in
Publication Data:

Zelazny, Roger.
  Blood of amber.

  I. Title.
PS3576.E43B58   1986   813'.54   86-3530

First Avon Printing: July 1987

FOR KIRBY McCAULEY

REFLECTIONS IN A CRYSTAL CAVE

My life had been relatively peaceful for eight years—not counting April thirtieths, when someone invariably tried to kill me. Outside of that, my academic career with its concentration on computer science went well enough and my four years' employment at Grand Design proved a rewarding experience, letting me use what I'd learned in a situation I liked while I labored on a project of my own on the side. I had a good friend in Luke Raynard, who worked for the same company, in sales. I sailed my little boat, I jogged regularly—

It all fell apart this past April 30, just when I thought things were about to come together. My pet project, Ghostwheel, was built; I'd quit my job, packed my gear and was ready to move on to greener shadows. I'd stayed in town this long only because that morbidly fascinating day was near, and this time I intended to discover who was behind the attempts on my life and why.

At breakfast that morning Luke appeared with a message from my former girlfriend, Julia. Her note said that she wanted to see me again. So I stopped by her place, where I found her dead, apparently killed by the same dog-like beast which then attacked me. I succeeded in destroying the creature. A quick search of the apartment before I fled the scene turned up a slim packet of strange playing cards, which I took along with me. They were too much like the magical Tarots of Amber and Chaos for a sorcerer such as myself not to be interested in them.

Yes. I am a sorcerer. I am Merlin, son of Corwin of Amber and Dara of the Courts of Chaos, known to local friends and acquaintances as Merle Corey: bright, charming, witty, athletic.... Go read Castiglione and Lord Byron for particulars, as I'm modest, aloof and reticent, as well.

The cards proved to be genuine magical objects, which seemed appropriate once I learned that Julia had been keeping company with an occultist named Victor Melman after we had broken up. A visit to this gentleman's studio resulted in his attempting to kill me in a ritual fashion. I was able to free myself from the constraints of the ceremony and question him somewhat, before local conditions and my enthusiasm resulted in his death. So much for rituals.

I'd learned enough from him to realize that he'd been but a cat's-paw. Someone else had apparently put him up to the sacrifice bit—and it seemed quite possible that the other person was the one responsible for Julia's death and my collection of memorable April thirtieths.

I had small time to reflect upon these matters, though, because I was bitten (yes, bitten) shortly thereafter by an attractive red-haired woman who materialized in Melman's apartment, following my brief telephone conversation with her in which I'd tried to pose as Melman. Her bite paralyzed me, but I was able to depart before it took full effect by employing one of the magical cards I'd found at Julia's place. It bore me into the presence of a sphinx, which permitted me to recover so that it could play that silly riddle game sphinxes love so well because they get to eat you when you lose. All I can say about it is that this particular sphinx was a bad sport.

Anyhow, I returned to the shadow Earth where I'd been making my home to discover that Melman's place had burned down during my absence. I tried phoning Luke, because I wanted to have dinner with him, and learned that he had checked out of his motel, leaving me a message indicating that he had gone to New Mexico on business and telling me where he'd be staying. The desk clerk also gave me a blue-stone ring Luke had left behind, and I took it with me to return when I saw him.

I flew to New Mexico, finally catching up with Luke in Santa Fe. While I waited in the bar for him to get ready for dinner, a man named Dan Martinez questioned me, giving the impression that Luke had proposed some business deal and that he wanted to be assured Luke was reliable and could deliver. After dinner, Luke and I went for a drive in the mountains. Martinez followed us and started shooting as we stood admiring the night. Perhaps he'd decided Luke was not reliable or couldn't deliver. Luke surprised me by drawing a weapon of his own and shooting Martinez. Then an even stranger thing happened. Luke called me by name —my real name, which I'd never told him—and cited my parentage and told me to get into the car and get the hell out. He emphasized his point by placing a shot in the ground near my feet. The matter did not seem open to discussion so I departed. He also told me to destroy those strange Trumps that had saved my life once already. And I'd learned on the way up that he'd known Victor Melman. . . .

I didn't go far. I parked downhill and returned on foot. Luke was gone. So was Martinez's body. Luke did not return to the hotel, that night or the next day, so I checked out and departed. The only person I was sure I could trust, and who actually might have some good advice for me, was Bill Roth. Bill was an attorney who lived in upstate New York, and he had been my father's best friend. I went to visit him, and I told him my story.

Bill got me to wondering even more about Luke. Luke, by the way, is a big, smart, red-haired natural athlete of uncanny prowess—and though we'd been friends for many years I knew next to nothing (as Bill pointed out) concerning his background.

A neighboring lad named George Hansen began hanging out near Bill's place, asking strange questions. I received an odd phone call, asking similar questions. Both interrogators seemed curious as to my mother's name. Naturally, I lied. The fact that my mother is a member of the dark aristocracy of the Courts of Chaos was none of their business. But the caller spoke my language, Thari, which made me curious enough to propose a meeting and a trade-off of information that evening in the bar of the local country club.

But my Uncle Random, King of Amber, called me home before that, while Bill and I were out hiking. George Hansen, it turned out, was following us and wanted to come along as we shifted away across the shadows of reality. Tough; he wasn't invited. I took Bill along because I didn't want to leave him with anyone acting that peculiar.

I learned from Random that my Uncle Caine was dead, of an assassin's bullet, and that someone had also tried to kill my Uncle Bleys but only succeeded in wounding him. The funeral service for Caine would be the following day.

I kept my date at the country club that evening, but my mysterious interrogator was nowhere in sight. All was not lost, however, as I made the acquaintance of a pretty lady named Meg Devlin—and, one thing leading to another, I saw her home and we got to know each other a lot better. Then, at a moment when I would have judged her thoughts to be anywhere but there, she asked me my mother's name. So, what the hell, I told her. It did not come to me until later that she might really have been the person I'd gone to the bar to meet.

Our liaison was terminated prematurely by a call from the lobby—from a man purportedly Meg's husband. I did what any gentleman would do. I got the hell out fast.

My Aunt Fiona, who is a sorceress (of a different style from my own), had not approved of my date. And apparently she approved even less of Luke, because she asked me whether I had a picture of him after I'd told her somewhat concerning him. I showed her a photo I had in my wallet, which included Luke in the group. I'd have sworn she recognized him from somewhere, though she wouldn't admit it. But the fact that she and her brother Bleys both disappeared from Amber that night would seem more than coincidental.

The pace of events was accelerated even more after that. A crude attempt at knocking off most of the family with a thrown bomb was made the next day, following Caine's funeral. The would-be assassin escaped. Later, Random was upset at a brief demonstration on my part of the power of the Ghostwheel, my pet project, my hobby, my avocation during those years at Grand Design. Ghostwheel is a—well, it started out as a computer that required a different set of physical laws to operate than those I'd learned in school. It involved what might be called magic. But I found a place where it could be built and operated, and I'd constructed it there. It was still programming itself when I'd left it. It seemed to have gone sentient, and I think it scared Random. He ordered me to go and turn it off. I didn't much like the idea, but I departed.

I was followed in my passage through Shadow; I was harassed, threatened and even attacked. I was rescued from a fire by a strange lady who later died in a lake. I was protected from vicious beasts by a mysterious individual and saved from a bizarre earthquake by the same person— who turned out to be Luke. He accompanied me to the final barrier, for a confrontation with Ghostwheel. My creation was a bit irritated with me and banished us by means of a shadow-storm—a thing it is not fun to be caught in, with or without an umbrella. I delivered us from the vicissitudes by means of one of the Trumps of Doom, as I'd dubbed the odd pasteboards from Julia's apartment.

We wound up outside a blue crystal cave, and Luke took me in. Good old Luke. After seeing to my needs he proceeded to imprison me. When he told me who he was, I realized that it was a resemblance to his father which had upset Fiona when she'd seen his photo. For Luke was the son of Brand, assassin and arch traitor, who had damn near destroyed the kingdom and the rest of the universe alone with it some years back. Fortunately, Caine had killed him before he'd accomplished his designs. Luke, I learned then, was the one who'd killed Caine, to avenge his father. (And it turned out he'd gotten the news of his father's death on an April thirtieth and had had a peculiar way of observing its anniversary over the years.) Like Random, he too had been impressed by my Ghostwheel, and he told me that I was to remain his prisoner, as I might become necessary in his efforts to gain control of the machine, which he felt would be the perfect weapon for destroying the rest of the family.

He departed to pursue the matter, and I quickly discovered that my powers were canceled by some peculiar property of the cave, leaving me with no one to talk to but you, Frakir, and no one here for you to strangle....

Would you care to hear a few bars of "Over the Rainbow"?

CHAPTER 1

I threw the hilt away after the blade had shattered. The weapon had done me no good against that blue sea of a wall in what I had taken to be its thinnest section. A few small chips of stone lay at my feet. I picked them up and rubbed them together. This was not the way out for me. The only way out seemed to be the way I had come in and it wasn't working.

I walked back to my quarters, meaning that section of the caves where I had cast my sleeping bag. I sat down on the bag, a heavy brown one, uncorked a wine bottle and took a drink. I had worked up a sweat hacking away at the wall.

Frakir stirred upon my wrist then, unwound herself partway and slithered into the palm of my left hand, to coil around the two blue chips I still held. She knotted herself about them, then dropped to hang and swing pendulum-like. I put the bottle aside and watched. The arc of her swing parelleled the lengthwise direction of the tunnel I now called home. The swinging continued for perhaps a full minute. Then she withdrew upward, halting when she came to the back of my hand. She released the chips at the

7

base of my third finger and returned to her normal hidden position about my wrist.

I stared. I raised the flickering oil lamp and studied the stones. Their color. . . .

Yes.

Seen against skin, they were similar in appearance to the stone in that ring of Luke's I had picked up at the New Line Motel some time ago. Coincidence? Or was there a connection? What had my strangling cord been trying to tell me? And where had I seen another such stone?

Luke's key ring. He'd a blue stone on it, mounted on a piece of metal. . . . And where might I have seen another?

The caverns in which I was imprisoned had the power to block the Trumps and my Logrus magic. If Luke carried stones from these walls about with him, there was probably a special reason. What other properties might they possess?

I tried for perhaps an hour to learn something concerning their nature, but they resisted my Logrus probes. Finally, disgusted, I pocketed them, ate some bread and cheese and took another swallow of wine.

Then I rose and made the rounds once more, inspecting my traps. I'd been a prisoner in this place for what seemed at least a month now. I had paced all these tunnels, corridors, grottoes, seeking an exit. None of them proved a way out. There were times when I had run manic through them and bloodied my knuckles upon their cold sides. There were times when I had moved slowly, seeking after cracks and fault lines. I had tried on several occasions to dislodge the boulder that barred the entranceway—to no avail. It was wedged in place, and I couldn't budge it. It seemed that I was in for the duration.

My traps. . . .

They were all as they had been the last time I had checked—deadfalls, boulders nature had left lying about in typical careless fashion, propped high and ready now to be released from their wedging when someone tripped any of the shadow-masked lengths of packing cord I'd removed from crates in the storeroom.

Someone?

Luke, of course. Who else? He was the one who'd imprisoned me. And if he returned—no, *when* he returned—the booby traps would be waiting. He was armed. He would have me at a disadvantage from the overhead position of the entrance if I merely waited for him below. No way. I would not be there. I would make him come in after me—and then—

Vaguely troubled, I returned to my quarters.

Hands behind my head, I lay there and reviewed my plans. The deadfalls could kill a man, and I did not want Luke dead. This had nothing to do with sentiment, though I had thought of Luke as a good friend until fairly recently —up until the time I learned that he had killed my Uncle Caine and seemed intent upon destroying the rest of my relatives in Amber as well. This was because Caine had killed Luke's father—my Uncle Brand—a man whom any of the others would gladly have done in also. Yes, Luke— or Rinaldo, as I now knew him—was my cousin, and he had a reason for engaging in one of our in-family vendettas. Still, going after everybody struck me as a bit intemperate.

But neither consanguinity nor sentiment bade me dismantle my traps. I wanted him alive because there were too many things about the entire situation that I did not understand and might never understand were he to perish without telling me.

Jasra . . . the Trumps of Doom . . . the means by which I had been tracked so easily through Shadow . . . the entire story of Luke's relationship with the painter and mad occultist Victor Melman . . . anything he knew about Julia and her death. . . .

I began again. I dismantled the deadfalls. The new plan was a simple one, and it drew upon something of which I believed Luke had no knowledge.

I moved my sleeping bag to a new position, in the tunnel just outside the chamber whose roof held the blocked entranceway. I shifted some of the food stores there, also. I was determined to remain in its vicinity for as much of the time as possible.

The new trap was a very basic thing: direct and just about unavoidable. Once I'd set it there was nothing to do but wait. Wait, and remember. And plan. I had to warn the others. I had to do something about my Ghostwheel. I needed to find out what Meg Devlin knew. I needed to ... lots of things.

I waited. I thought of Shadow storms, dreams, strange Trumps and the Lady in the Lake. After a long spell of drifting, my life had become very crowded in a matter of days. Then this long spell of doing nothing. My only consolation was that this time line probably outpaced most of the others that were important to me right now. My month here might only be a day back in Amber, or even less. If I could deliver myself from this place soon, the trails I wished to follow might still be relatively fresh.

Later, I put out the lamp and went to sleep. Sufficient light filtered through the crystal lenses of my prison, brightening and waning, for me to distinguish day from night in the outside world, and I kept my small series of routines in accord with its rhythms.

During the next three days I read through Melman's diary again—a thing heavy in allusion and low in useful information—and just about succeeded in convincing myself that the Hooded One, as he referred to his visitor and teacher, had probably been Luke. Except for a few references to androgyny, which puzzled me. References to the sacrifice of the Son of Chaos near the end of the volume were something I could take personally, in light of my present knowledge of Melman's having been set up to destroy me. But if Luke had done it, how to explain his ambiguous behavior on the mountain in New Mexico, when he had advised me to destroy the Trumps of Doom and had driven me away almost as if to protect me from something? And then he had admitted to several of the earlier attempts on my life, but denied the later ones. No reason to do that if he were indeed responsible for all of them. What else might be involved? Who else? And how? There were obviously missing pieces to the puzzle, but I felt as if they were minor, as if the smallest bit of new information and the slightest jiggling of the pattern would suddenly cause everything to fall into place, with the emerging picture to be something I should have seen all along.

I might have guessed that the visitation would be by night. I might have, but I didn't. Had it occurred to me, I would have changed my sleep cycle and been awake and alert. Even though I felt fairly confident of my trap's efficiency, every little edge is important in truly crucial matters.

I was deeply asleep, and the grating of rock upon rock was a distant thing. I stirred but slowly as the sounds continued, and it was several seconds more before the proper circuits closed and I realized what was occurring. Then I sat up, my mind still dusty, and moved into a crouch beside the wall of the chamber nearest the entranceway, knuckling my eyes, brushing back my hair, seeking lost alertness on sleep's receding shore.

The first sounds I heard must have accompanied the removal of the wedges, which apparently had entailed some rocking or tipping of the boulder. The continuing sounds were muffled, echoless—external.

So I ventured a quick glance into the chamber. There was no opened adit, showing stars. The overhead vibrations continued. The rocking sounds were now succeeded by a steady crunching, grating noise. A ball of light with a diffuse halo shone through the translucent stone of the chamber's roof. A lantern, I guessed. Too steady to be a torch. And a torch would be impractical under the circumstances.

A crescent of sky appeared, holding two stars near its nether horn. It widened, and I heard the heavy breathing and grunts of what I took to be two men.

My extremities tingled as I felt additional adrenaline doing its biological trick within me. I hadn't counted on Luke's bringing anyone with him. My foolproof plan might not be proof against this—meaning I was the fool.

The boulder rolled more quickly now, and there was not

even time for profanity as my mind raced, focused upon a course of action and assumed its appropriate stance.

I summoned the image of the Logrus and it took shape before me. I rose to my feet, still leaning against the wall, and began moving my arms to correspond with the random-seeming movements of two of the eidolon's limbs. By the time I achieved a satisfactory conjunction, the sounds from overhead had ceased.

The opening was now clear. Moments later the light was raised and moved toward it.

I stepped into the chamber and extended my hands. As the men, short and dark, came into view above me my original plan was canceled completely. They both carried unsheathed poignards in their right hands. Neither of them was Luke.

I reached out with my Logrus gauntlets and took hold of each of them by the throat. I squeezed until they collapsed within my grip. I squeezed a little longer, then released them.

As they dropped from sight I hooked the high lip of the entrance with my glowing lines of force and drew myself upward with them. As I reached the opening I paused to recover Frakir, who was coiled about its underside. That had been my trap. Luke, or anyone else, would have been passing through a noose to enter, a noose ready to tighten instantly upon anything moving through.

Now, though. . . .

A trail of fire ran down the slope to my right. The fallen lantern had shattered, its spilled fuel become a burning rivulet. The men I had choked lay sprawled at either hand. The boulder that had blocked this opening rested to the left and somewhat to the rear of me. I remained where I was— head and shoulders above the opening, resting on my elbows—with the image of the Logrus dancing between my eyes, the warm tingling of its power lines yet a part of my arms, Frakir moving from my left shoulder down to my biceps.

It had been almost too easy. I couldn't see Luke trusting a couple of lackeys to question, kill or transport me—

whichever of these had been their mission. That is why I had not emerged fully, but scanned the nighted environs from my vantage of relative security.

Prudent, for a change. For someone else shared the night with me. It was sufficiently dark, even with the dwindling fire trail, that my ordinary vision did not serve to furnish me this intelligence. But when I summon the Logrus, the mental set that grants me vision of its image permits me to view other nonphysical manifestations as well.

So it was that I detected such a construct beneath a tree to my left, amid shadows where I would not have seen the human figure before which it hovered. And a strange pattern at that, reminiscent of Amber's own; it turned like a slow pinwheel, extending tendrils of smoke-shot yellow light. These drifted toward me across the night and I watched, fascinated, knowing already what I would do when the moment came.

There were four big ones, and they came on slowly, probing. When they were within several yards of me they halted, gained slack, then struck like cobras. My hands were together and slightly crossed, Logrus limbs extended. I separated them with a single sweeping motion, tilting them slightly forward as I did so. They struck the yellow tendrils, casting them away to be thrown back upon their pattern. I felt a tingling sensation in my forearms as this occurred. Then, using my right-hand extension as if it were a blade, I struck at the now-wavering pattern as if it were a shield. I heard a short sharp cry as that image grew dim, and I struck again quickly, hauled myself out of my hole and started down the slope, my arm aching.

The image—whatever it had been—faded and was gone. By then, however, I could make out more clearly the figure leaning against the tree trunk. It appeared to be that of a woman, though I could not distinguish her features because of some small object she had raised and now held before her near to eye level. Fearing that it was a weapon, I struck at it with a Logrus extension, hoping to knock it from her hand.

I stumbled then, for there was a recoil which jolted my arm with considerable force. It would seem to have been a potent sorcerous object which I had struck. At least I had the pleasure of seeing the lady sway also. She uttered a short cry, too, but she hung on to the object.

A moment later a faint polychrome shimmering began about her form and I realized what the thing was. I had just directed the force of the Logrus against a Trump. I had to reach her now, if only to find out who she was.

But as I rushed ahead I realized that I could not get to her in time. Unless . . .

I plucked Frakir from my shoulder and cast her along the line of the Logrus force, manipulating her in the proper direction and issuing my commands as she flew.

From my new angle of view and by the faint rainbow halo that now surrounded her I finally saw the lady's face. It was Jasra, who had damn near killed me with a bite back in Melman's apartment. In a moment she would be gone, taking with her my chance of obtaining some answers on which my life might depend.

"Jasra!" I cried, trying to break her concentration.

It didn't work, but Frakir did. My strangling cord, glowing silver now, caught her about the throat, whipping out with a free end to lash tightly about the branch that hung near, to Jasra's left.

The lady began to fade, apparently not realizing that it was too late. She couldn't trump out without decapitating herself.

She learned it quickly. I heard her gurgling cry as she stepped back, grew solid, lost her halo, dropped her Trump and clawed at the cord encircling her throat.

I came up beside her, to lay my hand upon Frakir, who uncoiled one end from the tree limb and rewound it about my wrist.

"Good evening, Jasra," I said, jerking her head back. "Try the poison bite again and you'll need a neck brace. You understand?"

She tried to talk but couldn't. She nodded.

"I'm going to loosen my cord a bit," I said, "so you can answer my questions."

I eased Frakir's grip upon her throat. She began coughing, then, and gave me a look that would have turned sand to glass. Her magical construct had faded completely, so I let the Logrus slip away also.

"Why are you after me?" I asked. "What am I to you?"

"Son of perdition!" she said, and she tried to spit at me but her mouth must have been too dry.

I jerked lightly on Frakir and she coughed again.

"Wrong answer," I said. "Try again."

But she smiled then, her gaze shifting to a point beyond me. I kept the slack out of Frakir and chanced a glance. The air was beginning to shimmer, behind me and to the right, in obvious preparation to someone's trumping in.

I did not feel ready to take on an additional threat at this time, and so I dipped my free hand into my pocket and withdrew a handful of my own Trumps. Flora's was on top. Fine. She'd do.

I pushed my mind toward her, through the feeble light, beyond the face of the card. I felt her distracted attention, followed by a sudden alertness.

Then, *Yes . . .?*

"Bring me through! Hurry!" I said.

Is it an emergency? she asked.

"You'd better believe it," I told her.

Uh—okay. Come on.

I had an image of her in bed. It grew clearer, clearer. She extended her hand.

I reached out and took it. I moved forward just as I heard Luke's voice ring out, crying, "Stop!"

I continued on through, dragging Jasra after me. She tried to draw back and succeeded in halting me as I stumbled against the side of the bed. It was then I noted the dark-haired, bearded man regarding me with wide eyes from the bed's farther side.

"Who—? What—?" he began as I smiled bleakly and regained my balance.

Luke's shadowy form came into view beyond my prisoner. He reached forward and seized Jasra's arm, drawing her back away from me. She made a gurgling noise as the movement drew Frakir more tightly about her throat.

Damn! What now?

Flora rose suddenly, her face contorted, the scented lavender sheet falling away as she drove a fist forward with surprising speed.

"You bitch!" she cried. "Remember me?"

The blow fell upon Jasra's jaw, and I barely managed to free Frakir in time to keep from being dragged backward with her into Luke's waiting arms.

Both of them faded, and the shimmer was gone.

The dark-haired guy in the meantime had scrambled out of the bed and was snatching up articles of clothing. Once he had them all in his grasp he did not bother to don any, but simply held them in front of him and backed quickly toward the door.

"Ron! Where are you going?" Flora asked.

"Away!" he answered, and he opened the door and passed through it.

"Hey! Wait!"

"No way!" came the reply from the next room.

"Damn!" she said, glaring at me. "You have a way of messing up a person's life." Then, "Ron! What about dinner?" she called.

"I have to see my analyst," came his voice, followed shortly by the slamming of another door.

"I hope you realize what a beautiful thing you just destroyed," Flora told me.

I sighed. "When did you meet him?" I asked.

She frowned. "Well, yesterday," she replied. "Go ahead and smirk. These things are not always a mere function of time. I could tell right away that it was going to be something special. Trust someone crass like you or your father to cheapen a beautiful—"

"I'm sorry," I said. "Thanks for pulling me through. Of course he'll be back. We just scared the hell out of him. But how could he fail to return once he's known you?"

She smiled. "Yes you *are* like Corwin," she said. "Crass, but perceptive."

She rose and crossed to the closet, took out a lavender robe and donned it.

"What," she said, belting it about her, "was that all about?"

"It's a long story—"

"Then I'd better hear it over lunch. Are you hungry?" she asked.

I grinned.

"It figures. Come on."

She led me out through a French Provincial living room and into a large country kitchen full of tiles and copper. I offered to help her, but she pointed at a chair beside the table and told me to sit.

As she was removing numerous goodies from the refrigerator, I said, "First—"

"Yes?"

"Where are we?"

"San Francisco," she replied

"Why have you set up housekeeping here?"

"After I finished that business of Random's I decided to stay on. The town looked good to me again."

I snapped my fingers. I'd forgotten she'd been sent to determine the ownership of the warehouse where Victor Melman had had his apartment and studio, and where Brutus Storage had a supply of ammo that would fire in Amber.

"So who owned the warehouse?" I asked.

"Brutus Storage," she replied. "Melman rented from them."

"And who owns Brutus Storage?"

"J. B. Rand, Inc."

"Address?"

"An office in Sausalito. It was vacated a couple of months ago."

"Did the people who owned the place have a home address for the renter?"

"Just a post office box. It's been abandoned too."

I nodded. "I'd a feeling it would be something like that," I said. "Now tell me about Jasra. Obviously you know the lady."

She sniffed. "No lady," she said. "A royal whore is what she was when I knew her."

"Where?"

"In Kashfa."

"Where's that?"

"An interesting little shadow kingdom, a bit over the edge of the Golden Circle of those with which Amber has commerce. Shabby barbaric splendor and all that. It's kind of a cultural backwater."

"How is it you know it at all, then?"

She paused a moment in stirring something in a bowl.

"Oh, I used to keep company with a Kashfan nobleman I'd met in a wood one day. He was out hawking and I happened to have twisted my ankle—"

"Uh," I interjected, lest we be diverted by details. "And Jasra?"

"She was consort to the old king Menillan. Had him wrapped around her finger."

"What have you got against her?"

"She stole Jasrick while I was out of town."

"Jasrick?"

"My nobleman. Earl of Kronklef."

"What did His Highness Menillan think of these goings-on?"

"He never knew. He was on his deathbed at the time. Succumbed shortly thereafter. In fact, that's why she really wanted Jasrick. He was chief of the palace guard and his brother was a general. She used them to pull off a coup when Menillan expired. Last I heard, she was queen in Kashfa and she'd ditched Jasrick. Served him proper, I'd say. I think he had his eye on the throne, but she didn't care to share it. She had him and his brother executed for treason of one sort or another. He was really a handsome fellow. . . . Not too bright, though."

"Do the people of Kashfa have any—uh—unusual physical endowments?" I asked.

She smiled. "Well, Jasrick was one hell of a fellow. But I wouldn't use the word 'unusual' to—"

"No, no," I interrupted. "What I meant was some sort of anomaly of the mouth—retractable fangs or a sting or something of that sort."

"Un-uh," she said, and I could not tell whether her heightened coloring came from the heat of the stove. "Nothing like that. They're built along standard lines. Why do you ask?"

"When I told you my story back in Amber I omitted the part where Jasra bit me, and I was barely able to trump out because of some sort of poison she seemed to have injected. It left me numb, paralyzed and very weak for a long while."

She shook her head. "Kashfans can't do anything like that. But then, of course, Jasra is not a Kashfan."

"Oh? Where's she from?"

"I don't know. But she's a foreigner. Some say a slaver brought her in from a distant land. Others say she just wandered in herself one day and caught Menillan's eye. It was rumored she was a sorceress. I don't know."

"I do. That rumor's right."

"Really? Perhaps that's how she got Jasrick."

I shrugged. "How long ago was your—experience—with her?"

"Thirty or forty years, I'd guess."

"And she is still queen in Kashfa?"

"I don't know. It's been a long time since I've been back that way."

"Is Amber on bad terms with Kashfa?"

She shook her head. "No special terms at all, really. As I said, they're a bit out of the way. Not as accessible as a lot of other places, with nothing greatly desirable for trade."

"No real reason then for her to hate us?"

"No more than for hating anyone else."

Some delightful cooking odors began to fill the room. As I sat there sniffing them and thinking of the long, hot

shower I would head for after lunch, Flora said what I had
somehow known she would say.

"That man who dragged Jasra back. . . . He looked familiar. Who was he?"

"He was the one I told you about back in Amber," I
replied. "Luke. I'm curious whether he reminds you of
anyone."

"He seems to," she said, after a pause. "But I can't say
just who."

As her back was to me I said, "If you're holding anything that might break or spill if you drop it, please put it
down."

I heard something set to rest on the countertop. Then she
turned, a puzzled expression on her face.

"Yes?"

"His real name is Rinaldo, and he's Brand's son," I told
her. "I was his prisoner for over a month in another
shadow. I just now escaped."

"Oh, my," she whispered. Then, "What does he want?"

"Revenge," I answered.

"Against anyone in particular?"

"No. All of us. But Caine, of course, was first."

"I see."

"Please don't burn anything," I said. "I've been looking
forward to a good meal for a long time."

She nodded and turned away. After a while she said,
"You knew him for a pretty long time. What's he like?"

"He always seemed to be a fairly nice guy. If he's crazy,
like his dad, he hid it well."

She uncorked a wine bottle, poured two glasses and
brought them over. Then she began serving the meal.

After a few bites she paused with her fork half raised
and stared at nothing in particular.

"Who'd have thought the son of a bitch would repro-
duce?" she remarked.

"Fiona, I think," I told her. "The night before Caine's
funeral she asked me whether I had a photo of Luke. When
I showed her one I could tell that something was bothering
her, but she wouldn't say what."

"And the next day she and Bleys were gone," Flora said. "Yes. Now I think of it, he does look somewhat the way Brand did when he was very young—so long ago. Luke seems bigger and heavier, but there is a resemblance."

She resumed eating.

"By the way, this is very good," I said.

"Oh, thanks." She sighed then. "That means I have to wait till you're finished eating to hear the whole story."

I nodded, because my mouth was full. Let the empire totter. I was starved.

CHAPTER 2

Showered, trimmed, manicured and garbed in fresh-conjured finery, I got a number out of Information and placed a call to the only Devlin listed in Bill Roth's area. The voice of the woman who answered did not possess the proper timbre, though I still recognized it.

"Meg? Meg Devlin?" I said.

"Yes," came the reply. "Who is this?"

"Merle Corey."

"Who?"

"Merle Corey. We spen an interesting night together some time back—"

"I'm sorry," she said. "There must be some mistake."

"If you can't talk freely now I can call whenever you say. Or you can call me."

"I don't know you," she said, and she hung up.

I stared at the receiver. If her husband were present I'd assumed she'd play it a bit cagey but would at least give some indication that she knew me and would talk another time. I had held off on getting in touch with Random because I'd a feeling he'd summon me back to Amber immediately, and I'd wanted to talk to Meg first. I certainly

22

couldn't spare the time to go and visit her. I could not understand her response, but for now at least I was stuck with it. So I tried the only other thing that occurred to me. I got hold of Information again and obtained the number for Bill's next-door neighbors, the Hansens.

It was answered on the third ring—a woman's voice I recognized as Mrs. Hansen's. I had met her in the past, though I had not seen her on my most recent trip to the area.

"Mrs. Hansen," I began. "It's Merle Corey."

"Oh, Merle.... You were just up here a while ago, weren't you?"

"Yes. Couldn't stay long, though. But I did finally get to meet George. Had several long talks with him. In fact, I'd like to speak with him right now if he's handy."

The silence ran several beats too long before she responded.

"George.... Well, George is over at the hospital just now, Merle. Is it something you could tell me?"

"Oh, it's not urgent," I said. "What happened to George?"

"It—it's nothing real bad. He's just an outpatient now, and today's his day to get checked over and pick up some medication. He had a—sort of—breakdown last month. Has a couple days' worth of amnesia, and they can't seem to figure what caused it."

"I'm sorry to hear that."

"Well, the X-rays didn't show any damage—like he'd hit his head or anything. And he seems okay now. They say he'll probably be fine. But they want to keep an eye on him a little longer. That's all." Suddenly, as if struck by inspiration, she asked, "How'd he seem when you were talking with him, anyway?"

I'd seen it coming, so I didn't hesitate.

"He seemed fine when I talked with him," I answered. "But of course I hadn't known him before, so I couldn't tell whether he was acting any different."

"I see what you mean," she said. "Do you want him to call you back when he gets in?"

"No. I'm going to be going out," I said, "and I'm not sure when I'll be getting back. It was nothing really important. I'll get in touch again one of these days."

"Okay, then. I'll tell him you called."

"Thanks. G'bye."

That one I'd almost expected. After Meg. George's behavior had been overtly weird, at the end there. What had bothered me was that he'd seemed to know who I really was and to know about Amber—and he even wanted to follow me through a Trump. It was as if he and Meg had both been subjected to some strange manipulation.

Jasra came to mind immediately in this regard. But then she was Luke's ally, it seemed, and Meg had warned me against Luke. Why would she do that if Jasra were controlling her in some fashion? It didn't make sense. Who else did I know who might be capable of causing such phenomena?

Fiona, for one. But then she'd been party to my later return to this shadow from Amber and had even picked me up after my evening with Meg. And she'd seemed just as puzzled about the course of events as I was.

Shit. Life is full of doors that don't open when you knock, equally spaced amid those that open when you don't want them to.

I went back and knocked on the bedroom door, and Flora told me to come in. She was seated before a mirror, applying makeup.

"How'd it go?" she asked.

"Not too well. Totally unsatisfactory, actually." I summarized the results of my calls.

"So what are you going to do now?" she inquired.

"Get in touch with Random," I said, "and bring him up to date. I've got a feeling he'll call me back to hear it all. So I wanted to say good-bye, and thanks for helping me. Sorry if I broke up your romance."

She shrugged, her back still to me, as she studied herself in the mirror.

"Don't worry—"

I did not hear the remainder of her sentence, though she

continued talking. My attention was snatched away by what seemed the beginning of a Trump contact. I made myself receptive and waited. The feeling grew stronger but the caller's presence did not become manifest. I turned away from Flora.

"Merle, what is it?" I heard her say then.

I raised one hand to her as the feeling intensified. I seemed to be staring down a long black tunnel with nothing at its farther end.

"I don't know," I said, summoning the Logrus and taking control of one of its limbs. "Ghost? Is that you? Are you ready to talk?" I asked.

There was no reply. I felt a chill as I remained receptive, waiting. I had never experienced anything quite like this before. I'd a strong feeling that if I but moved forward I would be transported somewhere. Was this a challenge? A trap? Whatever, I felt that only a fool would accept such an invitation from the unknown. For all I knew, it might deliver me back to the crystal cave.

"If there is something you want," I said, "you are going to have to make yourself known and ask. I've given up on blind dates."

A sense of presence trickled through, then, but no intimations of identity.

"All right," I said. "I'm not coming and you have no message. The only other thing I can think of is that you're asking to come to me. If that's the case, come ahead."

I extended both of my apparently empty hands, my invisible strangling cord writhing into position in my left, an unseen Logrus death bolt riding my right. It was one of those times when courtesy demanded professional standards.

A soft laughter seemed to echo within the dark tunnel. It was purely a mental projection, however, cold and genderless.

Your offer is, of course, a trick, came to me then. *For you are not a fool. Still, I grant your courage, to address the unknown as you do. You do not know what you face, yet you await it. You even invite it.*

"The offer is still good," I said.

I never thought of you as dangerous.

"What do you want?"

To regard you.

"Why?"

There may come a time when I will face you on different terms.

"What terms?"

I feel that our purposes will be crossed.

"Who are you?"

Again, the laughter.

No. Not now. Not yet. I would merely look upon you, and observe your reactions.

"Well? Have you seen enough?"

Almost.

"If our purposes are crossed, let the conflict be now," I said. "I'd like to get it out of the way so I can get on with some important business."

I appreciate arrogance. But when the time comes the choice will not be yours.

"I'm willing to wait," I said, as I cautiously extended a Logrus limb out along the dark way.

Nothing. My probe encountered nothing. . . .

I admire your performance. Here!"

Something came rushing toward me. My magical extension informed me that it was soft—too soft and loose to do me any real harm—a large, cool mass showing bright colors. . . .

I stood my ground and extended through it—beyond, far, farther—reaching for the source. I encountered something tangible but yielding: a body perhaps, perhaps not; too—too big to snap back in an instant.

Several small items, hard and of sufficiently low mass, recommended themselves to my lightning search. I seized upon one, tore it free of whatever held it and called it to me.

A wordless impulse of startlement reached me at the same time as the rushing mass and the return of my Logrus summoning.

It burst about me like fireworks: flowers, flowers, flowers. Violets, anemones, daffodils, roses. . . . I heard Flora gasp as hundreds of them rained into the room. The contact was broken immediately. I was aware that I held something small and hard in my right hand, and the heady odors of the floral display filled my nostrils.

"What the hell," said Flora, "happened?"

"I'm not sure," I answered, brushing petals from my shirtfront. "You like flowers? You can have these."

"Thanks, but I prefer a less haphazard arrangement." she said, regarding the bright mound that lay at my feet. "Who sent them?"

"A nameless person at the end of a dark tunnel."

"Why?"

"Down payment on a funeral display, maybe. I'm not sure. The tenor of the whole conversation was somewhat threatening."

"I'd appreciate it if you'd help me pick them up before you go."

"Sure," I said.

"There are vases in the kitchen and the bathroom. Come on."

I followed her and collected several. On the way, I studied the object I had brought back from the other end of the sending. It was a blue button mounted in a gold setting, a few navy blue threads still attached. The cut stone bore a curved, four-limbed design. I showed it to Flora and she shook her head.

"It tells me nothing," she said.

I dug into my pocket and produced the chips of stone from the crystal cave. They seemed to match. Frakir stirred slightly when I passed the button near her, then lapsed again into quiescence, as if having given up on warning me about blue stones when I obviously never did anything about them.

"Strange," I said.

"I'd like some roses on the night table," Flora told me, "and a couple of mixed displays on the dresser. You know, no one's ever sent *me* flowers this way. It's a rather intriguing introduction. Are you sure they were for you?"

I growled something anatomical or theological and gathered rosebuds.

Later, as we sat in the kitchen drinking coffee and musing, Flora remarked, "This thing's kind of spooky."

"Yes."

"Maybe you ought to discuss it with Fi after you've talked with Random."

"Maybe."

"Speaking of whom, shouldn't you be calling Random?"

"Maybe."

"What do you mean, 'maybe'? He's got to be warned."

"True. But I've a feeling that being safe won't get any questions answered for me."

"What do you have in mind, Merle?"

"Do you have a car?"

"Yes, I just got it a few days back. Why?"

I withdrew the button and the stones from my pocket, spread them on the table and regarded them again. "It just occurred to me while we were picking up flowers where I might have seen another of these."

"Yes?"

"There is a memory I must have been blocking, because it was very distressing: Julia's appearance when I found her. I seem to recall now that she had on a pendant with a blue stone. Maybe it's just coincidence, but—"

She nodded. "Could be. But even so, the police probably have it now."

"Oh, I don't want the thing. But it reminds me that I didn't really get to look over her apartment as well as I might have if I hadn't had to leave in a hurry. I want to see it again before I go back to Amber. I'm still puzzled as to how that—creature—got in."

"What if the place has been cleaned out? Or rented again?"

I shrugged. "Only one way to find out."

"Okay, I'll drive you there."

A few minutes later we were in her car and I was giving her directions. It was perhaps a twenty-minute drive beneath a sunny late-afternoon sky, stray clouds passing. I spent much of the time making certain preparations with Logrus forces, and I was ready by the time we reached the proper area.

"Turn here and go around the block," I said, gesturing. "I'll show you where to park if there's a place."

There was, close to the spot where I'd parked on that day.

When we were stopped beside the curb she glanced at me. "Now what? Do we just go up to the place and knock?"

"I'm going to make us invisible," I told her, "and I'm going to keep us that way till we're inside. You'll have to stay close to me in order for us to see each other, though."

She nodded.

"Dworkin did it for me once," she said, "when I was a child. Spied on a lot of people then." She chuckled. "I'd forgotten."

I put the finishing touches to the elaborate spell and laid it upon us, the world growing dimmer beyond the windshield as I did. It was as if I regarded our surroundings through gray sunglasses as we slipped out the passenger side of the car. We walked slowly up to the corner and turned right.

"Is this a hard spell to learn?" she asked me. "It seems a very handy one to know."

"Unfortunately, yes," I said. "Its biggest drawback is that you can't just do it at a moment's notice if you don't have it hanging ready—and I didn't. So, starting from scratch, it takes about twenty minutes to build."

We turned up the walk to the big old house.

"Which floor?" she asked me.

"Top."

We climbed to the front door and found it locked. No doubt they were more particular about such matters these days.

"Break it?" Flora whispered.

"Too noisy," I answered.

I placed my left hand upon the doorknob and gave Frakir a silent command. She unwound two turnings of her coil from about my wrist, coming into view as she moved across the lock plate and slithered into the keyhole. There followed a tightening, a stiffening and several rigid movements.

A soft click meant the bolt was drawn, and I turned the knob and pulled gently. The door opened. Frakir returned to bracelethood and invisibility.

We entered, closing the door quietly behind us. We were not present in the wavery mirror. I led Flora up the stairs.

There were soft voices from one of the rooms on the second floor. That was all. No wind. No excited dogs. And the voices grew still before we reached the third floor.

I saw that the entire door to Julia's apartment had been replaced. It was slightly darker than the other and it sported a bright new lock. I tapped upon it gently and we waited. There was no response, but I knocked again after perhaps half a minute and we waited again.

No one came. So I tried it. It was locked, but Frakir repeated her trick and I hesitated. My hand shook as I recalled my last visit. I knew her mutilated corpse was no longer lying there. I knew no killer beast was waiting to attack me. Yet the memory held me for several seconds.

"What's the matter?" Flora whispered.

"Nothing," I said, and I pushed the door open.

The place had been partly furnished, as I recalled. The part that had come with it remained—the sofa and end tables, several chairs, a larger table—but all Julia's own stuff was gone. There was a new rug on the floor, and the floor itself had been buffed recently. It did not appear that the place had been re-let, as there were no personal items of any sort about.

We entered and I closed the door, dropping the spell that had cloaked us as I began my circuit through the rooms. The place brightened perceptibly as our magic veils faded.

"I don't think you're going to find anything," Flora said. "I can smell wax and disinfectant and paint. . . ."

I nodded.

"The more mundane possibilities seem to be excluded," I said. "But there is something else I want to try."

I calmed my mind and called up the Logrus-seeing. If there were any remaining traces of a magical working, I hoped I could spot them in this fashion. I wandered slowly then, through the living room, regarding everything from every possible angle. Flora moved off, conducting her own investigation, which consisted mainly in looking under everything. The room flickered slightly for me as I scanned at those wavelengths where such a manifestation was most likely to be apparent—at least, that was the best way to describe the process in this shadow.

Nothing, large or small, escaped my scrutiny. But nothing was revealed to it. After long minutes I moved into the bedroom.

Flora must have heard my sudden intake of breath, because she was into the room and at my side in seconds, and staring at the chest of drawers before which I stood.

"Something in it?" she inquired, reaching forward, then withdrawing her hand.

"No. Behind it," I said.

The chest of drawers had been moved in the course of purging the apartment. It used to occupy a space several feet farther to the right. That which I now saw was visible to its left and above it, with more of it obviously blocked to my sight. I took hold of the thing and pushed it back to the right, to the position it had formerly occupied.

"I still don't see anything," Flora said.

I reached out and caught hold of her hand, extending the Logrus force so that she, too, saw what I saw.

"Why"—she raised her other hand and traced the faint rectangular outline on the wall—"it looks like a . . . doorway," she said.

I studied it—a dim line of faded fire. The thing was obviously sealed and had been for some time. Eventually it would fade completely and be gone.

"It *is* a doorway," I answered.

She pulled me back into the other room to regard the opposite side of the wall.

"Nothing here," she observed. "It doesn't go through."

"Now you've got the idea," I said. "It goes somewhere else."

"Where?"

"Wherever the thing that killed Julia came from."

"Can you open it?"

"I am prepared to stand in front of it for as long as I have to," I told her, "and try."

I returned to the other room and studied it once again.

"Merlin," she said, as I released her hand and raised mine before me, "don't you think this is the point where you should get in touch with Random, tell him exactly what has been happening and perhaps have Gérard standing next to you if you succeed in opening that door?"

"I probably should," I agreed, "but I'm not going to."

"Why not?"

"Because he might tell me not to."

"He might be right, too."

I lowered my hands and turned toward her. "I have to admit you have a point," I said. "Random has to be told everything, and I've probably put it off too long already. So here is what I would like you to do: Go back to the car and wait. Give me an hour. If I'm not out by then, get in touch with Random, tell him everything I told you and tell him about this, too."

"I don't know," she said. "If you don't show, Random's going to be mad at me."

"Just tell him I insisted and there was nothing you could do. Which is actually the case, if you stop to think about it."

She pursed her lips. "I don't like leaving you—though I'm not anxious to stay either. Care to take along a hand grenade?"

She raised her purse and began to open it.

"No. Thanks. Why do you have it, anyway?"

She smiled. "I always carry them in this shadow. They sometimes come in handy. But okay, I'll go wait."

She kissed me lightly on the cheek and turned away.

"And try to get hold of Fiona," I said, "if I don't show. Tell her the whole story, too. She might have a different angle on this."

She nodded and departed. I waited until I heard the door close, then focused my attention fully upon the bright rectangle. Its outline seemed fairly uniform, with only a few slightly thicker, brighter areas and a few finer, dimmer ones. I traced the lines slowly with the palm of my right hand at a height of about an inch above the wall's surface. I felt a small prickling, a heatlike sensation as I did this. Predictably, it was greater above the brighter areas. I took this as an indication that the seal was slightly less perfect in these spots. Very well. I would soon discover whether the thing could be forced, and these would be my points of attack.

I twisted my hands deeper into the Logrus until I wore the limbs I desired as fine-fingered gauntlets, stronger than metals, more sensitive than tongues in the places of their power. I moved my right hand to the point nearest it, on a level with my hip. I felt the pulse of an old spell when I touched that spot of greater brightness. I narrowed my extension as I pushed, making it finer and finer until it slipped through. The pulsing then became a steady thing. I repeated the exercise on a higher area to my left.

I stood there, feeling the force that had sealed it, my fine filament extensions throbbing within its matrix. I tried moving them, first upward, then down. The right one slid a little farther than the left, in both directions, before a tightness and resistance halted it. I summoned more force from the body of the Logrus, which swam specterlike within and before me, and I poured this energy into the gauntlets, the pattern of the Logrus changing form again as I did so. When I tried once more to move it, the right one slid downward for perhaps a foot before the throbbing trapped it; when I pushed it upward it rose nearly to the top. I tried again on the left. It moved all the way to the top, but it only passed perhaps six inches below the starting point when I drew it downward.

I breathed deeply and felt myself beginning to perspire. I pumped more power into the gauntlets and forced their extensions farther downward. The resistance was even greater there, and the throbbing passed up my arms and into the very center of my being. I paused and rested, then raised the force to an even higher level of intensity. The Logrus writhed again and I pushed both hands all the way to the floor, then knelt there panting before I began working my way along the bottom. The portal was obviously meant never to be opened again. There was no artistry for this, only brute force.

When my forces met in the middle, I withdrew and regarded the work. To the right, to the left and along the bottom, the fine red lines had now become broad fiery ribbons. I could feel their pulsation across the distance that separated us.

I stood and raised my arms. I began to work along the top, starting at the corners, moving inward. It was easier than it had been earlier. The forces from the opened areas seemed to add a certain pressure, and my hands just flowed to the middle. When they met I seemed to hear something like a soft sighing sound. I dropped them and considered my work. The entire outline flared now. But more than that. It seemed almost as if the bright line were flowing, around and around. . . .

I stood there for several minutes, regrouping, relaxing, settling. Working up my nerve. All I knew was that the door would lead to a different shadow. That could mean anything. When I opened it something could, I suppose, leap out and attack me. But then, it had been sealed for some time. More probably any trap would be of a different sort. Most likely, I would open it and nothing would happen. I would then have a choice of merely looking around from where I stood or entering. And there probably wouldn't be very much to see, just standing there, looking. . . .

So I extended my Logrus members once again, taking hold of the door at either side, and I pushed. A yielding occurred on the side to my right, so I released my hold on the left. I continued my pressure on the right and the whole thing suddenly swung inward and away. . . .

I was looking down a pearly tunnel, which appeared to widen after a few paces. Beyond that was a ripple effect, as of distant heat patterns above the road on a hot summer day. Patches of redness and indeterminate dark shapes swam within it. I waited for perhaps half a minute, but nothing approached.

I prepared Frakir for trouble. I maintained my Logrus connection. I advanced, extending probes before me. I passed within.

A sudden change in the pressure gradient at my back caused me to cast a quick glance in that direction. The doorway had closed and dwindled, now appearing to me in the distance as a tiny red cube. My several steps could, of course, have borne me a great distance also, should the rules of this space so operate.

I continued, and a hot wind flowed toward me, engulfed me, stayed with me. The sides of my passageway receded, the prospect before me continued to shimmer and dance, and my pace became more labored, as if I were suddenly walking uphill. I heard something like a grunt from beyond the place where my vision misbehaved, and my left Logrus probe encountered something that it jolted slightly. Frakir began to throb simultaneous with my sensing an aura of menace through the probe. I sighed. I hadn't expected this was going to be easy. If I'd been running the show I wouldn't have let things go with just sealing the door.

"All right, asshole! Hold it right there!" a voice boomed from ahead.

I continued to trudge forward.

It came again. "I said halt!"

Things began to swim into place as I advanced, and suddenly there were rough walls to my right and left and a roof overhead, narrowing, converging—

A huge rotund figure barred my way, looking like a purple Buddha with bat ears. Details resolved themselves as I drew nearer: protruding fangs, yellow eyes that seemed to be lidless, long red claws on its great hands and feet. It was seated in the middle of the tunnel and made no effort to rise. It wore no clothing, but its great swollen belly rested upon its knees, concealing its sex. Its voice had been gruffly masculine, however, and its odor generically foul.

"Hi," I said. "Nice day, wasn't it?"

It growled and the temperature seemed to rise slightly. Frakir had grown frantic and I calmed her mentally.

The creature leaned forward and with one bright nail inscribed a smoking line in the stone of the floor. I halted before it.

"Cross that line, sorcerer, and you've had it," it said.

"Why?" I asked.

"Because I said so."

"If you're collecting tolls," I suggested, "name the price."

It shook its head. "You can't buy your way past me."

"Uh—what makes you think I'm a sorcerer?"

It opened the dingy cavern of its face, displaying even more lurking teeth than I'd suspected, and it did something like the rattling of a tin sheet way down deep in back.

"I felt that little probe of yours," it said. "It's a sorcerer's trick. Besides, nobody but a sorcerer could have gotten to the place where you're standing."

"You do not seem to possess a great deal of respect for the profession."

"I eat sorcerers," it told me.

I made a face, thinking back over some of the old farts I've known in the business.

"To each, his, her or its own, I guess," I told it. "So what's the deal? A passage is no good unless you can get through it. How do I get by here?"

"You don't."

"Not even if I answer a riddle?"

"That won't do it for me," it said. But a small gleam came into its eye. "Just for the hell of it, though, what's green and red and goes round and round and round?" it asked.

"You know the sphinx!"

"Shit!" it said. "You've heard it."

I shrugged. "I get around."

"Not here you don't."

I studied it. It had to have some special defense against magical attacks if it were set to stop sorcerers. As for physical defense it was fairly imposing. I wondered how fast it was. Could I just dive past and start running? I decided that I did not wish to experiment along that line.

"I really do have to get through," I tried. "It's an emergency."

"Tough."

"Look, what do you get out of this, anyway? It seems like a pretty crummy job, sitting here in the middle of a tunnel."

"I love my work. I was created for it."

"How come you let the sphinx come and go?"

"Magical beings don't count."

"Hm."

"And don't try to tell me you're really a magical being, and then pull some sorcerous illusion. I can see right through that stuff."

"I believe you. What's your name, anyhow?"

It snorted. "You can call me Scrof, for conversational purposes. Yourself?"

"Call me Corey."

"Okay, Corey. I don't mind sitting here bullshitting with you, because that's covered by the rules. It's allowed. You've got three choices and one of them would be real stupid. You can turn around and go back the way you came and be none the worse for wear. You can also camp right where you are for as long as you like and I won't lift a finger so long as you behave. The dumb thing to do would be to cross this line I've drawn. Then I'd terminate you. This is the Threshold and I am the Dweller on it. I don't let anybody get by."

"I appreciate your making it clear."

"It's part of the job. So what'll it be?"

I raised my hands and the lines of force twisted like knives at each fingertip. Frakir dangled from my wrist and began to swing in an elaborate pattern.

Scrof smiled. "I not only eat sorcerers, I eat their magic, too. Only a being torn from the primal Chaos can make that claim. So come ahead, if you think you can face that."

"Chaos, eh? Torn from the primal Chaos?"

"Yep. There's not much can stand against it."

"Except maybe a Lord of Chaos," I replied, as I shifted my awareness to various points within my body. Rough work. The faster you do it the more painful it is.

Again, the rattling of the tin sheet.

"You know what the odds are against a Chaos Lord coming this far to go two out of three with a Dweller?" Scrof said.

My arms began to lengthen and I felt my shirt tear across my back as I leaned forward. The bones in my face shifted about and my chest expanded and expanded. . . .

"One out of one should be enough," I replied, when the transformation was complete.

"Shit," Scrof said as I crossed the line.

CHAPTER 3

I stood just within the mouth of the cave for some time, my left shoulder hurting and my right leg sore also. If I could get the pain under control before I retransformed myself there was a chance that much of it would fade during the anatomical reshuffling. The process itself would probably leave me pretty tired, however. It takes a lot of energy, and switching twice this close together could be somewhat prostrating, following my bout with the Dweller. So I rested within the cave into which the pearly tunnel had eventually debouched, and I regarded the prospect before me.

Far down and to my left was a bright blue and very troubled body of water. White-crested waves expired in kamikaze attacks on the gray rocks of the shore; a strong wind scattered their spray and a piece of rainbow hung within the mist.

Before me and below me was a pocked, cracked and steaming land which trembled periodically, as it swept for well over a mile toward the high dark walls of an amazingly huge and complex structure, which I immediately christened Gormenghast. It was a hodgepodge of architec-

39

tural styles, bigger even than the palace at Amber and somber as all hell. Also, it was under attack.

There were quite a few troops in the field before the walls, most of them in a distant nonscorched area of more normal terrain and some vegetation, though the grasses were well trampled and many trees shattered. The besiegers were equipped with scaling ladders and a battering ram, but the ram was idle at the moment and the ladders were on the ground. What appeared to have been an entire village of outbuildings smoldered darkly at the wall's base. Numerous sprawled figures were, I assumed, casualties.

Moving my gaze even farther to the right, I encountered an area of brilliant whiteness beyond that great citadel. It looked to be the projecting edge of a massive glacier, and gusts of snow or ice crystals were whipped about it in a fashion similar to the sea mists far to my left.

The wind seemed a constant traveler through these parts. I heard it cry out high above me. When I finally stepped outside to look upward, I found that I was only about halfway up a massive stony hillside—or low mountainside, depending on how one regards such matters—and the whining note of the wind came down even more loudly from those broken heights. There was also a *thump* at my back, and when I turned I could no longer locate the cave mouth. My journey along the route from the fiery door had been completed once I exited the cave, and its spell had apparently clamped down and closed the way immediately. I supposed that I could locate the outline upon the steep wall if I wanted to, but at the moment I had no such desire. I made a little pile of stones before it, and then I looked about again, studying details.

A narrow trail curved off to my right and back among some standing stones. I headed in that direction. I smelled smoke. Whether it was from the battle site or the area of vulcanism below I could not tell. The sky was a patchwork of cloud and light above me. When I halted between two of the stones and turned to regard the scene below once again, I saw that the attackers had formed themselves into new groups and that the ladders were being borne toward the walls. I also saw what looked like a tornado rise on the far side of the citadel and begin a slow counterclockwise movement about the walls. If it continued on its route it would eventually reach the attackers. Neat trick. Fortunately it was their problem and not mine.

I worked my way back into a stony declivity and settled myself upon a low ledge. I began the troublesome shape-shifting work, which I paced to take me half an hour or so. Changing from something nominally human to something rare and strange—perhaps monstrous to some, perhaps frightening—and then back again is a concept some may find repugnant. They shouldn't. We all of us do it every day in many different ways, don't we?

When the transformation was completed I lay back, breathing deeply, and listened to the wind. I was sheltered from its force by the stones and only its song came down to me. I felt vibrations from distant tremors of the earth and chose to take them as a gentle message, soothing.... My clothes were in tatters, and for the moment I was too tired to summon a fresh outfit. My shoulder seemed to have lost its pain, and there was only the slightest twinge in my leg, fading, fading.... I closed my eyes for a few moments.

Okay, I'd made it through, and I'd a strong feeling that the answer to the matter of Julia's killer lay in the besieged citadel below. Offhand, I didn't see any easy way into the place at the moment, to make inquiry. But that was not the only way I might proceed. I decided to wait where I was, resting, until it grew dark—that is, if things here proceeded in a normal dark-light fashion. Then I'd slip downstairs, kidnap one of the besiegers and question him. Yes. And if it didn't get dark? Then I'd think of something else. Right now, though, just drifting felt best....

For how long I dozed, I was uncertain. What roused me was the clicking of pebbles, from somewhere off to the right. I was instantly alert, though I didn't stir. There was no effort at stealth, and the pattern of approaching sounds —mainly slapping footfalls, as of someone wearing loose sandals—convinced me that only a single individual was moving in this direction. I tensed and relaxed my muscles and drew a few deep breaths.

A very hairy man emerged from between two of the stones to my right. He was about five and a half feet in height, very dirty, and he wore a dark animal skin about his loins; also, he had on a pair of sandals. He stared at me for several seconds before displaying the yellow irregularities of his smile.

"Hello. Are you injured?" he asked, in a debased form of Thari that I did not recall ever having heard before.

I stretched to make sure and then stood. "No," I replied. "Why do you ask that?"

The smile persisted. "I thought maybe you'd had enough of the fighting below and decided to call it quits."

"Oh, I see. No, it's not exactly like that. . . ."

He nodded and stepped forward. "Dave's my name. What's yours?"

"Merle," I said, clasping his grimy hand.

"Not to worry, Merle," he told me. "I wouldn't turn in anybody who decided to take a walk from a war, unless maybe there was a reward—and there ain't on this one. Did it myself years ago and never regretted it. Mine was goin' the same way this one seems to be goin', and I had sense enough to get out. No army's ever taken that place down there, and I don't think one ever will."

"What place is it?"

He cocked his head and squinted, then shrugged. "Keep of the Four Worlds," he said. "Didn't the recruiter tell you anything?"

I sighed. "Nope," I said.

"Wouldn't have any smokin' stuff on you, would you?"

"No," I answered, having used all my pipe tobacco back in the crystal cave. "Sorry."

I moved past him to a point where I could look downward from between the stones. I wanted another look at the Keep of the Four Worlds. After all, it was the answer to a riddle as well as the subject of numerous cryptic references in Melman's diary. Fresh bodies were scattered all over before its walls, as if cast about by the whirlwind, which was now circling back toward the point whence it had risen. But a small party of besiegers had apparently made it to the top of the wall despite this. And a fresh party had formed below and was headed for the ladders. One of its members bore a banner I could not place, but which seemed vaguely familiar—black and green, with what might be a couple of heraldic beasts having a go at each other. Two ladders were still in place, and I could see some fierce fighting going on behind the battlements.

"Some of the attackers seem to have gotten in," I said.

Dave hurried up beside me and stared. I immediately moved upwind.

"You're right," he acknowledged. "Now, that's a first. If they can get that damn gate open and let the others in they might even have a chance. Never thought I'd live to see it."

"How long ago was it," I asked, "when the army you were with attacked the place?"

"Must be eight, nine—maybe ten years," he muttered. "Those guys must be pretty good."

"What's it all about?" I asked.

He turned and studied me. "You really don't know?"

"Just got here," I said.

"Hungry? Thirsty?"

"As a matter of fact, yes."

"Come on, then." He took hold of my arm and steered me back between the stones, then led me along a narrow trail.

"Where are we headed?" I asked.

"I live nearby. I make it a point to feed deserters, for old times' sake. I'll make an exception for you."

"Thanks."

The trail split after a short while, and he took the right-hand branch, which involved some climbing. Eventually this led us to a series of rocky shelves, the last of which receded for a considerable distance. There were a number of clefts at its rear, into one of which he ducked. I followed him a short distance along it, and he halted before a low cave mouth. A horrible odor of putrefaction drifted forth, and I could hear the buzzing of flies within.

"This is my place," he announced. "I'd invite you in, but it's a little—uh—"

"That's okay," I said. "I'll wait."

He ducked inside, and I realized that my appetite was rapidly vanishing, especially when it came to anything he might have stored in that place.

Moments later he emerged, a duffel bag slung over his shoulder. "Got some good stuff in here," he announced.

I started walking back along the cleft. "Hey! Where you headed?"

"Air," I said. "I'm going back out on the shelf. It's a bit close back there."

"Oh. Okay," he said, and he fell into step behind me.

He had two unopened bottles of wine, several canteens of water, a fresh-looking loaf of bread, some tinned meat, a few firm apples and an uncut head of cheese in the bag, I discovered, after we'd seated ourselves on a ledge out in the open and he'd gestured for me to open the thing and serve myself. Having prudently remained upwind, I took some water and an apple for openers.

"Place has a stormy history," he stated, withdrawing a small knife from his girdle and cutting himself a piece of cheese. "I'm not sure who built it or how long it's been there."

When I saw that he was about to dig the cork out of a wine bottle with the knife I halted him and essayed a small and surreptitious Logrus sending. The response was quick, and I passed him the corkscrew immediately. He handed me the entire bottle after he'd uncorked it and opened the other for himself. For reasons involving public health I was grateful, though I wasn't in the mood for that much wine.

"That's what I call being prepared," he said, studying the corkscrew. "I've needed one of these for some time. . . ."

"Keep it," I told him. "Tell me more about that place. Who lives there? How did you come to be part of an invading army? Who's attacking it now?"

He nodded and took a swig of wine.

"The earliest boss of the place that I know of was a wizard named Sharu Garrul. The queen of my country departed suddenly and came here." He paused and stared off into the distance for a time, then snorted. "Politics! I don't even know what the given reason for the visit was at the time. I'd never heard of the damned place in those days. Anyhow, she stayed a long while and people began to wonder: Was she a prisoner? Was she working out an alliance? Was she having an affair? I gather she sent back messages periodically, but they were the usual bland crap that didn't say anything—unless of course there were also secret communications folks like me wouldn't have heard about. She had a pretty good-sized retinue with her, too, with an honor guard that was not just for show. These guys were very tough veterans, even though they dressed pretty. So it was kind of debatable what was going on at that point."

"A question, if I may," I said. "What was your king's part in all this? You didn't mention him, and it would seem he ought to know—"

"Dead," he announced. "She made a lovely widow, and there was a lot of pressure on her to remarry. But she just took a succession of lovers and played the different factions off against each other. Usually her men were military leaders or powerful nobles, or both. She'd left her son in charge when she made this trip, though."

"Oh, so there was a prince old enough to sit in control?"

"Yes. In fact, he started the damned war. He raised troops and wasn't happy with the muster, so he got in touch with a childhood friend, a man generally considered an outlaw, but who commanded a large band of mercenaries. Name of Dalt—"

"Stop!" I said.

My mind raced as I recalled a story Gérard had once told me, about a strange man named Dalt who had led a private army against Amber, unusually effectively. Benedict himself had had to be recalled to oppose him. The man's forces had been defeated at the foot of Kolvir, and

Dalt himself severely wounded. Though no one ever saw
his body, it was assumed he would have died of such injuries. But there was more.

"Your home," I said. "You never named it. Where are
you from, Dave?"

"A place called Kashfa," he replied.

"And Jasra was your queen?"

"You've heard of us. Where're you from?"

"San Francisco," I said.

He shook his head. "Don't know the place."

"Who does? Listen, how good are your eyes?"

"What do you mean?"

"A little while ago, when we looked down on the fighting, could you make out the flag the attackers were carrying?"

"Eyes ain't what they used to be," he said.

"It was green and black with some sort of animals on
it."

He whistled. "A lion rending a unicorn, I'll bet. Sounds
like Dalt's."

"What is the significance of that device?"

"He hates them Amberites, is what it means. Even went
up against them once."

I tasted the wine. Not bad.

The same man, then....

"You know why he hates hem?" I asked.

"I understand they killed his mother," he said. "Had
something to do with border wars. They get real complicated. I don't know the details."

I pried open a tin of meat, broke off some bread and
made myself a sandwich.

"Please go ahead with your story," I said.

"Where was I?"

"The prince got hold of Dalt because he was concerned
about his mother, and he needed more troops in a hurry."

"That's right, and I was picked up for Kashfan service
about that time—foot soldier. The prince and Dalt led us
through dark ways till we came to that place below. Then
we did just what them guys downstairs were doing."

"And what happened?"

He laughed. "Went bad for us at first," he said. "I think it's somehow easy for whoever's in charge down there to control the elements—like that twister you saw a while ago. We got an earthquake and a blizzard and lightning. But we pressed on to the walls anyhow. Saw my brother scalded to death with boiling oil. That's when I decided I'd had enough. I started running and climbed on up here. Nobody chased me, so I waited around and watched. Probably shouldn't have, but I didn't know how things would go. More of the same, I'd figgered. But I was wrong, and it was too late to go back. They'd have whacked off my head or some other valuable parts if I did."

"What happened?"

"I got the impression that the attack forced Jasra's hand. She'd apparently been planning to do away with Sharu Garrul all along and take over the place herself. I think she'd been setting him up, gaining his confidence before she struck. I believe she was a little afraid of the old man. But when her army appeared on the doorstep she had to move, even though she wasn't ready. She took him on in a sorcerous duel while her guard held his men at bay. She won, though I gather she was somewhat injured. Mad as hell, too, at her son—for bringing in an army without her ordering it. Anyway, her guard opened the gates to them, and she took over the Keep. That's what I meant about no army taking the place. That one was an inside job."

"How did you learn all this?"

"Like I said, when deserters head this way I feed 'em and get the news."

"You gave me the impression that there have been other attempts to take the place. These would have had to be after she'd taken over."

He nodded and took another drink of wine.

"Yup. There was apparently a coup back in Kashfa, with both her and her kid away—a noble named Kasman, bother of one of her dead lovers, a fellow named Jasrick. This Kasman took over, and he wanted her and the prince out of the way. Must've attacked this place half a dozen times. Never could get in. Finally resigned himself to a standoff, I think. She sent her son off somewhere later, maybe to raise another army and try to win back her throne. I don't know. That was long ago."

"What about Dalt?"

"They paid him off with some loot from the Keep— there was apparently a lot of good stuff in there—and he took his troops and went back to wherever he hangs out."

I took another sip of wine myself and cut off a piece of the cheese. "How come you've stayed around all these years? It seems like a hard life."

He nodded. "Truth of it is, I don't know the way home. Those were strange trails they brought us in on. I thought I knew where they were, but when I went lookin' I couldn't never find 'em. I suppose I could have just taken off, but then I'd probably get lost more than ever. Besides, I know I can make out here. A few weeks and those outbuildings will be rebuilt and the peasants will move back in, no matter who wins. And they think I'm a holy man, prayin' up here and meditatin'. Any time I wander down that way they come out for a blessin' and give me enough food and drink to hold me for a long while."

"Are you a holy man?" I asked.

"I just pretend," he said. "Makes them happy and keeps me fed. Don't go tellin' that, though."

"Of course not. They wouldn't believe me, anyway."

He laughed again. "You're right."

I got to my feet and walked back along the trail a little way, so that I could see the Keep once again. The ladders were on the ground, and I beheld even more scattered dead. I saw no signs of the struggle within.

"Is the gate open yet?" Dave called.

"No. I don't think the ones who got in were sufficient to the task."

"Is that green and black banner anywhere in sight?"

"I can't see it anywhere."

He rose and came over, carrying both bottles. He passed me mine and we both took a drink. The ground troops began to fall back from the area before the wall.

"Think they're giving up or re-forming for another rush?" he asked me.

"Can't say yet," I told him.

"Whichever it is, there should be a lot of good loot down there tonight. Stick around and you'll have all you can carry."

"I'm curious," I said, "why Dalt would be attacking again, if he's on good terms with the queen and her son."

"I think it's just the son," he said, "and he's gone. The old lady's supposed to be a real bitch. And after all, the guy *is* a mercenary. Maybe Kasman hired him to go after her."

"Maybe she's not even in there," I said, having no idea how this time stream ran, but thinking of my recent encounter with the lady. The image of it, though, caused a strange train of thought. "What's the prince's name, anyway?" I asked.

"Rinaldo," he answered. "He's a big red-haired guy."

"She's his mother!" I said involuntarily.

He laughed. "That's how you get to be a prince," he said. "Have the queen be your mother."

But then, that would mean. . . .

"Brand!" I said. Then, "Brand of Amber."

He nodded. "You've heard the story."

"Not really. Just that much," I replied. "Tell it to me."

"Well, she snared herself an Amberite — the prince called Brand," he said. "Rumor had it they met over some magical operation and it was love at first blood. She wanted to keep him, and I've heard it said they actually were married in a secret ceremony. But he wasn't interested in the throne of Kashfa, though he was the only one she might have been willing to see on it. He traveled a lot, was away for long stretches of time. I've heard it said that he was responsible for the Days of Darkness years ago, and that he died in a great battle between Chaos and Amber at that time, at the hands of his kinsmen."

"Yes," I said, and Dave gave me a strange look, half puzzlement, half scrutiny. "Tell me more about Rinaldo," I said quickly.

"Not much to say," he replied. "She bore him, and I've heard she taught him something of her Arts. He didn't know his father all that well, Brand being away so much. Kind of a wild kid. Ran away any number of times and hung out with a brand of outlaws—"

"Dalt's people?" I asked.

He nodded. "Rode with them, they say—even though his mother'd placed bounties on many of their heads at that time."

"Wait a minute. You say that she really hated these outlaws and mercenaries—"

"'Hate' may be the wrong word. She'd never bothered about them before, but when her son got friendly with them I think she just got mad."

"She thought they were a bad influence?"

"No, I think she didn't like it that he'd run to them and they'd take him in whenever he had a falling out with her."

"Yet you say that she saw Dalt paid off out of the Keep's treasure and allowed him to ride away, after they'd forced her hand against Sharu Garrul."

"Yup. Big argument at the time, too, between Rinaldo and his mom, over just that point. And she finally gave in. That's the way I heard it from a couple of guys who were there. One of the few times the boy actually stood up to her and won, they say. In fact, that's why the guys deserted. She ordered all witnesses to their argument executed, they told me. They were the only ones managed to get away."

"Tough lady."

"Yup."

We walked on back to the area where we'd been seated and ate some more food. The song of the wind rose in pitch and a storm began out at sea. I asked Dave about big dog-like creatures, and he told me that packs of them would probably be feasting on the battle's victims tonight. They were native to the area.

"We divide the spoils," he said. "I want the rations, the wine and any valuables. They just want the dead."

"What good are the valuables to you?" I said.

He looked suddenly apprehensive, as if I were considering the possibility of robbing him.

"Oh, it don't really amount to much. It's just that I've always been a thrifty person," he said, "and I make it sound more important than it is."

"You never can tell," he added.

"That's true," I agreed.

"How'd you get here anyway, Merle?" he asked quickly, as if to get my mind off the subject of his loot.

"Walked," I said.

"That don't sound right. Nobody comes here willingly."

"I didn't know I was coming here. Don't think I'll be staying long either," I said, as I saw him take up the small knife and begin toying with it. "No sense going below and begging after hospitality at a time like this."

"That's true," he remarked.

Was the old coot actually thinking of attacking me, to protect his cache? He could be more than a little mad by now, living up here alone in his stinking cave, pretending to be a saint.

"Would you be interested in returning to Kashfa," I said, "if I could set you on the right trail?"

He gave me a crafty look. "You don't know that much about Kashfa," he said, "or you wouldn't have been asking me all those questions. Now you say you can send me home?"

"I take it you're not interested?"

He sighed. "Not really, not any more. It's too late now. This is my home. I enjoy being a hermit."

I shrugged. "Well, thanks for feeding me, and thanks for all the news." I got to my feet.

"Where you going now?" he asked.

"I think I'll look around some, then head for home." I backed away from that small lunatic glow in his eyes.

He raised the knife, his grip tightened on it. Then he lowered it and cut another piece of cheese.

"Here, you can take some of the cheese with you if you want," he said.

"No, that's okay. Thanks."

"Just trying to save you some money. Have a good trip."

"Right. Take it easy."

I heard his chuckling all the way back to the trail. Then the wind drowned it.

I spent the next several hours reconnoitering. I moved around in the hills. I descended into the steaming, quaking lands. I walked along the seashore. I passed through the rear of the normal-seeming area and crossed the neck of the ice field. In all of this, I stayed as far from the Keep itself as possible. I wanted to fix the place as firmly in mind as I could, so that I could find my way back through Shadow rather than crossing a threshold the hard way. I saw several packs of wild dogs on my journey, but they were more intent upon the battle's corpses than anything that moved.

There were oddly inscribed boundary stones at each to-pographical border, and I found myself wondering whether they were mapmakers' aids or something more. Finally, I wrestled one from the burning land over about fifteen feet into a region of ice and snow. I was knocked down almost immediately by a heavy tremor; I was able to scramble away in time, however, from the opening of a crevice and the spewing of geysers. The hot area claimed that small slice of the cold land in less than half an hour. Fortunately, I moved quickly to get out of the way of any further tur-moil, and I observed the balance of these phenomena from a distance. But there was more to come.

I crouched back among the rocks, having reached the foothills of the range from which I had started by crossing through a section of the volcanic area. There, I rested and watched for a time while that small segment of terrain rearranged itself and the wind smeared smoke and steam across the land. Rocks bounced and rolled; dark carrion birds went out of their way to avoid what had to be some interesting thermals.

Then I beheld a movement which I first assumed to be seismic in origin. The boundary stone I had shifted rose slightly and jogged to the side. A moment later, however, and it was elevated even farther, appearing almost as if it had been levitated slightly above the ground. Then it drifted across the blasted area, moving in a straight line at a uniform speed, until—as nearly as I could judge—it had recovered its earlier position. And there it settled. Moments later the turmoil recommenced, and this time it was a jolting shrug of the ice sheet, jerking back, reclaiming the invaded area.

I called up my Logrus sight, and I was able to make out a dark glow surrounding the stone. This was connected by a long, straight, steady stream of light of the same general hue, extending from a high rear tower of the Keep. Fascinating. I would have given a lot for a view of the interior of that place.

Then, born with a sigh, maturing to a whistle, a whirlwind rose from the disputed area, growing, graying, swaying, to advance suddenly toward me like the swung proboscis of some cloudy, sky-high elephant. I turned and climbed higher, weaving my way amid rocks and around the shoulders of hillsides. The thing pursued, as if there were an intelligence guiding its movements. And the way it hung together while traversing that irregular terrain indicated an artificial nature, which in this place most likely meant magic.

It takes some time to determine an appropriate magical defense, and even more time to bring it into being. Unfortunately, I was only about a minute ahead of the posse, and that margin was probably dwindling.

When I spotted the long narrow crevice beyond the next turning, jagged as a limb of lightning, I paused only an instant to peer into its depth, and then I was descending, my tattered garments lashed about me, the windy tower a rumbling presence at my back. . . .

The way ran deep and so did I, following its jogs, its twistings. The rumble rose to a roar, and I coughed at the cloud of dust that engulfed me. A hailstorm of gravel assailed me. I threw myself flat then, about eight feet below the surface of the land, and covered my head with my arms, for I believed that the thing was about to pass directly above me.

I muttered warding spells as I lay there, despite their

minuscule parrying effect at this distance against such an energy-intensive manifestation.

I did not jump up when the silence came. It could be that the tornado's driver had withdrawn support and collapsed the funnel on seeing that I might be out of reach. It could also be the eye of the storm, with more to come, by and by.

While I did not jump up, I did look up, because I hate to miss educational opportunities.

And there was the face—or, rather, the mask—at the center of the storm, regarding me. It was a projection, of course, larger than life and not fully substantial. The head was cowled; the mask was full and cobalt bright and strongly reminiscent of the sort worn by goalies in ice hockey; there were two vertical breathing slits from which pale smoke emerged—a touch too theatrical for my taste; a lower series of random punctures was designed to give the impression of a sardonically lopsided mouth. A distorted sound of laughter came down to me from it.

"Aren't you overdoing it a bit?" I said, coming up into a crouch and raising the Logrus between us. "For a kid on Halloween, yes. But we're all adults here, aren't we? A simple domino would probably serve—"

"You moved my stone!" it said.

"I've a certain academic interest in such matters," I offered, easing myself into the extensions. "Nothing to get upset about. Is that you, Jasra? I—"

The rumbling began again, softly at first, then building once more.

"I'll make a deal," I said. "You call off the storm, and I'll promise not to move any more markers."

Again, the laughter as the storm sounds rose. "Too late," came the reply. "Too late for you. Unless you're a lot tougher than you look."

What the hell! The battle is not always to the strong, and nice guys tend to win because they're the ones who get to write their memoirs. I'd been fiddling with the Logrus projections against the insubstantiality of the mask until I found the link, the opening leading back to its source. I stabbed through it—a thing on the order of an electrical discharge—at whatever lay behind.

There came a scream. The mask collapsed, the storm collapsed, and I was on my feet and running again. When whatever I'd hit recovered I did not want to be in the same place I had been because that place might be subject to sudden disintegration.

I had a choice of cutting off into Shadow or seeking an even faster path of retreat. If a sorcerer were to tag me as I started shadow-slipping I could be followed. So I dug out my Trumps and shuffled forth Random's. I rounded the next turning of the way then, and I would have had to halt there anyway, I saw, because it narrowed to a width impossible for me to pass. I raised the card and reached with my mind.

There followed contact, almost immediately. But even as the images solidified I felt a probe. I was certain that it was my blue-masked nemesis seeking me once more.

But Random came clear, seated before a drum set, sticks in hand. He set aside the drumsticks and rose.

"It's about time," he said, and he extended his hand.

Even as I reached I felt something rushing toward me. As our fingers touched and I stepped forward, they burst about me like a giant wave.

I passed through into the music room in Amber. Random had opened his mouth to speak again when the cascade of flowers fell upon us.

Brushing violets from his shirtfront, he regarded me. "I'd rather you said it with words," he remarked.

CHAPTER 4

Portrait of the artists, purposes crossed, temperature falling. . . .

Sunny afternoon, and walking through small park following light lunch, us, prolonged silences and monosyllabic responses to conversational sallies indicating all's not well at other end of communication's taut line. Upon bench, seated then, facing flower beds, souls catch up with bodies, words with thoughts. . . .

"Okay, Merle. What's the score?" she asks.

"I don't know what game you're talking about, Julia."

"Don't get cute. All I want's a straight answer."

"What's the question?"

"That place you took me, from the beach, that night. . . . Where was it?"

"It was—sort of a dream."

"Bullshit!" She turns sideways to face me fully, and I must meet those flashing eyes without my face giving anything away. "I've been back there, several times, looking for the way we took. There is no cave. There's nothing! What happened to it? What's going on?"

"Maybe the tide came in and—"

"Merle! What kind of an idiot do you take me for? That walk we took isn't on the maps. Nobody around here's ever heard of anything like those places. It was geographically impossible. The times of day and the seasons kept shifting. The only explanation is supernatural or paranormal—whatever you want to call it. What happened? You owe me an answer and you know it. What happened? Where were you?"

I look away, past my feet, past the flowers.

"I—can't say."

"Why not?"

"I—" What could I say? It was not only that telling her of Shadow would disturb, perhaps destroy, her view of reality. At the heart of my problem lay the realization that it would also require telling her how I knew this, which would mean telling her who I am, where I am from, what I am—and I was afraid to give her this knowledge. I told myself that it would end our relationship as surely as telling her nothing would; and if it must end either way, I would rather we parted without her possessing this knowledge. Later, much later, I was to see this for the rationalization it was; my real reason for denying her the answers she desired was that I was not ready to trust her, or anyone, so close to me as I really am. Had I known her longer, better—another year, say—I might have answered her. I don't know. We never used the word "love," though it must have run through her mind on occasion, as it did through mine. It was, I suppose, that I didn't love her enough to trust her, and then it was too late. So, "I can't tell you," were my words.

"You have some power that you will not share."

"Call it that, then."

"I would do whatever you say, promise whatever you want promised."

"There is a reason, Julia."

She is on her feet, arms akimbo. "And you won't even share that."

I shake my head.

"It must be a lonely world you inhabit, magician, if even those who love you are barred from it."

At that moment it seems she is simply trying her last trick for getting an answer from me. I screw my resolve yet tighter. "I didn't say that."

"You didn't have to. It is your silence that tells me. If you know the road to Hell too, why not head that way? Good-bye!"

"Julia. Don't. . . ."

She chooses not to hear me.

Still life with flowers. . . .

Awakening. Night. Autumn wind beyond my window. Dreams. Blood of life without the body . . . swirling. . . .

I swung my feet out of bed and sat rubbing my eyes, my temples. It had been sunny and afternoon when I'd finished telling Random my story, and he'd sent me to get some shuteye afterward. I was suffering from shadow lag and felt completely turned around at the moment, though I was not certain exactly what the hour might be.

I stretched, got up, repaired myself and donned fresh clothing. I knew that I would not be able to get back to sleep; also, I was feeling hungry. I took a warm cloak with me as I departed my quarters. I felt like going out rather than raiding the larder. I was in the mood for some walking, and I hadn't been outside the palace and into town in—years, I guessed.

I made my way downstairs, then cut through a few chambers and a big hall, connecting up at the rear with a corridor I could have followed all the way from the stair if I'd cared to, but then I'd have missed a couple of tapestries I'd wanted to say hello to: an idyllic sylvan scene, with a couple making out following a picnic lunch; and a hunting scene of dogs and men pursuing a magnificent stag, which looks as if it might yet have a chance of getting away, if it will dare a stupendous leap that lies ahead. . . .

I passed through and made my way up the corridor to a postern, where a bored-looking guard named Jordy suddenly strove to seem attentive when he heard me coming. I stopped to pass the time with him and learned that he didn't get off duty till midnight, which was almost two hours away.

"I'm heading down into town," I said. "Where's a good place to eat this time of night?"

"What've you got a taste for?"

"Seafood," I decided.

"Well, Fiddler's Green—about two thirds of the way down the Main Concourse—is very good for seafood. It's a fancy place . . ."

I shook my head. "I don't want a fancy place," I said.

"The Net's still supposed to be good—down near the corner of the Smiths and Ironmongers Street. It's not real fancy."

"But you wouldn't go there yourself?"

"Used to," he replied. "But a number of the nobles and big merchants discovered it recently. I'd feel kind of uncomfortable there these days. It's gotten sort of clubby."

"Hell! I don't want conversation or atmosphere. I just want some nice fresh fish. Where would you go for the best?"

"Well, it's a long walk. But if you go all the way down to the docks, at the base of the cove, it's a little to the west. . . . But maybe you shouldn't. It's kind of late, and that isn't the best neighborhood after dark."

"Is that by any chance Death Alley?"

"They do sometimes call it that, sir, as bodies are occasionally found there of a morning. Maybe you'd better go to the Net, seeing as you're alone."

"Gérard took me through that area once, during the day. I think I could find my way around it, all right. What's the name of the place?"

"Uh, Bloody Bill's."

"Thanks. I'll say hi to Bill for you."

He shook his head. "Can't. It was renamed after the manner of his demise. His cousin Andy runs it now."

"Oh. What was it called before?"

"Bloody Sam's," he said.

Well, what the hell. I bade him a good night and set out

walking. I took the path to the short stairway down the slope, which led to the walkway through a garden and over to a side gate, where another guard let me out. It was a cool night with the breezed smells of autumn burning down the world about me. I drew it into my lungs and sighed it out again as I headed for the Main Concourse, the distant, almost-forgotten, slow clopping sounds of hoofs on cobbles coming to me like something out of dream or memory. The night was moonless but filled with stars, and the concourse below flanked by globes of phosphorescent liquid set atop high poles, long-tailed mountain moths darting about them.

When I reached the avenue I strolled. A few closed carriages rolled by as I passed along the way. An old man walking a tiny green dragon on a chain leash touched his hat to me as I passed and said, "Good evening." He had seen the direction from which I had come, though I was sure he did not recognize me. My face is not that well-known about town. My spirits loosened a bit after a time, and I felt a spring come into my step.

Random had not been as angry as I'd thought he might. Since Ghostwheel had not been stirring up any trouble, he had not charged me to go after it immediately and try again for a shutdown. He had merely told me to think about it and come up with the best course of action we might pursue. And Flora had been in touch earlier and told him who Luke was—a thing that seemed to have eased his mind somehow, knowing the identity of the enemy. Though I'd asked, he would not tell me what plans he might have formulated for dealing with him. He did allude to the recent dispatch of an agent to Kashfa, though, to obtain certain unspecified information. The thing that seemed to trouble him the most, actually, was the possibility that the outlaw Dalt was still to be numbered among the living.

"Something about that man . . ." Random began.

"What?" I'd asked.

"For one thing, I saw Benedict run him through. That generally tends to terminate a person's career."

"Tough son of a bitch," I said. "Or damn lucky. Or both."

"If he is the same man, he's the son of the Desacratrix. You've heard of her?"

"Deela," I said. "Wasn't that her name? Some sort of religious fanatic? Militant?"

Random nodded. "She caused a lot of trouble out around the periphery of the Golden Circle—mostly near Begma. You ever been there?"

"No."

"Well, Begma's the nearest point on the circle to Kashfa, which is what makes your story particularly interesting. She'd raided a lot in Begma and they couldn't handle her by themselves. They finally reminded us of the protection alliance we have with almost all the Circle kingdoms—and Dad decided to go in personally and teach her a lesson. She'd burned one Unicorn shrine too many. He took a small force, defeated her troops, took her prisoner and hanged a bunch of her men. She escaped, though, and a couple of years later when she was all but forgotten she came back with a fresh force and started the same crap all over. Begma screamed again, but Dad was busy. He sent Bleys in with a large force. There were several inconclusive engagements—they were raiders, not a regular army —but Bleys finally cornered them and wiped them out. She died that day, leading her troops."

"And Dalt's her son?"

"That's the story, and it makes some sense, because he did everything he could to harass us for a long time. He was after revenge, pure and simple, for his mother's death. Finally, he put together a fairly impressive fighting force and tried to raid Amber. Got a lot farther than you'd think, right up to Kolvir. But Benedict was waiting, his pet regiment at his back. Benedict cut them to pieces, and it sure looked as if he'd wounded Dalt mortally. A few of his men were able to carry him off the field, so we never saw the body. But hell! Who cared?"

"And you think he could be the same guy who was Luke's friend when he was a kid—and later?"

"Well, the age is about right and he seems to hail from the same general area. I suppose it's possible."

I mused as I strolled. Jasra hadn't really liked the guy, according to the hermit. So what was his part in things now? Too many unknowns, I decided. It would take knowledge rather than reasoning to answer that one. So let it ride and go enjoy dinner. . . .

I continued on down the concourse. Near to its farther end I heard laughter and saw where some hardy drinkers still occupied a few tables at a sidewalk cafe. One of them was Droppa, but he didn't spot me and I passed on. I did not feel like being amused. I turned onto Weavers Street, which would take me over to where West Vine wound its way up from the harbor district. A tall masked lady in a silver cloak hurried by and into a waiting carriage. She glanced back once and smiled beneath her domino. I was certain that I didn't know her, and I found myself wishing I did. It was a pretty smile. Then a gust of wind brought me the smokesmell of someone's fireplace and rattled a few dead leaves as it went by. I wondered where my father was.

Down along the street then and left on West Vine. . . . Narrower here than the concourse, but still wide; a greater distance between lights, but still sufficiently illuminated for night travelers. A pair of horsemen clopped slowly by, singing a song I did not recognize. Something large and dark passed overhead a bit later, to settle upon a roof across the street. A few scratching noises came from that direction, then silence. I followed a curve to the right, then another to the left, entering what I knew to be a long series of switchbacks. My way grew gradually steeper. A harbor breeze came up at some point a little later, bearing me my first salt sea smells of the evening. A short while afterward—two turns, I believe—and I had a view of the sea itself, far below: bobbing lights on a sparkling, swelling slickness over black, pent by the curving line of bright dots, Harbor Road. To the east the sky was powdered slightly. A hint of horizon appeared at the edge of the world. I thought I caught a glimpse of the distant light of Cabra minutes later, then lost it again with another turning of the way.

A puddle of light like spilled milk pulsed on the street to

my right, outlining a ghostly gridwork of cobbles at its farthest downhill reach; the stippled pole above it might advertise some spectral barbershop; the cracked globe at its top still showed a faint phosphorescence, skull-on-a-stick style, reminding me of a game we used to play as kids back in the Courts. A few lighted footprints proceeded downhill away from it, faint, fainter, gone. I passed on, and across the distance I heard the cries of sea birds. Autumn's smells were submerged in ocean's. The powdered light beyond my left shoulder rose higher above the water, drifted forward across the wrinkled face of the deep. Soon. . . .

My appetite grew as I walked. Ahead, I beheld another dark-cloaked stroller on the other side of the street, a slight glowing at the edges of the boots. I thought of the fish I would soon be eating and hurried, breasting the figure and passing. A cat in a doorway paused at licking her asshole to watch me go by, hind leg held vertical the while. Another horseman passed, this one headed up the hill. I heard the fringes of an argument between a man and a woman from upstairs in one of the darkened buildings. Another turning and the shoulder of the moon came into sight like some magnificent beast surfacing, shrugging droplets from bright bathic grottoes. . . .

Ten minutes later I had reached the port district and found my way over to Harbor Road, its lack of all but occasional globes supplemented by window spillage, a number of buckets of burning pitch and the glow of the now-risen moon. The smells of salt and sea-wrack were more intense here, the road more cluttered with trash, the passersby more colorfully garbed and noisier than any on the concourse, unless you counted Droppa. I made my way to the rear of the cove, where the sounds of the sea came to me more strongly: the rushing, building advances of waves, then their crashing and splashing out beyond the breakwater; the gentler falls and slopping withdrawals nearer at hand; the creaking of ships, the rattling of chains, the bumping of some smaller vessel at pier or moor post. I wondered where the Starburst, my old sailboat, might be now.

I followed the curve of the road over to the western shore of the harbor. A pair of rats chased a black cat across my path as I wandered briefly, checking several sidestreets for the one I sought. The smells of barf as well as solid and liquid human waste mingled with other odors here, and I heard the cries, crashes and thuds of a struggle from somewhere nearby, leading me to believe that I was in the proper neighborhood. From somewhere distant a buoy bell rattled; from somewhere nearby I heard an almost bored-sounding string of curses preceding a pair of sailors who rounded the nearest corner to my right, reeling, staggered on past me, grinning, and broke into song moments later, receding. I advanced and checked the sign on that corner. SEABREEZE LANE, it read.

That was it, the stretch commonly called Death Alley. I turned there. It was just a street like any other. I didn't see any corpses or even collapsed drunks for the first fifty paces, though a man in a doorway tried to sell me a dagger and a mustachioed stock character offered to fix me up with something young and tight. I declined both, and learned from the latter that I wasn't all that far from Bloody Bill's. I walked on. My occasional glances showed me three dark-cloaked figures far to the rear which, I supposed, could be following me; I had seen them back on Harbor Road too. Also, they might not. In that I was not feeling particularly paranoid, I reflected that they could be anybody going anywhere and decided to ignore them. Nothing happened. They kept to themselves, and when I finally located Bloody Bill's and entered they passed on by, crossing the street and going into a small bistro a little farther down along the way.

I turned and regarded Bill's. The bar was to my right, tables to my left, suspicious-looking stains on the floor. A board on the wall suggested I give my order at the bar and say where I was sitting. The day's catch was chalked beneath this.

So I went over and waited, collecting glances, until a heavy-set man with gray and amazingly shaggy brows came over and asked what I wanted. I told him the blue sea

scut and pointed at an empty table to the rear. He nodded
and shouted my order back through a hole in the wall, then
asked me whether I wanted a bottle of Bayle's Piss to go
with it. I did, he got it for me, and a glass, uncorked it and
passed it over. I paid up there, headed back to the table I
had chosen and seated myself with my back to the wall.

Oil flames flickered through dirty chimneys in brackets
all about the place. Three men—two young, one middle-
aged—played cards at the corner table in the front and
passed a bottle. An older man sat alone at the table to my
left, eating. He had a nasty-looking scar running both
above and below his left eye, and there was a long wicked
blade about six inches out of its scabbard resting on the
chair to his right. He, too, had his back to the wall. Men
with musical instruments rested at another table: between
numbers, I guessed. I poured some of the yellow wine into
my glass and took a sip: a distinctive taste I remembered
from across the years. It was okay for quaffing. Baron
Bayle owned a number of vineyards about thirty miles to
the east. He was the official vintner to the Court, and his
red wines were generally excellent. He was less successful
with the whites, though, and often wound up dumping a lot
of second-rate stuff onto the local market. It bore his emblem and a picture of a dog—he liked dogs—so it was
sometimes called Dog Piss and sometimes Bayle's Piss,
depending on who you talked to. Dog lovers sometimes
take offense at the former appellation.

About the time my food arrived I noticed that two young
men near the front of the bar were glancing in my direction
more than occasionally, exchanging a few indistinguishable
words and laughing and smiling a lot. I ignored them and
turned my attention to my meal. A little later the scarred
man at the next table said softly, without leaning or looking
toward me, his lips barely moving, "Free advice. I think
those two guys at the bar noticed you're not wearing a
blade, and they've marked you for trouble."

"Thanks," I said.

Well. . . . I was not overly concerned about my ability to
deal with them, but given a choice I'd rather avoid the

occasion entirely. If all that it required was a visible blade, that was easily remedied.

A moment's meditation and the Logrus danced before me. Shortly thereafter, I was reaching through it in search of the proper weapon—neither too long nor too heavy, properly balanced, with a comfortable grip—with a wide dark belt and scabbard. It took me close to three minutes, partly because I was so fussy about it, I suppose—but hell, if prudence required one, I wanted comfort—and partly because it is harder reaching through Shadow in the vicinity of Amber than it is almost anywhere else.

When it came into my hands I sighed and mopped my brow. Then I brought it up slowly from beneath the table, belt and all, drew it about half a foot from its scabbard, to follow a good example, and placed it on the seat to my right. The two guys at the bar caught the performance and I grinned back at them. They had a quick consultation, and this time they weren't laughing. I poured myself a fresh glass of wine and drank it off at a single draught. Then I returned to my fish, about which Jordy had been right. The food here was very good.

"Neat trick, that," the man at the next table said. "I don't suppose it's an easy one to learn?"

"Nope."

"It figures. Most good things aren't, or everybody'd do 'em. They may still go after you, though, seeing as you're alone. Depends on how much they drink and how reckless they get. You worried?"

"Nope."

"Didn't think so. But they'll hit someone tonight."

"How can you tell?"

He looked at me for the first time and grinned a nasty grin. "They're generic, like wind-up toys. See you around."

He tossed a coin onto the table, stood, buckled on his sword belt, picked up a dark, feathered hat and headed for the door.

"Take care."

I nodded.

" 'Night."

As he passed out of the place the two guys began whispering again, this time glancing after him rather than at me. Some decision reached, they rose and departed quickly. For a moment I was tempted to follow, but something restrained me. A little later, I heard the sounds of a scuffle from up the street. Not too long after that, a figure appeared in the doorway, hovered a moment, then fell forward. It was one of the two drinkers. His throat had been cut.

Andy shook his head and dispatched his waiter to inform the local constabulary. Then he took hold of the body by the heels and dragged it outside, so as not to impede the flow of customers.

Later, when I was ordering another fish, I asked Andy about the occurrence. He smiled grimly.

"It is not good to mess with an emissary of the Crown," he said. "They tend to pick them tough."

"That guy who was sitting next to me works for Random?"

He studied my face, then nodded. "Old John worked for Oberon, too. Whenever he passes through he eats here."

"I wonder what sort of mission he was on?"

He shrugged. "Who knows? But he paid me in Kashfan currency, and I know he ain't from Kashfa."

As I worked on my second platter I pondered that one. Whatever it was that Random had wanted from Kashfa was probably on its way to the castle right now, unless of course it was unavailable. It would almost have to concern Luke and Jasra. I wondered what it was, and of what benefit it might be.

I sat there for a long while after that, thinking, and the place was a lot less noisy than it had been for most of an hour, even when the musicians began a fresh set. Had it been John the guys had been watching all along, with both of us misinterpreting their gazes as directed toward me? Or had they simply decided to go after the first person who left alone? I realized from these reflections that I was beginning to think like an Amberite again—seeking plots everywhere—and I hadn't been back all that long. Something in the atmosphere, I guessed. Probably it was a good thing that my mind was moving along these lines once more, since I was involved in so much already and it seemed an investment in self-preservation.

I finished my glass of wine and left the bottle on the table with a few drinks still in it. It occurred to me that I shouldn't be fogging my senses any further, all things considered. I rose and buckled on my sword belt.

As I passed the bar Andy nodded. "If you run into anyone from the palace," he said softly, "you might mention that I didn't know that was going to happen."

"You knew them?"

"Yeah. Sailors. Their ship came in a couple of days ago. They've been in trouble here before. Blow their pay fast, then look for some more the quick way."

"Do you think they might be professionals at—removing people?"

"Because of John's being what he is, you mean? No. They got caught once too often, mainly for being stupid. Sooner or later they were bound to run into someone who knew what he was doing and end up this way. I don't know anyone who'd hire them for something serious."

"Oh, he got the other one too?"

"Yep. Up the street a way. So you might mention that they just happened to be in the wrong place at the wrong time."

I stared at him and he winked.

"I saw you down here with Gérard, several years ago. I make it a point never to forget a face that might be worth remembering."

I nodded. "Thanks. You serve a good meal."

Outside, it was cooler than it had been earlier. The moon hung higher and the sea was noisier. The street was deserted in my immediate vicinity. Loud music poured from one of the places back toward Harbor Street, with accompanying sounds of laughter. I glanced within as I passed it and saw where a tired-looking woman on a small stage appeared to be giving herself a gynecological examination. From somewhere nearby I heard a sound of breaking glass. A drunk reeled toward me from between two buildings, one hand outstretched. I walked on. The wind sighed amid masts in the harbor, and I found myself wishing Luke were at my side—like in the old days, before things got complicated—someone of my own age and cast of mind to talk to. All my relatives here had too many centuries of cynicism or wisdom for us to see things and feel them in much the same way.

Ten paces later, Frakir pulsed wildly upon my wrist. In that there was no one anywhere near me at that moment, I did not even draw my new blade. I threw myself flat, then rolled toward the shadows to my right. Simultaneous with this, I heard a *thunk* from the side of the building across the street. The first glance I could spare in that direction showed me an arrow protruding from a wall, its height and position such that had I not taken the dive it might well have hit me. Its angle also indicated that I had just cast myself in the direction from which it had been discharged.

I raised myself enough to draw my blade and looked to my right. There were no opened windows or doors in the immediately adjacent building, a darkened place, its front wall only about six feet away now. But there was a gap between it and the buildings on either side, and geometry told me that the arrow had come from the open area ahead of me.

I rolled again, bringing myself up beside the low, roofed porch which ran the full width of the place. I scrambled up onto it before I rose fully. Staying near the wall I advanced, cursing the slowness silence demanded. I was almost near enough to the opening to be able to rush any archer who might step out, before he could release another arrow. The possibility of his circling and catching me from behind did pass through my mind, though, and I flattened myself against the wall, blade extended forward, and cast quick glances behind as I moved. Frakir writhed into my left hand and hung ready.

If I reached the corner and no one emerged I was uncertain what I would do next. The situation seemed to demand a magical offensive. But unless the spells were already hung—and I'd been remiss in this—one can seldom spare the attention it requires in life-and-death situations. I halted. I controlled my breathing. I listened. . . .

He was being careful, but I heard faint sounds of movement from the roof, coming forward. But this did not preclude another, or even several, being around the corner. I had no idea how many persons might be involved in this ambush, though it was beginning to strike me as a little too sophisticated for a simple robbery. In such a case, I doubted there would be only one. And their forces might be split several ways. I held my position, my mind racing. When the attack came, it would be concerted, I was certain of that. I imagined an archer around the corner, arrow nocked, waiting for a signal. The one on the roof would most likely have a blade. I guessed at blades for any others, too. . . .

I pushed aside any questions as to who might be after me and how they had located me here—if it were indeed me, personally, whom they were after. Such considerations made no difference at this point. I would be just as dead were they random thugs seeking my purse as I would be if they were assassins, should they succeed in the present enterprise.

Again. A sound from above. Someone was directly overhead. Any moment now. . . .

With a shuffling noise and a great cry a man leaped from the roof to the street before me. His shout was apparently the signal to the archer, also, for there was immediate movement at the corner of the building, accompanied by the sounds of rapid footfalls from the building's other corner, to my rear.

Before his feet even struck the ground I had cast Frakir at the man from the roof with a command to kill. And I was rushing the archer before he had even rounded the corner completely, my blade already swinging. My cut passed through his bow, his arm and his lower abdomen. On the minus side, there was a man with a drawn blade

right behind him and someone was running toward me
along the porch.

I placed my left foot upon the folding archer's chest and
propelled him backward into the man behind him. I used
the recoiling momentum from the push to spin, my blade
sweeping through a wide, wild parry which I had to adjust
immediately to stop a head cut from the man who had
crossed the porch. As I riposted to his chest and had my
own cut parried I became peripherally aware of the one
from the roof kneeling now in the street and tearing at his
throat, in evidence that Frakir was doing her job.

The man somewhere to my rear made my back feel very
exposed. I had to do something fast or his blade would be
in me within seconds. So. . . .

Rather than riposting, I pretended to stumble, actually
gathering my weight, positioning myself.

He lunged, cutting downward. I sprang to the side and
thrust with a twisting movement of my body. If he were
able to adjust the angle of that cut as I moved I would feel
it in seconds. Dangerous, but I couldn't see any other
choice.

Even as my blade entered his chest I did not know
whether he had connected with me. Not that it mattered
now. Either he had or he hadn't. I had to keep moving until
I stopped or was stopped.

I used my blade like a lever, turning him as I continued
my counterclockwise movement, him at its center, hoping
to position him between that fourth man and myself.

The maneuver was partly successful. It was too late to
interpose my skewered and sagging adversary fully, but in
time at least to cause a small collision between him and the
other. Time enough, I hoped, as the other stumbled to the
side, stepping down from the porch. All I needed do now
was wrench my blade free, and it would be one-on-one.

I yanked at it. . . .

Damn, damn, damn. The thing was wedged into bone
and wouldn't come free. And the other man had regained
his footing. I kept turning the body to keep it between us

while with my left hand I tried to free my most recent
adversary's own blade from his still-clenched right fist.

Ditto the damns. It was locked in a death grip, his
fingers like metal cables about the haft.

The man in the street gave me a nasty smile while moving his blade about, looking for an opening. It was then
that I caught the flash of the blue-stone ring he wore, answering my question as to whether it was me in particular
who had been sought, here, tonight.

I bent my knees as I moved and positioned my hands
low upon the dead man's body.

Situations such as this are, for me, sometimes video-
taped into memory—a total absence of conscious thought
and a great mass of instant perceptions—timeless, yet only
subject to serial review when the mind indulges in later
replay.

There were cries from various places along the street,
from within and without. I could hear people rushing in my
direction. There was blood on the boards all around me,
and I recall cautioning myself not to slip on it. I could see
the archer and his bow, both of them broken, on the ground
past the far edge of the porch. The garroted swordsman
was sprawled in the street, off to the right of the man who
menaced me now. The body I steered and positioned had
become dead weight. To my small relief I saw that no more
attackers had emerged from anywhere to join the final man
I faced. And that man was sidestepping and feinting, getting ready to make his rush.

Okay. Time.

I propelled the corpse toward my attacker with all my
strength an did not wait to observe the result of my action.
The risk I was about to take granted me no time for such
indulgence.

I dove into the street and did a shoulder roll past the
supine figure, who had dropped his blade in trying to use
his hands against Frakir. As I moved I heard the sound of
some impact followed by a grunt from above and somewhere to the rear, indicating that I had been at least partly

on target when I'd pushed the dead man toward the other. How effectively this would serve me still remained to be seen.

My right hand snaked out as I went by, catching the hilt of the fallen man's blade. I rolled to my feet, facing back in the direction from which I had come, extending the blade, crossing my legs and springing backward. . . .

Barely in time. He was upon me with a strong series of attacks, and I backed away fast, parrying wildly. He was still smiling, but my first riposte slowed his advance and my second one stopped it.

I settled and stood my ground. He was strong, but I could see that I was faster. There were people near at hand now, watching us. A few shouts of useless advice reached me. To which of us it was directed, I could not say. It didn't matter, though. He stood for a few moments as I began to press my attack, and then he began to give ground, slowly, and I was sure that I could take him.

I wanted him alive, though, which would make things a little more difficult. That blue-stoned ring flashing and retreating before me held a mystery to which he had the answer, and I needed that answer. Therefore, I had to keep pressing him, to wear him down. . . .

I tried turning him, a little at a time, as subtly as I could. I was hoping to press him into stumbling over the dead man to his rear. It almost worked, too.

When his rear foot fell upon the arm of the sprawled man, he shifted his weight forward to maintain his balance. In one of those instants of inspiration on which one must act immediately without thinking, he turned this movement into a rush, seeing that my blade was out of line in preparation for the heavy rush I was about to give him as he stumbled. Wrong of me to have anticipated that much, I guess.

He beat my blade cross-body with a heavy swing, throwing his own weapon way out of line also and bringing us *corps á corps,* with him turning in the same direction I was facing and unfortunately providing him with the opportunity to drive his left fist into my right kidney with the full force of his momentum.

Immediately, his left foot shot out to trip me, and the impact of the blow as we came together showed me that he was going to succeed. The best thing I could manage was to catch hold of my cloak with my left hand, spinning it out and dragging it back, entangling both our blades as we fell, while I tried hard to turn on the way down, so as to land on top of him. I did not succeed in falling upon him. We came down side by side, still facing each other, and the guard of someone's blade—my own, I think—hit me hard in the ribs on my left side.

My right hand was caught beneath me and my left was still tangled in my cloak. His left was free, though, and high. He clawed at my face with it, and I bit his hand but couldn't hold it. In the meantime, I finally managed to drag my own left hand free and I thrust it into his face. He turned his head away, tried to knee me and hit my hip, then thrust stiff fingers toward my eyes. I caught his wrist and held it. Both of our right hands were still pinned and our weights seemed about equal. So all that I had to do was squeeze.

The bones of his wrist crunched within my grip, and for the first time he cried out. Then I simply pushed him away, rolled into a kneeling position and started to rise, dragging him up along with me. End of the game. I had won.

He slumped suddenly against me. For a moment, I thought it a final trick, and then I saw the blade protruding from his back, the hand of the grim-faced man who had put it there already tightening to pull it out again.

"You son of a bitch!" I cried in English—though I'm sure the meaning came through—and I dropped my burden and drove my fist into the stranger's face, knocking him over backward, his blade remaining in place. "I needed him!"

I caught hold of my former adversary and raised him into the most comfortable position I could manage.

"Who sent you?" I asked him. "How did you find me?"

He grinned weakly and dribbled blood. "No freebies here," he said. "Ask somebody else," and he slumped forward and got blood on my shirtfront.

I drew the ring from his finger and added it to my collection of goddamned blue stones. Then I rose and glared at the man who had stabbed him. Two other figures were helping him to his feet.

"Just what the hell did you do that for?" I asked, advancing upon them.

"I saved your damn life," the man growled.

"The hell you did! You might have just cost me it! I needed that man alive!"

Then the figure to his left spoke, and I recognized the voice. She placed her hand lightly upon the arm I did not even realize I had raised to strike the man again.

"He did it on my orders," she said. "I feared for your life, and I did not understand that you wanted him prisoner."

I stared at her pale proud features within the dark cloak's raised cowl. It was Vinta Bayle, Caine's lady, whom I had last seen at the funeral. She was also the third daughter of the Baron Bayle, to whom Amber owed many a bibulous night.

I realized that I was shaking slightly. I drew a deep breath and caught control of myself.

'I see," I said at last. "Thank you."

"I am sorry," she told me.

I shook my head. "You didn't know. What's done is done. I'm grateful to anybody who tries to help me."

"I can still help you," she said. "I might have misread this one, but I believe you may still be in danger. Let's get away from here."

I nodded. "A moment, please."

I went and retrieved Frakir from about the neck of the other dead man. She disappeared quickly into my left sleeve. The blade I had been using fit my scabbard after a fashion, so I pushed it home and adjusted the belt, which had pulled around toward the rear.

"Let's go," I said to her.

The four of us strode back toward Harbor Street. Interested bystanders got out of our way quickly. Someone was probably already robbing the dead behind us. Things fall apart; the center cannot hold. But what the hell, it's home.

CHAPTER 5

Walking, with the Lady Vinta and two servingmen of the House of Bayle, my side still hurting from its encounter with a sword hilt, beneath a moonbright, starbright sky, through a sea mist, away from Death Alley. Lucky, actually, that a bump on the side was all I acquired in my engagement with those who would do me harm. How they had located me so quickly upon my return, I could not say. But it seemed as if Vinta might have some idea about this, and I was inclined to trust her, both because I knew her somewhat and because she had lost her man, my Uncle Caine, to my former friend Luke, from whose party anything involving a blue stone seemed to have its origin.

When we turned onto a seaward side way off Harbor Street, I asked her what she had in mind.

"I thought we were heading for Vine," I said.

"You know you are in danger," she stated.

"I guess that's sort of obvious."

"I could take you to my father's place up in town," she said, "or we could escort you back to the palace, but someone knows you are here and it didn't take long to reach you."

"True."

"We have a boat moored down this way. We can sail along the coast and reach my father's country place by morning. You will have disappeared. Anyone seeking you in Amber will be foiled."

"You don't think I'd be safe back in the palace?"

"Perhaps," she said. "But your whereabouts may be known locally. Come with me and this won't be the case."

"I'll be gone and Random will learn from one of the guards that I was heading for Death Alley. This will cause considerable consternation and a huge brouhaha."

"You can reach him by Trump tomorrow and tell him that you're in the country—if you have your cards with you."

"True. How did you know where to find me this evening? You can't persuade me that we met by coincidence."

"No, we followed you. We were in the place across the way from Bill's."

"You anticipated tonight's happenings?"

"I saw the possibility. If I'd known everything, of course I'd have prevented it."

"What's going on? What do you know about all of this, and what's your part in it?"

She laughed, and I realized it was the first time I had ever heard her do it. It was not the cold, mocking thing I would have guessed at from Caine's lady.

"I want to sail while the tide is high," she said, "and you want a story that will take all night. Which will it be, Merlin? Security or satisfaction?"

"I'd like both, but I'll take them in order."

"Okay," she said, then turned to the smaller of the two men, the one I had hit. "Jarl, go home. In the morning, tell my father that I decided to go back to Arbor House. Tell him it was a nice night and I wanted to sail, so I took the boat. Don't mention Merlin."

The man touched his cap to her. "Very good, m'lady."

He turned and headed back along the way we had come.

"Come on," she said to me then, and she and the big fellow—whose name I later learned was Drew—led me

down among the piers to where a long sleek sailboat was
tied up. "Do much sailing?" she asked me.

"Used to," I said.

"Good enough. You can give us a hand."

Which I did. We didn't talk much except for business
while we were getting unbuttoned and rigged and casting
off. Drew steered and we worked the sails. Later, we were
able to take turns for long spells. The wind wasn't tricky.
In fact, it was just about perfect. We slid away, rounded the
breakwater and made it out without any problems. Having
stowed our cloaks, I saw that she wore dark trousers and a
heavy shirt. Very practical, as if she'd planned for something like this ahead of time. The belt she stowed bore a
real, full-length blade, not some jeweled dagger. And just
from watching the way she moved, I'd a feeling she might
be able to use the thing pretty well. Also, she reminded me
of someone I couldn't quite place. It was more a matter of
mannerisms of gesture and voice than it was of appearance.
Not that it mattered. I had more important things to think
about as soon as we settled into routine and I had a few
moments to stare across the dark waters and do some quick
reviewing.

I was familiar with the general facts of her life, and I
had encountered her a number of times at social gatherings.
I knew she knew that I was Corwin's son and that I had
been born and raised in the Courts of Chaos, being half of
that bloodline which was linked anciently with Amber's
own. In our conversation the last time we met, it became
apparent that she was aware that I had been off in Shadow
for some years, going native and trying to pick up something of an education. Presumably, Uncle Caine had not
wanted her ignorant of family matters—which led me to
wonder how deeply their relationship might have run. I'd
heard that they had been together for several years. So I
wondered exactly how much she knew about me. I felt
relatively safe with her, but I had to decide how much I
was willing to tell her in exchange for the information she
obviously possessed concerning those who were after me
locally. This, because I had a feeling it would probably be a

trade-off. Other than doing a favor for a member of the family, which generally comes in handy, there was no special reason for her having an interest in me personally. Her motivation in the whole matter pretty much had to be a desire for revenge, so far as I could see, for Caine's killing. With this in mind, I was willing to deal. It is always good to have an ally. But I had to decide how much I was willing to give her of the big picture. Did I want her messing around in the entire complex of events that surrounded me? I doubted it, even as I wondered how much she would be asking. Most likely she just wanted to be in on the kill, whatever that might be. When I glanced over to where moonlight accentuated the planes of her angular face, it was not difficult to superimpose a mask of Nemesis upon those features.

Out from shore, riding the sea breeze east, passing the great rock of Kolvir, the lights of Amber like jewels in her hair, I was taken again by an earlier feeling of affection. Though I had grown up in darkness and exotic lighting amid the non-Euclidean paradoxes of the Courts, where beauty was formed of more surreal elements, I felt more and more drawn to Amber every time I visited her, until at last I realized she was a part of me, until I began to think of her, too, as home. I did not want Luke storming her slopes with riflemen, or Dalt performing commando raids in her vicinity. I knew that I would be willing to fight them to protect her.

Back on the beach, near the place where Caine had been laid to rest, I thought I saw a flash of prancing whiteness, moving slowly, then quickly, then vanishing within some cleft of the slope. I would have said it was a Unicorn, but with the distance and the darkness and the quickness of it all, I could never be certain.

We picked up a perfect wind a little later, for which I was grateful. I was tired, despite my day-long slumber. My escape from the crystal cave, my encounter with the Dweller, and the pursuit by the whirlwind and its masked master all flowed together in my mind as the nearly continuous action that they were. And now the postadrenal reaction from my latest activity was settling in. I wanted nothing more than to listen to the lapping of the waves while I watched the black and craggy shoreline slide by to port or turned to regard the flickering sea to starboard. I did not want to think, I did not want to move. . . .

A pale hand upon my arm.

"You're tired," I heard her say.

"I guess so," I heard myself say.

"Here's your cloak. Why don't you put it on and rest? We're holding steady. The two of us can manage easily now. We don't need you."

I nodded as I drew it about me. "I'll take you up on that. Thanks."

"Are you hungry or thirsty?"

"No. I had a big meal back in town."

Her hand remained on my arm. I looked up at her. She was smiling. It was the first time I had seen her smile. With the fingertips of her other hand she touched the bloodstain on my shirtfront.

"Don't worry. I'll take care of you," she said.

I smiled back at her because it seemed she wanted me to. She squeezed my shoulder and left me then, and I stared after her and wondered whether there were some element I had omitted from my earlier equation concerning her. But I was too tired now to solve for a new unknown. My thinking machinery was slowing, slowing. . . .

Back braced against the port gunwale, rocked gently by the swells, I let my head nod. Through half-closed eyes I saw the dark blot she had indicated upon my white shirtfront. Blood. Yes, blood. . . .

"First blood!" Despil had cried. "Which is sufficient! Have you satisfaction?"

"No!" Jurt had shouted. "I barely scratched him!" and he spun on his stone and waved the triple claws of his *trisp* in my direction as he prepared to have at me again.

The blood oozed from the incision in my left forearm and formed itself into beads which rose into the air and drifted away from me like a handful of scattered rubies. I

raised my *fandon* into a high guard position and lowered
my *trisp*, which I held far out to the right and angled forward. I bent my left knee and rotated my stone 90 degrees
on our mutual axis. Jurt corrected his own position immediately and dropped a half-dozen feet. I turned another 90
degrees, so that each of us seemed to be hanging upside
down in relation to the other.

"Bastard son of Amber!" he cried, and the triple lances
of light raked toward me from his weapon, to be shattered
into bright, mothlike fragments by the sweep of my *fandon,* to fall, swirling, downward into the Abyss of Chaos
above which we rode.

"Up yours," I replied, and squeezed the haft of my *trisp,*
triggering the pulsed beams from its three hair-fine blades.
I extended my arm above my head as I did so, slashing at
his shins.

He swept the beams away with his *fandon,* at almost the
full extent of their eight-foot effective range. There is
about a three-second recharge pause on a *trisliver,* but I
feinted a dead cut toward his face, before which he raised
fand reflexively, and I triggered the *trisp* for a swirl cut at
his knees. He broke the one-second pulse in low *fand,* triggered a thrust at my face and spun over backward through a
full 360, counting on the recharge time to save his back
and coming up, *fandon* high, to cut at my shoulder.

But I was gone, circling him, dropping and rotating
erect. I cut at his own exposed shoulder but was out of
range. Despil, on his beachball-sized stone, was circling
also, far to my right, while my own second—Mandor—
high above, was dropping quickly. We clung to our small
stones with shapeshifted feet, there on an outer current of
Chaos, drifting, as at the whirlpool's rim. Jurt rotated to
follow me, keeping his left forearm—to which the *fandon*
is attached, elbow and wrist—horizontal, and executing a
slow circular movement with it. Its three-foot length of
filmy mesh, *mord*-weighted at the bottom, glittered in the
balefire glow, which occurred at random intervals from
many directions. He held his *trisp* in middle attack position, and he showed his teeth but was not smiling as I

moved and he moved at opposite ends of the diameter of a ten-foot circle which we described over and over, looking for an opening.

I tilted the plane of my orbit and he adjusted his own immediately to keep me company. I did it again, and so did he. Then I did the dive—90 degrees forward, *fandon* raised and extended—and I turned my wrist and dropped my elbow, angling my raking cut upward beneath his guard.

He cursed and cut, but I scattered his light, and three dark lines appeared upon his left thigh. The *trisliver* only cuts to a depth of about three quarters of an inch through flesh, which is why the throat, eyes, temples, inner wrists and femoral arteries are particularly favored targets in a serious encounter. Still, enough cuts anywhere and you eventually wave good-bye to your opponent as he spins downward in a swarm of red rubbles into that place from whence no traveler returns.

"Blood!" Mandor cried, as the beads formed upon Jurt's leg and drifted. "Is there satisfaction, gentlemen?"

"I'm satisfied," I answered.

"I'm not!" Jurt replied, turning to face me as I drifted to his left and rotated to my right. "Ask me again after I've cut his throat!"

Jurt had hated me from sometime before he had learned to walk, for reasons entirely his own. While I did not hate Jurt, liking him was totally beyond my ability. I had always gotten along reasonably well with Despil, though he tended to take Jurt's side more often than my own. But that was understandable. They were full brothers, and Jurt was the baby.

Jurt's *trisp* flashed and I broke the light and riposted. He scattered my beams and spun off to the side. I followed. Our *trisps* flared simultaneously, and the air between us was filled with flakes of brilliance as both attacks were shattered. I struck again, this time low, as soon as I had recharge. His came in high, and again both attacks died in *fand*. We drifted nearer.

"Jurt," I said, "if either of us kills the other, the survivor will be outcast. Call it off."

"It will be worth it," he said. "Don't you think I've thought about it?"

Then he slashed an attack at my face. I raised both arms reflexively, *fandon* and *trisp*, and triggered an attack as shattered light showered before me. I heard him scream.

When I lowered my *fandon* to eye level I saw that he was bent forward, and his *trisp* was drifting away. So was his left ear, trailing a red filament that quickly beaded itself and broke apart. A flap of scalp had also come loose, and he was trying to press it back into place.

Mandor and Despil were already spiraling in.

"We declare the duel ended!" they were shouting, and I twisted the head of my *trisp* into a safety-lock position.

"How bad is it?" Despil asked me.

"I don't know."

Jurt let him close enough to check, and a little later Despil said, "He'll be all right. But Mother is going to be mad."

I nodded. "It was his idea," I said.

"I know. Come on. Let's get out of here."

He helped Jurt steer toward an outcropping of the Rim, *fandon* trailing like a broken wing. I lingered behind. Sawall's son Mandor, my stepbrother, put his hand on my shoulder.

"You didn't even mean him that much," he said. "I know."

I nodded and bit my lip. Despil had been right about the Lady Dara, our mother, though. She favored Jurt, and somehow he'd have her believing this whole thing was my fault. I sometimes felt she liked both of her sons by Sawall, the old Rim Duke she'd finally married after giving up on Dad, better than me. I'd once overheard it said that I reminded her of my father, whom I'd been told I resembled more than a little. I wondered again about Amber and about other places, out in Shadow, and felt my customary twinge of fear as this recalled to me the writhing Logrus, which I knew to be my ticket to other lands. I knew that I was going to try it sooner than I had originally intended.

"Let's go see Suhuy," I said to Mandor, as we rose up out of the Abyss together. "There are more things I want to ask him."

When I finally went off to college I did not spend a lot of time writing home.

"... home," Vinta was saying, "pretty soon now. Have a drink of water," and she passed me a flask.

I took several long swallows and handed it back. "Thanks."

I stretched my cramped muscles and breathed the cold sea air. I looked for the moon and it was way back behind my shoulder.

"You were really out," she said.

"Do I talk in my sleep?"

"No."

"Good."

"Bad dreams?"

I shrugged. "Could be worse."

"Maybe you made a little noise, right before I woke you."

"Oh."

Far ahead I saw a small light at the end of a dark promontory. She gestured toward it.

"When we've passed the point," she said, "we will come into sight of the harbor at Baylesport. We'll find breakfast there, and horses."

"How far is it from Arbor House?"

"About a league," she replied. "An easy ride."

She stayed by me in silence for a while, watching the coastline and the sea. It was the first time we had simply sat together, my hands unoccupied and my mind free. And my sorcerer's sense was stirred in that interval. I felt as if I were in the presence of magic. Not some simple spell or the aura of some charmed object she might be bearing, but something very subtle. I summoned my vision and turned it upon her. There was nothing immediately obvious, but prudence suggested I check further. I extended my inquiry through the Logrus. . . .

"Please don't do that," she said.

I had just committed a faux pas. It is generally considered somewhat gauche to probe a fellow practitioner in such a fashion.

"I'm sorry," I said. "I didn't realize you were a student of the Art."

"I am not," she answered, "but I am sensitive to its operations."

"In that case, you would probably make a good one."

"My interests lie elsewhere," she said.

"I thought perhaps someone had laid a spell upon you," I stated. "I was only trying to—"

"Whatever you saw," she said, "belongs. Let it be."

"As you would. Sorry."

She must have known I couldn't let it rest at that, though, when unknown magic represents possible danger. So she went on, "It is nothing that can do you harm, I assure you. Quite the contrary."

I waited, but she did not have anything further to say on the matter. So I had to let it drop, for the moment. I shifted my gaze back to the lighthouse. What was I getting into with her, anyhow? How had she even known that I was back in town, let alone that I would visit Death Alley when I did? She must have known that the question would occur to me, and if there was to be good faith on both our parts she should be willing to explain it.

I turned back toward her, and she was smiling again.

"The wind changes in the lee of the light," she said, and she rose. "Excuse me. I've work to do."

"May I give you a hand?"

"In a bit. I'll call you when I need you."

I watched her move away, and as I did I had the eerie feeling that she was watching me also, no matter where she was looking. I realized, too, that this feeling had been with me for some time, like the sea.

* * *

By the time we had docked and put everything in order and headed up a hill along a wide cobbled way toward an inn with smoke snaking from its chimney, the sky was growing pale in the east. After a hearty breakfast, morning's light lay full upon the world. We walked then to the livery stable where three quiet mounts were obtained for the ride to her father's estate.

It was one of those clear crisp autumn days which become rarer and dearer as the year winds down. I finally felt somewhat rested, and the inn had had coffee—which is not that common in Amber, outside the palace—and I enjoy my morning cup. It was good to move through the countryside at a leisurely pace and to smell the land, to watch the moisture fade from sparkling fields and turning leaves, to feel the wind, to hear and watch a flock of birds southbound for the Isles of the Sun. We rode in silence, and nothing happened to break my mood. Memories of sorrow, betrayal, suffering and violence are strong but they do fade, whereas interludes such as this, when I close my eyes and regard the calendar of my days, somehow outlast them, as I see myself riding with Vinta Bayle under morning skies where the houses and fences are stone and stray seabirds call, there in the wine country to the east of Amber, and the scythe of Time has no power in this corner of the heart.

When we arrived at Arbor House we gave the horses into the care of Bayle's grooms, who would see to their eventual return to town. Drew departed for his own quarters then, and I walked with Vinta to the huge hilltop manor house. It commanded far views of rocky valleys and hillsides where the grapes were grown. A great number of dogs approached and tried to be friendly as we made our way to the house, and once we had entered their voices still reached us on occasion. Wood and wrought iron, gray flagged floors, high beamed ceilings, clerestory windows, family portraits, a couple of small tapestries of salmon, brown, ivory and blue, a collection of old weapons showing a few touches of oxidation, soot smudges on the gray stone about the hearth. . . . We passed through the big front hall and up a stair.

"Take this room," she said, opening a darkwood door, and I nodded as I entered and looked about. It was spacious, with big windows looking out over the valley to the south. Most of the servants were at the Baron's place in town for the season. "There is a bath in the next room," she told me, indicating a door to my left.

"Great. Thanks. Just what I need."

"So repair yourself as you would." She crossed to the window and looked downward. "I'll meet you on that terrace in about an hour, if that is agreeable."

I went over and looked down upon a large flagged area, well shaded by ancient trees—their leaves now yellow, red and brown, many of them dotting the patio—the place bordered by flower beds, vacant now, a number of tables and chairs arranged upon it, a collection of potted shrubs well disposed among them.

"Fine."

She turned toward me. "Is there anything special you would like?"

"If there is any coffee about, I wouldn't mind another cup or two when I meet you out there."

"I'll see what I can do."

She smiled and seemed to sway slightly toward me for a moment. It almost seemed in that instant as if she wanted me to embrace her. But if she did not, it could be slightly awkward. And under the circumstances I wanted no familiarity with her anyway, having no idea as to the sort of game she was playing. So I returned her smile, reached out and squeezed her arm, said, "Thank you," and stepped away. "I guess I'll see about that bath now."

I saw her to the door and led her out.

It was good to get my boots off. It was far better to soak, for a long, warm time.

Later, in fresh-conjured attire, I made my way downstairs and located a side door that led off the kitchen onto the patio. Vinta, also scrubbed and refitted, in brown rid-

ing pants and a loose tan blouse, sat beside a table at the
east end of the patio. Two places were set upon it, and I
saw a coffeepot and a tray of fruit and cheeses. I crossed
over, leaves crunching beneath my feet, and sat down.

"Did you find everything to your satisfaction?" she
asked me.

"Entirely," I replied.

"And you've notified Amber of your whereabouts?"

I nodded. Random had been a bit irritated at my taking
off without letting him know, but then he had never told me
not to. He was less irritated, however, when he learned that
I hadn't gone all that far, and he even acknowledged finally
that perhaps I had done a prudent thing in disappearing
following such a peculiar attack. "Keep your eyes open and
keep me posted," were his final words.

"Good. Coffee?"

"Please."

She poured and gestured toward the tray. I took an apple
and took a bite.

"Things have begun happening," she said ambiguously,
as she filled her own cup.

"I can't deny it," I acknowledged.

"And your troubles have been manifold."

"True."

She took a sip of coffee. "Would you care to tell me
about them?" she finally said.

"They're a little too manifold," I replied. "You said
something last night about your story being a long one,
too."

She smiled faintly. "You must feel you have no reason to
trust me more than necessary at this point," she said. "I can
see that. Why trust anyone you don't have to when something dangerous is afoot, something you do not completely
understand? Right?"

"It does strike me as a sound policy."

"Yet I assure you that your welfare is of the highest
concern to me."

"Do you think I may represent a means of getting at
Caine's killer?"

"Yes," she said, "and insofar as they may become your killers I would like to get at them."

"Are you trying to tell me that revenge is not your main objective?"

"That's right. I would rather protect the living than avenge the dead."

"But that part becomes academic if it's the same individual in both cases. Do you think it is?"

"I am not certain," she said, "that it was Luke who sent those men after you last night."

I placed my apple beside my cup and took a long drink of coffee. "Luke?" I said. "Luke who? What do you know of any Luke?"

"Lucas Raynard," she said steadily, "who trained a band of mercenaries in the Pecos Wilderness in northern New Mexico, issued them supplies of a special ammunition that will detonate in Amber, and sent them all home with it to await his orders to muster and be transported here—to attempt something your father once tried years ago."

"Holy shit!" I said.

That *would* explain a lot—like Luke's showing up in fatigues back at the Hilton in Santa Fe, with his story about liking to hike around in the Pecos, with that round of peculiar ammunition I'd found in his pocket; and all the other trips he'd been making there—more, actually, than seemed absolutely necessary on his sales route. . . . That angle had never occurred to me, but it made a lot of sense in light of everything I'd since learned.

"Okay," I acknowledged, "I guess you know Luke Raynard. Mind telling me how you came by this?"

"Yes."

"Yes?"

"Yes, I mind. I'm afraid I'm going to have to play this game your way and trade you information a piece at a time. Now that I think of it, it will probably make me feel more comfortable too. How does that sound to you?"

"Either one of us can call it quits at any time?"

"Which stops the trading, unless we can negotiate it."

"All right."

"So you owe me one. You just returned to Amber the other day. Where had you been?"

I sighed and took another bite of the apple. "You're fishing," I said finally. "That's a big question. I've been to a lot of places. It all depends on how far back you want to go."

"Let's take it from Meg Devlin's apartment to yesterday," she said.

I choked on a piece of apple. "Okay, you've made the point—you have some damn good sources of information," I observed. "But it has to be Fiona for that one. You're in league with her some way, aren't you?"

"It's not your turn for a question," she said. "You haven't answered mine yet."

"Okay, Fi and I came back to Amber after I left Meg's place. The next day Random sent me on a mission, to turn off a machine I'd built called Ghostwheel. I failed in this but I ran into Luke along the way. He actually helped me out of a tight spot. Then, following a misunderstanding with my creation, I used a strange Trump to take both Luke and myself to safety. Luke subsequently imprisoned me in a crystal cave—"

"Aha!" she said.

"I should stop here?"

"No, go on."

"I was a prisoner for a month or so, though it amounted to only a few days, Amber time. I was released by a couple of fellows working for a lady named Jasra, had an altercation with them and with the lady herself and trumped out to San Francisco, to Flora's place. There, I revisited an apartment where a murder had occurred—"

"Julia's place?"

"Yes. In it, I discovered a magical gateway which I was able to force open. I passed through it to a place called the Keep of the Four Worlds. A battle was in progress there, the attackers probably being led by a fellow named Dalt, of some small notoriety hereabouts at one time. Later, I was pursued by a magical whirlwind and called names by a masked wizard. I trumped out and came home—yesterday."

"And that's everything?"

"In capsule form, yes."

"Are you leaving out anything?"

"Sure. For instance, there was a Dweller on the threshold of the gateway, but I was able to get by."

"No, that's part of the package. Anything else?"

"Mm. Yes, there were two peculiar communications, ending in flowers."

"Tell me about them."

So I did.

She shook her head when I'd finished. "You've got me there," she said.

I finished my coffee and the apple. She refilled my cup.

"Now it's my turn," I said. "What did you mean by that 'Aha!' when I mentioned the crystal cave?"

"It was blue crystal, wasn't it? And it blocked your powers."

"How'd you know?"

"It was the color of the stone in the ring you took from that man last night."

"Yes."

She got to her feet and moved around the table, stood a moment, then pointed to the vicinity of my left hip.

"Would you empty that pocket onto the table, please?"

I smiled. "Sure. How'd you know?"

She didn't answer that one, but then it was a different question. I removed the assortment of blue stones from my pocket—the chips from the cave, the carved button I'd snatched, the ring—and placed them upon the table.

She picked up the button, studied it, then nodded.

"Yes, that's one also," she stated.

"One what?"

She ignored the query and dipped her right forefinger into a bit of spilled coffee within her saucer. She then used it to trace three circles around the massed stones, widdershins. Then she nodded again and returned to her seat. I'd summoned the vision in time to see her build a cage of force about them. Now, as I continued to watch, it seemed as if they were exhaling faint wisps of blue smoke that remained within the circle.

"I thought you said you weren't a sorcerer."

"I'm not," she replied.

"I'll save the question. But continue answering the last one. What is the significance of the blue stones?"

"They have an affinity for the cave, and for each other," she told me. "A person with very little training could hold one of them and simply begin walking, following the slight psychic tugging. It would eventually lead him to the cave."

"Through Shadow, you mean?"

"Yes."

"Intriguing, but I fail to see any great value to it."

"But that is not all. Ignore the pull of the cave, and you will become aware of secondary tuggings. Learn to distinguish the signature of the proper stone, and you can follow its bearer anywhere."

"That does sound a little more useful. Do you think that's how those guys found me last night, because I had a pocket full of the things?"

"Probably, from a practical standpoint, they helped. Actually though, in your case, they should not even have been necessary at this point."

"Why not?"

"They have an additional effect. Anyone who has one in his possession for a time becomes attuned to the thing. Throw it away and the attunement remains. You can still be tracked then, just as if you had retained the stone. You would possess a signature of your own."

"You mean that even now, without them, I'm marked?"

"Yes."

"How long does it take to wear off?"

"I am not certain that it ever does."

"There must be some means of deattunement."

"I do not know for certain, but I can think of a couple of things that would probably do it."

"Name them."

"Walking the Pattern of Amber or negotiating the

Logrus of Chaos. They seem almost to break a person apart and do a reassemblement into a purer form. They have been known to purge many strange conditions. As I recall, it was the Pattern that restored your father's memory."

"Yes—and I won't even ask you how you know about the Logrus—you may well be right. As with so much else in life, it seems enough of a pain in the ass to be good for me. So, you think they could be zeroing in on me right now, with or without the stones?"

"Yes."

"How do you know all this?" I asked.

"I can sense it—and that's an extra question. But I'll give you a free one in the interests of expedition."

"Thanks. I guess it's your turn now."

"Julia was seeing an occulist named Victor Melman before she died. Do you know why?"

"She was studying with him, looking for some sort of development—at least, that's what I was told by a guy who knew her at the time. This was after we broke up."

"That is not exactly what I meant," she said. "Do you know why she desired this development?"

"Sounds like an extra question to me, but maybe I owe you one. The fellow I'd spoken with told me that I had scared her, that I'd given her to believe that I possessed unusual abilities, and that she was looking for some of her own in self-defense."

"Finish it," she said.

"What do you mean?"

"That's not a complete answer. *Did* you actually give her cause to believe that and to be afraid of you?"

"Well, I guess I did. Now my question: How could you possibly know anything about Julia in the first place?"

"I was there," she answered. "I knew her."

"Go ahead."

"That's it. Now it's my turn."

"That's hardly complete."

"But it's all you're getting on that one. Take it or leave it."

"According to our agreement I can call it quits over that."

"True. Will you?"

"What do you want to know next?"

"Did Julia develop the abilities she sought?"

"I told you that we'd stopped seeing each other before she got involved in that sort of thing. So I have no way of knowing."

"You located the portal in her apartment from which the beast that slew her had presumably emerged. Two questions now—not for you to answer for me, just for you to think over: Why would anyone want her dead in the first place? And does it not seem a very peculiar way to have gone about it? I can think of a lot simpler ways of disposing of a person."

"You're right," I agreed. "A weapon is a hell of a lot easier to manage than magic any day. As for why, I can only speculate. I had assumed it was a trap for me, and that she had been sacrificed as part of the package—my annual April thirtieth present. Do you know about them, too?"

"Let's save that business for later. You are obviously aware that sorcerers have styles, the same as painters, writers, musicians. When you succeeded in locating that gateway in Julia's apartment, was there anything about it which we might refer to as the author's signature?"

"Nothing special that I can recall. Of course, I was in a hurry to force it. I wasn't there to admire the aesthetics of the thing. But no, I can't associate it with anyone with whose work I am familiar. What are you getting at?"

"I just wondered whether it were possible that she might have developed some abilities of her own along these lines, and in the course of things opened that gateway herself and suffered those consequences."

"Preposterous!"

"All right. I am just trying to turn up some reasons. I take it then that you never saw any indication that she might possess latent abilities for sorcery?"

"No, I can't recall any instances."

I finished my coffee, poured a refill.

"If you don't think Luke is after me now, why not?" I asked her then.

"He set up some apparent accidents for you, years ago."

"Yes. He admitted that recently. He also told me that he quit doing it after the first few times."

"That is correct."

"You know, it's maddening—not knowing what you know and what you do not."

"That is why we're talking, isn't it? It was your idea to go about it this way."

"It was not! You suggested this trade-off!"

"This morning, yes. But the idea was originally yours, some time ago. I am thinking of a certain telephone conversation, at Mr. Roth's place—"

"You? That disguised voice on the phone? How could that be?"

"Would you rather hear about that or about Luke?"

"That! No, Luke! Both, damn it!"

"So it would seem there is a certain wisdom in keeping to the format we've agreed upon. There is much to be said for orderliness."

"Okay, you've made another point. Go on about Luke."

"It seemed to me, as an observer, that he quit that business as soon as he got to know you better."

"You mean back about the time we became friendly—that wasn't just an act?"

"I couldn't tell for sure then—and he certainly countenanced the years of attacks on you—but I believe that he actually sabotaged some of them."

"Who was behind them after he quit?"

"A red-haired lady with whom he seemed to be associated."

"Jasra?"

"Yes, that was her name—and I still don't know as much about her as I'd like to. Do you have anything there?"

"I think I'll save that for a big one," I said.

For the first time, she directed a narrow-eyed, teeth-clenched expression toward me.

"Can't you see that I'm trying to help you, Merlin?"

"Really, what I see is that you want information I have," I said, "and that's okay. I'm willing to deal because you seem to know things I want, too. But I've got to admit that your reasons are murky to me. How the hell did you get to Berkeley? What were you doing calling me at Bill's place? What is this power of yours you say isn't sorcery? How—"

"That's three questions," she said, "and the beginning of a fourth. Would you prefer to write them all out, and have me do the same for you? Then we can both go off to our rooms and decide which ones we want to answer?"

"No," I replied. "I'm willing to play the game. But you are aware of my reason for wanting to know these things. It's a matter of self-preservation to me. I thought at first that you wanted information that would help you to nail the man who killed Caine. But you said no, and you didn't give me anything to put in its place."

"I did, too! I want to protect you!"

"I appreciate the sentiment. But why? When it comes down to it, you hardly know me."

"Nevertheless, that is my reason and I don't feel like going behind it. Take it or leave it."

I got to my feet and began pacing the patio. I didn't like the thought of giving away information that could be vital to my security, and ultimately that of Amber—though I had to admit I was getting a pretty good return for what I'd given. Her stuff did sound right. For that matter, the Bayles had a long history of loyalty to the Crown, for whatever that was worth. The thing that bothered me the most, I decided, was her insistence that it was not actually revenge that she was after. Apart from this being a very un-Amberlike attitude, if she were any judge at all as to what would go over with me she need but have agreed that blood was what she wanted in order to make her concern intelligible. I would have bought it without looking any further. And what did she offer in its place? Airy nothings and classified motives. . . .

Which could well mean she was telling the truth. Disdaining the use of a workable lie and offering something more cumbersome in its place would seem the mark of genuine honesty. And she did, apparently, have more answers that I wanted—

I heard a small rattling sound from the table. I thought at first that she might be drumming on it with her fingertips as a sign of her irritation with me. But when I glanced back I saw that she was sitting perfectly still, not even looking at me.

I drew nearer, seeking the source. The ring, the pieces of blue stone and even the button were jiggling about on the tabletop, as of their own accord.

"Something you're doing?" I asked.

"No," she replied.

The stone in the ring cracked and fell out of its setting.

"What, then?"

"I broke a link," she said. "I believe something may be trying to reestablish it and failing."

"Even so, if I'm still attuned they don't need them in order to locate me, do they?"

"There may be more than one party involved," she observed. "I think I should have a servant ride back to town and throw the things into the ocean. If someone wished to follow them there, fine."

"The chips should just lead back to the cave, and the ring to the dead man," I said. "But I'm not ready to throw the button away."

"Why not? It represents a big unknown."

"Exactly. But these things would have to work both ways, wouldn't they? That would mean that I could learn to use the button to find my way to the flower thrower."

"That could be dangerous."

"And not doing it could prove more dangerous in the long run. No, you can throw the rest of them into the sea, but not the button."

"All right. I'll keep it pent for you."

"Thanks. Jasra is Luke's mother."

"You're joking!"

"Nope."

"That explains why he didn't lean on her directly about

the later April thirtieths. Fascinating! It opens up a whole
new lane of speculation."

"Care to share them?"

"Later, later. In the meantime, I'll take care of these
stones right now."

She scooped them all out of the circle and they seemed,
for a moment, to dance in her hand. She stood.

"Uh—the button?" I said.

"Yes."

She put the button into her pocket and kept the others in
her hand.

"You're going to get attuned yourself if you keep the
button that way, aren't you?"

"No," she said, "I won't."

"Why not?"

"There's a reason. Excuse me while I find a container
for the others, and someone to transport them."

"Won't that person get attuned?"

"It takes a while."

"Oh."

"Have some more coffee—or something."

She turned and left. I ate a piece of cheese. I tried to
figure out whether I'd gotten more answers or more new
questions during the course of our conversation. I tried to
fit some of the new pieces into the old puzzle.

"Father?"

I turned, to see who had spoken. There was no one in
sight.

"Down here."

A coin sized disk of light lay within a nearby flower
bed, otherwise empty save for a few dry stalks and leaves.
The light caught my attention when it moved slightly.

"Ghost?" I asked.

"Uh-huh," came the reply from among the leaves. "I
was waiting to catch you when you were alone. I'm not
sure I trust that woman."

"Why not?"

"She doesn't scan right, like other people. I don't know

what it is. But that's not what I wanted to talk to you about."

"What then?"

"Uh—well, did you mean what you said about not really intending to turn me off?"

"Jeez! After all the sacrifices I made for you! Your education and everything. . . . And lugging all your damn components out to a place like that where you'd be safe! How can you ask me that?"

"Well, I heard Random tell you to do it—"

"You don't do everything you're told either, do you? Especially when it comes to assaulting me when I just wanted to check out a few programs? I deserve a little more respect than that!"

"Uh—yeah. Look, I'm sorry."

"You ought to be. I went through a lot of crap because of you."

"I looked for you for several days, and I couldn't find you."

"Crystal caves are no fun."

"I don't have much time now. . . ." The light flickered, faded almost to the point of vanishing, returned to full brilliance. "Will you tell me something fast?"

"Shoot."

"That fellow who was with you when you came out this way—and when you left—the big red-haired man?"

"Luke. Yes?"

The light grew dimmer again.

"Is it okay to trust him?" Ghost's voice came faintly, weakly.

"No!" I shouted. "That would be damn stupid!"

Ghost was gone, and I couldn't tell whether he'd heard my answer.

"What's the matter?" Vinta's voice, from above me.

"Argument with my imaginary playmate," I called out.

Even from that distance I could see the expression of puzzlement on her face. She sought in all directions about the patio and then, apparently persuading herself that I was indeed alone, she nodded.

"Oh," she said. Then, "I'll be along in a little while."

"No hurry," I answered.

Where shall wisdom be found, and where is the place of understanding? If I knew, I'd walk over and stand there. As it was, I felt as if I stood in the midst of a large map, surrounded by vague areas wherein were penned the visages of particularly nasty-looking random variables. A perfect place for a soliloquy, if one had anything to say.

I went back inside to use the john. All that coffee.

CHAPTER 6

Well, maybe.

With Julia, I mean.

I sat alone in my room, thinking by candlelight.

Vinta had stirred a few sunken memories to the surface.

It was later on, when we weren't seeing much of each other. . . .

I'd met Julia first in a Computer Science course I was taking. We'd started seeing each other occasionally, just coffee after class and like that, at first. Then more and more frequently, and pretty soon it was serious.

Now it was ending as it had started, a little more each time. . . .

I felt her hand on my shoulder as I was leaving the supermarket with a bag of groceries. I knew it was her and I turned and there was no one there. Seconds later, she hailed me from across the parking lot. I went over and said hello, asked her if she were still working at the software place where she'd been. She said that she wasn't. I recalled that she was wearing a small silver pentagram on a chain about her neck. It could easily—and more likely should—have been hanging down inside her blouse. But of course I wouldn't have seen it then, and her body language indicated that she wanted me to see it. So I ignored it while we exchanged a few generalities, and she turned me down on dinner and a movie, though I asked after several nights.

"What are you doing now?" I inquired.

"I'm studying a lot."

"What?"

"Oh, just—different things. I'll surprise you one of these days."

Again, I didn't bite, though an over-friendly Irish setter approached us about then. She placed her hand on its head and said, "Sit!" and it did. It became still as a statue at her side, and remained when we left later. For all I know, there's a dog skeleton still crouched there, near the cart return area, like a piece of modern sculpture.

It didn't really seem that important at the time. But in retrospect, I wondered....

We had ridden that day, Vinta and I. Seeing my growing exasperation of the morning, she must have felt a break was in order. She was right. Following a light lunch, when she made the suggestion that we take a ride about the estate, I agreed readily. I had wanted a little more time in which to think before continuing our cross-examination and discourse game. And the weather was good, the countryside attractive.

We made our way along a curling trail through arbors, which led at length into the northern hills from where we were afforded long views across the rugged and cross-hatched land down to the sun-filled sea. The sky was full of winds and wisps of cloud, passing birds.... Vinta seemed to have no special destination in mind, which was all right with me. As we rode, I recalled a visit to a Napa Valley winery, and the next time we drew rein to rest the horses I asked her, "Do you bottle the wine here at the estate? Or is that done in town? Or in Amber?"

"I don't know," she said.

"I thought you grew up here."

"I never paid attention."

I bit back a remark about patrician attitudes. Unless she

were joking, I couldn't see how she'd fail to know something like that.

She caught my expression, though, and added immediately, "We've done it various ways at various times. I've been living in town for several years now. I'm not sure where the principal bottling has been done recently."

Nice save, because I couldn't fault it. I hadn't intended my question as any sort of trap, but felt as if I had just touched on something. Possibly from the fact that she didn't let it go at that. She went on to say that they shipped large casks all over the place and often sold them in that fashion. On the other hand, there were smaller customers who wanted the product bottled. . . . I stopped listening after a time. On the one hand, I could see it, coming from a vinter's daughter. On the other, it was all stuff I could have made up myself on the spot. There was no way for me to check on any of it. I got the feeling that she was trying to snow me, to cover something. But I couldn't figure what.

"Thanks," I said when she paused for breath, and she gave me a strange look but took the hint and did not continue.

"You have to speak English," I said in that language, "if the things you told me earlier are true,"

"Everything I told you is true," she replied, in unaccented English.

"Where'd you learn it?"

"On the shadow Earth where you went to school."

"Would you care to tell me what you were doing there?"

"I was on a special mission."

"For your father? For the Crown?"

"I'd rather not answer you at all than lie to you."

"I appreciate that. Of course, I must speculate."

She shrugged.

"You said you were in Berkeley?" I asked.

A hesitation, then, "Yes."

"I don't remember ever seeing you around."

Another shrug. I wanted to grab her and shake her. Instead I said, "You knew about Meg Devlin. You said you were in New York—"

"I believe you're getting ahead of me on questions."

"I didn't know we were playing the game again. I thought we were just talking."

"All right, then: Yes."

"Tell me one more thing and perhaps I can help you."

She smiled. "I don't need any help. You're the one with problems."

"May I, anyway?"

"Go ahead and ask. Every time you question me you tell me things I wish to know."

"You knew about Luke's mercenaries. Did you visit New Mexico, too?"

"Yes, I've been there."

"Thanks," I said.

"That's all?"

"That's all."

"You've come to some conclusion?"

"Perhaps."

"Care to tell me what it is?"

I smiled and shook my head.

I left it at that. A few oblique queries on her part as we rode on led me to believe that I had her wondering what I might have guessed or suddenly seen. Good. I was determined to let it smolder. I needed something to balance her reticence on those points about which I was most curious, to lead hopefully to a full trade of information. Besides, I *had* reached a peculiar conclusion concerning her. It was not complete, but if it were correct I would require the rest of the answer sooner or later. So it was not exactly as if I were setting up a bluff.

The afternoon was golden, orange, yellow, red about us, with an autumn-damp smell behind the cool nips of the breezes. The sky very blue, like certain stones. . . .

Perhaps ten minutes later I asked her a more neutral question. "Could you show me the road to Amber?"

"You don't know it?"

I shook my head. "I've never been this way before. All I know is that there are overland routes coming through here that lead to the Eastern Gate."

"Yes," she said. "A bit farther to the north, I believe. Let's go find it."

She headed back to a road we had followed for a time earlier and we turned right on it, which seemed logical. I did not remark on her vagueness, though I expected a comment from her before too long in that I had not elaborated on my plans and I'd a feeling she was hoping that I would.

Perhaps three quarters of a mile later we came to a crossroads. There was a low stone marker at the far left corner giving the distance to Amber, the distance back to Baylesport, the distance to Baylecrest in the east and to a place called Murn, straight ahead.

"What's Murn?" I asked.

"A little dairy village."

No way I could check that, without traveling six leagues.

"You plan on riding back to Amber?" she asked.

"Yes."

"Why not just use a Trump?"

"I want to get to know the area better. It's my home. I like it here."

"But I explained to you—about the danger. The stones have marked you. You can be tracked."

"That doesn't mean I *will* be tracked. I doubt that whoever sent the ones I met last night would even be aware this soon that they'd found me and failed. They'd still be lurking about if I hadn't decided to go out for dinner. I'm sure I have a few days' grace in which to remove the markings you spoke of."

She dismounted and let her horse nibble a few blades of grass. I did the same. Dismounted, that is.

"You're probably right. I just don't like to see you taking *any* chances," she said. "When are you planning on heading back?"

"I don't know. I suppose that the longer I wait the more likely it is that the person behind last night's business will get restless and maybe send more muscle."

She took hold of my arm and turned, so that she was

suddenly pressed against me. I was somewhat surprised by the act, but my free arm automatically moved to hold the lady as it tends to on such occasions.

"You weren't planning on leaving now, were you? Because if you are, I'm going with you."

"No," I answered truthfully. Actually, I'd been thinking of departing the following morning, following a good night's sleep.

"When, then? We still have a lot of things to talk about."

"I think we've pushed the question-and-answer business about as far as you're willing to let it go."

"There are some things—"

"I know."

Awkward, this. Yes, she was desirable. And no, I didn't care to have anything to do with her that way. Partly because I felt she wanted something else as well—what, I wasn't sure—and partly because I was certain she possessed a peculiar power to which I did not wish to expose myself at intimate range. As my Uncle Suhuy used to say, speaking technically as a sorcerer, "If you don't understand it, don't screw around with it." And I had a feeling that anything beyond a friendly acquaintanceship with Vinta could well turn into a duel of energies.

So I kissed her quickly to stay friendly and disengaged myself.

"Maybe I'll head back tomorrow," I told her.

"Good. I was hoping you'd spend the night. Perhaps several. I will protect you."

"Yes, I'm still very tired," I said.

"We'll have to feed you a good meal and build up your strength."

She brushed my cheek with her fingertips then, and I suddenly realized that I did know her from somewhere. Where? I couldn't say. And that, too, frightened me. More than a little. As we mounted and headed back toward Arbor House I began making my plans for getting out of there that night.

So, sitting in my room, sipping a glass of my absent

host's wine (the red) and watching the candles flicker in the breeze from an opened window, I waited—first for the house to grow quiet (which it had), then for a goodly time to pass. My door was latched. I had mentioned how tired I felt several times during dinner, and then I had retired early. I am not so egotistically male that I feel myself constantly lusted after, but Vinta had given indication that she might stop by and I wanted the excuse of heavy sleeping. Least of all did I wish to offend her. I had problems enough without turning my strange ally against me.

I wished I still had a good book about, but I'd left my last one at Bill's place, and if I were to summon it now I did not know but that Vinta might sense the sending, just as Fiona had once known I was creating a Trump, and come pounding on the door to see what the hell was going on.

But no one came pounding, and I listened to the creakings of a quiet house and the night sounds without. The candles shortened themselves and the shadows on the wall behind the bed ebbed and flowed like a dark tide beyond their swaying light. I thought my thoughts and sipped my wine. Pretty soon. . . .

An imagining? Or had I just heard my name whispered from some undetectable place?

"Merle. . . ."

Again.

Real, but—

My vision seemed to swim for a moment, then I realized it for what it was: a very weak Trump contract.

"Yes," I said, opening and extending. "Who is it?"

"Merle, baby. . . . Give me a hand or I've had it. . . ."

Luke!

"Right here," I said, reaching, reaching, as the image grew clear, solidified.

He was leaning, his back against a wall, shoulders slumped, head hanging.

"If this is a trick, Luke, I'm ready for it," I told him. I rose quickly and, crossing to the table where I had laid my blade, I drew it and held it ready.

"No trick. Hurry! Get me out of here!"

He raised his left hand. I extended my left hand and caught hold of it. Immediately he slumped against me, and I staggered. For an instant I thought it was an attack, but he was dead weight and I saw that there was blood all over him. He still clutched a bloody blade in his right hand.

"Over here. Come on."

I steered him and supported him for several paces, then deposited him on the bed. I pried the blade from his grip, then placed it along with mine on a nearby chair.

"What the hell happened to you?"

He coughed and shook his head weakly. He drew several deep breaths, then, "Did I see a glass of wine," he asked, "as we passed a table?"

"Yeah. Hold on."

I fetched it, brought it back, propped him and held it to his lips. It was still over half full. He sipped it slowly, pausing for deep breaths.

"Thanks," he said when he'd finished, then his head turned to the side.

He was out. I took his pulse. It was fast but kind of weak.

"Damn you, Luke!" I said. "You've got the worst timing. . . ."

But he didn't hear a word. He just lay there and bled all over the place.

Several curses later I had him undressed and was going over him with a wet towel to find out where, under all that blood, the injuries lay. There was a nasty chest wound on the right, which might have hit the lung. His breathing was very shallow, though, and I couldn't tell. If so, I was hoping he'd inherited the regenerative abilities of Amber in full measure. I put a compress on it and laid his arm on top to hold it in place while I checked elsewhere. I suspected he had a couple of fractured ribs, also. His left arm was broken above the elbow and I set it and splinted it, using loose slats from a chair I'd noticed in the back of the closet earlier, and I strapped it to him. There were over a dozen lacerations and incisions of various degrees of severity on his thighs, right hip, right arm and shoulder, his back. None of them, fortunately, involved arterial bleeding. I cleaned all of these and bound them, which left him looking like an illustration in a first-aid handbook. Then I checked his chest wound again and covered him up.

I wondered about some of the Logrus healing techniques I knew in theory but had never had a chance to practice. He was looking pretty pale, so I decided I had better try them. When I'd finished, some time later, it seemed as if his color had returned to his face. I added my cloak to the blanket which covered him. I took his pulse again and it felt stronger. I cursed again, just to stay in practice, removed our blades from the chair and sat down on it.

A little later my conversation with Ghostwheel returned to trouble me. Had Luke been trying to do a deal with my creation? He'd told me he wanted Ghost's power, to prosecute his designs against Amber. Then Ghost had asked me earlier today whether Luke was to be trusted, and my answer had been emphatically negative.

Had Ghost terminated negotiations with Luke in the fashion I saw before me?

I fetched forth my Trumps and shuffled out the bright circle of the Ghostwheel. I focused on it, setting my mind for contact, reaching out, calling, summoning.

Twice I felt near to something—agitated—during the several minutes I devoted to the effort. But it was as if we were separated by a sheet of glass. Was Ghost occupied? Or just not inclined to talk with me?

I put my cards away. But they had served to push my thoughts into another channel.

I gathered Luke's gory clothing and did a quick search. I turned up a set of Trumps in a side pocket, along with several blank cards and a pencil—and yes, they seemed to be rendered in the same style as the ones I had come to call the Trumps of Doom. I added to the packet the one depicting myself, which Luke had been holding in his hand when he had trumped in.

His were a fascinating lot. There was one of Jasra, and one of Victor Melman. There was also one of Julia, and a partly completed one of Bleys. There was one for the crystal cave, another for Luke's old apartment. There were several duplicated from the Trumps of Doom themselves, one for a palace I did not recognize, one for one of my old pals, one for a rugged-looking blond guy in green and black, another of a slim, russet-haired man in brown and black, and one of a woman who resembled this man so closely it would seem they must be related. These last two, strangely, were done in a different style; even by a different hand, I'd say. The only unknown one I felt relatively certain about was the blond fellow, who, from his colors, I would assume to be Luke's old friend Dalt, the mercenary. There were also three separate attempts at something resembling Ghostwheel—none of them, I would guess, completely successful.

I heard Luke growl something, and I saw that his eyes were open and darting.

"Take it easy," I said. "You're safe."

He nodded and closed his eyes. A few moments later, he opened them again.

"Hey! My cards," he said weakly.

I smiled. "Nice work," I remarked. "Who did them?"

"Me," he answered. "Who else?"

"Where'd you learn?"

"My dad. He was real good at it."

"If you can do them, you must have walked the Pattern."

He nodded.

"Where?"

He studied me a moment, then performed a weak shrug and winced. "Tir-na Nog'th."

"Your father took you, saw you through it?"

Again, a nod.

Why not push it, since I seemed to be on a roll? I picked up a card.

"And here's Dalt," I said. "You used to be Cub Scouts together, didn't you?"

He did not reply. When I looked up I saw narrowed eyes and a furrowed brow.

"I've never met him," I added. "But I recognize the colors, and I know he's from out your way—around Kashfa."

Luke smiled. "You always did your homework back in school, too," he said.

"And usually on time," I agreed. "But with you I've been running late. Like, I can't find a Trump for the Keep of the Four Worlds. And here's someone I don't know."

I picked up the slim lady's card and waved it at him.

He smiled. "Gettin' weak and losin' my breath again," he said. "You been to the Keep?"

"Yep."

"Recently?"

I nodded.

"Tell you what," he said at last. "Tell me what you saw at the Keep and how you learned some of that stuff about me and I'll tell you who she is."

I thought quickly. I could say things so that I probably wouldn't be telling him anything he didn't already know.

So, "The other way around," I said.

"Okay. The lady," he stated, "is Sand."

I stared so hard that I felt the beginnings of a contact. I smothered it.

"The long-lost," he added.

I raised the card depicting the man who resembled her. "Then this must be Delwin," I said.

"Right."

"You didn't do these two cards. They're not your style, and you probably wouldn't have known what they looked like to begin with."

"Perceptive. My father drew them, back in the time of the troubles—for all the good it did him. They wouldn't help him either."

"Either?"

"They weren't interested in helping me, despite their disaffection with this place. Count them as out of the game."

"This place?" I said. "Where do you think you are, Luke?"

His eyes widened. He cast his gaze about the room. "The camp of the enemy," he answered. "I had no choice. These are your quarters in Amber, right?"

"Wrong," I replied.

"Don't bait me, Merle. You've got me. I'm your prisoner. Where am I?"

"Do you know who Vinta Bayle is?"

"No."

"She was Caine's mistress. This is her family's place, way out in the country. She's just up the hall somewhere. Might even stop by. I think she's got a crush on me."

"Uh-oh. She a tough lady?"

"Very."

"What you doing making out with her this soon after the funeral? That's hardly decent."

"Huh! If it weren't for you there wouldn't have been any funeral."

"Don't give me that indignation crap, Merle. If it had been *your* dad, Corwin, he'd killed, wouldn't you have gone after him?"

"That's not fair. My father wouldn't have done all those things Brand did."

"Maybe, maybe not. But supposing he had? Even then. Wouldn't you have gone after Caine?"

I turned away. "I don't know," I said finally. "It's too damned hypothetical."

"You'd have done it. I know you, Merle. I'm sure you would have."

I sighed. "Maybe," I said. "Well, okay. Maybe I might have. But I would have stopped there. I wouldn't have gone after the others too. I don't want to make you feel any worse than you do about it, but your old man was psycho; you must know that. And you're not. I know you as well as you know me. I've been thinking about this for some time. You know, Amber recognizes the personal vendetta. You've got an arguable case there for one. And the death didn't even occur within Amber, if Random were really looking for an out for you."

"Why should he be?"

"Because I'd be vouching for your integrity in other matters."

"Come on, Merle—"

"You've got a classic vendetta defense—a son avenging his father's death."

"I don't know. . . . Hey, you trying to get out of telling me the stuff you promised to?"

"No, but—"

"So you made it to the Keep of the Four Worlds. What did you learn there and how did you learn it?"

"Okay. You think about what I said, though," I replied.

His expression remained unchanged.

Then, "There was an old hermit named Dave," I began.

Luke fell asleep before I finished. I just let my voice trail off and sat there. After a time, I rose and located the wine bottle and poured a little into the glass, since Luke had drunk most of mine. I took it with me to the window and stared down and out across the patio, where the wind was rattling leaves. I wondered about what I'd said to Luke. It wasn't a full picture I'd given him, partly because I hadn't had time to go into it thoroughly, mainly because he hadn't seemed interested. But even if Random did let him off the hook officially in the matter of Caine's death, Julian or Gérard would probably be looking to kill him under the same vendetta code I'd been talking about. I didn't really know what to do. I was obliged to tell Random about him, but I'd be damned if I'd do it yet. There were still too many things I had to learn from him, and getting at him might be a lot harder if he were a prisoner back in Amber. Why had he ever gotten himself born as Brand's son, anyway?

I returned to the bedside seat, near which I had left our weapons and Luke's Trumps. I moved these items across the room, to where I seated myself in the more comfortable chair I had occupied earlier. I studied his cards again. Amazing. A whole bunch of history in my hand. . . .

When Oberon's wife Rilga had shown less hardihood than many by aging rapidly and retiring to a reclusive life

at a country shrine, he had gone off and remarried, somewhat to the chagrin of their children—Caine, Julian and
Gérard. But to confuse genealogists and sticklers for family
legality, he had done it in a place where time flowed far
more rapidly than in Amber. Interesting arguments both for
and against the bigamous nature of his marriage to Harla
may be made. I'm in no position to judge. I had the story
from Flora years ago, and in that she'd never gotten along
too well with Delwin and Sand, the offspring of that union,
she was inclined to the pro-bigamy interpretation. I'd never
seen pictures of Delwin or Sand until now. There weren't
any hanging around the palace, and they were seldom
mentioned. But they had lived in Amber for the relatively
short time Harla was queen there. Following her death,
they grew unhappy with Oberon's policies toward her
homeland—which they visited often—and after a time
they departed, vowing not to have anything to do with
Amber again. At least that's the way I'd heard it. There
could easily have been all sorts of sibling politicking involved, too. I don't know.

But here were two missing members of the royal family,
and obviously Luke had learned of them and approached
them, hoping to revive old resentments and gain allies. He
admitted that it hadn't worked. Two centuries is a long
time to hold a grudge at high pitch. That's about how long
it had been since their departure, as I understood it. I wondered fleetingly whether I should get in touch with them,
just to say hello. If they weren't interested in helping Luke
I didn't suppose they'd be interested in helping the other
side either, now they were aware there was another side. It
did seem proper that I should introduce myself and pay my
respects, as a family member they'd never met. I decided
that I would do it sometime, though the present moment
was hardly appropriate. I added their Trumps to my own
collection, along with good intentions.

And then there was Dalt—a sworn enemy of Amber, I
gathered. I studied his card again, and I wondered. If he
were indeed such a good friend of Luke's, perhaps I should
let him know what had happened. He might even know of

the circumstances involved and mention something I could use. In fact, the more I thought about it—recalling his recent presence at the Keep of the Four Worlds—the more tempting it became to try to reach him. It seemed possible I could even pick up something about what was now going on in that place.

I gnawed a knuckle. Should I or shouldn't I? I couldn't see any harm that could come of it. I wasn't planning on giving anything away. Still, there were a few misgivings.

What the hell, I decided finally. Nothing ventured. . . .

Hello, hello. Reaching out through the suddenly cold card. . . .

A startled moment somewhere, and the sense of an *Aha!*

Like a portrait come to life, my vision stirred.

"Who are you?" the man asked, hand on hilt, blade half drawn.

"My name is Merlin," I said, "and we've a mutual acquaintance named Rinaldo. I wanted to tell you that he'd been badly injured."

By now, we both hovered between our two realities, solid and perfectly clear to each other. He was bigger than I'd thought from his representation, and he stood at the center of a stone-walled room, a window to his left showing a blue sky and a limb of cloud. His green eyes, at first wide, were now narrowed and the set of his jaw seemed a bit truculent.

"Where is he?" he inquired.

"Here. With me," I answered.

"How fortunate," he replied, and the blade was in his hand and he moved forward.

I flipped the Trump away, which did not sever the contact. I had to summon the Logrus to do that—and it fell between us like the blade of a guillotine and jerked me back as if I had just touched a live wire. My only consolation was that Dalt had doubtless felt the same thing.

"Merle, what's going on?" Luke's voice came hoarsely. "I saw—Dalt. . . ."

"Uh, yeah. I just called him."

He raised his head slightly. "Why?"

"To tell him about you. He's your friend, isn't he?"

"You asshole!" he said. "He's the one that did this to me!"

Then he began coughing and I rushed to his side.

"Get me some water, huh?" he said.

"Coming up."

I went off to the bathroom and fetched him a glass. I propped him and he sipped it for a time.

"Maybe I should have told you," he said finally. "Didn't think—you'd play games—that way, though—when you don't know—what's going on. . . ."

He coughed again, drank more water.

"Hard to know what to tell you—and what not to," he continued, a while later.

"Why not tell me everything?" I suggested.

He shook his head slightly. "Can't. Probably get you killed. More likely both of us."

"The way things have been going, it seems as if it could happen whether you tell me or not."

He smiled faintly and took another drink.

"Parts of this thing are personal," he said then, "and I don't want anyone else involved."

"I gather that your trying to kill me every spring for a while there was kind of personal, too," I observed, "yet somehow I felt involved."

"Okay, okay," he said, slumping back and raising his right hand. "I told you I cut that out a long time ago."

"But the attempts went on."

"They weren't my doing."

Okay, I decided. Try it. "It was Jasra, wasn't it?"

"What do you know about her?"

"I know she's your mother, and I gather this is her war too."

He nodded. "So you know. . . . All right. That makes it easier." He paused to catch his breath. "She started me doing the April thirtieth stuff for practice. When I got to know you better and quit, she was mad."

"So she continued it herself?"

He nodded.

"She wanted you to go after Caine," I said.

"So did I."

"But the others? She's leaning on you about them, I'll bet. And you're not so sure they have it coming."

Silence.

"Are you?" I said.

He shifted his gaze away from my own and I heard his teeth grind together.

"You're off the hook," he said at last. "I've no intention of hurting you. I won't let her do it either."

"And what about Bleys and Random and Fiona and Flora and Gérard and—"

He laughed, which cost him a wince and a quick clutch at his chest.

"They've nothing to worry about from us," he said, "right now."

"What do you mean?"

"Think," he told me. "I could have trumped back to my old apartment, scared hell out of the new tenants and called an ambulance. I could be in an emergency room right now."

"Why aren't you?"

"I've been hurt worse than this, and I've made it. I'm here because I need your help."

"Oh? For what?"

He looked at me, then looked away again. "She's in bad trouble, and we've got to rescue her."

"Who?" I asked, already knowing the answer.

"My mother," he replied.

I wanted to laugh, but I couldn't when I saw the expression on his face. It took real balls to ask me to help rescue the woman who'd tried to kill me—not once, but many times—and whose big aim in life seemed to be the destruction of my relatives. Balls, or—

"I've no one else to turn to," he said.

"If you talk me into this one, Luke, you'll deserve the Salesman of the Year Award," I said. "But I'm willing to listen."

"Throat's dry again," he said.

I went and refilled the glass. As I returned with it, it seemed there was a small noise in the hall. I continued listening while I helped Luke to a few more sips.

He nodded when he was finished, but I had heard another sound by then. I raised my finger to my lips and glanced at the door. I put down the glass, rose and crossed the room, retrieving my blade as I did so.

Before I reached the door, however, there was a gentle knock.

"Yes?" I said, advancing to it.

"It's me," came Vinta's voice. "I know that Luke is in there, and I want to see him."

"So you can finish him off?" I said.

"I told you before that that is not my intention."

"Then you're not human," I said.

"I never claimed I was."

"Then you're not Vinta Bayle," I said.

There followed a long silence, then, "Supposing I'm not?"

"Then tell me who you are."

"I can't."

"Then meet me halfway," I said, drawing upon all of my accumulated guesswork concerning her, "and tell me who you were."

"I don't know what you mean."

"Yes, you do. Pick one—any one. I don't care."

There was another silence, then, "I dragged you from the fire," she said, "but I couldn't control the horse. I died in the lake. You wrapped me in your cloak. . . ."

That was not an answer I had anticipated. But it was good enough.

With the point of my weapon I raised the latch. She pushed the door open and glanced at the blade in my hand.

"Dramatic," she remarked.

"You've impressed me," I said, "by the perils with which I am beset."

"Not sufficiently, it would seem." She entered, smiling.

"What do you mean?" I asked.

"I didn't hear you ask him anything about the blue

stones and what he might have homing in on you as a consequence of your attunement."

"You've been eavesdropping."

"A lifetime habit," she agreed.

I turned toward Luke and introduced her. "Luke, this is Vinta Bayle—sort of."

Luke raised his right hand, his eyes never leaving her face. "I just want to know one thing," he began.

"I'll bet you do," she replied. "Am I going to kill you or aren't I? Keep wondering. I haven't decided yet. Do you remember the time you were low on gas north of San Luis Obispo and you discovered your wallet was missing? You had to borrow money from your date to get back home. She had to ask you twice, before you paid her back."

"How could you know that?" he whispered.

"You got in a fight with three bikers one day," she went on. "You almost lost an eye when one of them wrapped a chain around your head. Seems to have healed up nicely. Can't see the scar—"

"And I won," he added.

"Yes. Not too many people can pick up a Harley and throw it like you did."

"I have to know," he said, "how you learned these things."

"Maybe I'll tell you that too, sometime," she said. "I just mentioned them to keep you honest. Now I'm going to ask you some questions, and your life is going to depend on giving me honest answers. Understand—"

"Vinta," I interrupted, "you told me that you weren't interested in killing Luke."

"It's not at the top of my list," she replied, "but if he's in the way of what is, he goes."

Luke yawned. "I'll tell you about the blue stones," he muttered. "I don't have anybody on a blue-stone detail after Merle now."

"Might Jasra have someone tracking him that way?"

"Possible. I just don't know."

"What about the ones who attacked him in Amber last night?"

"First I've heard of it," he said, and he closed his eyes.

"Look at this," she ordered, removing the blue button from her pocket.

He opened his eyes and squinted at it.

"Recognize it?"

"Nope," he said, and closed his eyes again.

"And you don't mean Merle any harm now?"

"That's right," he answered, his voice drifting off.

She opened her mouth again and I said, "Let him sleep. He's not going anywhere."

She gave me an almost angry look, then nodded. "You're right," she said.

"So what are you going to do now—kill him while he's out?"

"No," she replied. "He was telling the truth."

"And does it make a difference?"

"Yes," she told me, "for now."

CHAPTER 7

I actually did get a fairly decent night's sleep despite everything, including a distant dogfight and a lot of howling. Vinta had been disinclined to continue at questions and answers, and I hadn't wanted her bothering Luke any more. I persuaded her to leave and let us rest. I sacked out on the comfortable chair, with my feet propped on the other one. I was hoping to continue my conversation with Luke in private. I remember chuckling right before I fell asleep as I tried to decide which of them I distrusted less.

I was awakened by the first brightening of the sky and a few arguments of birds. I stretched several times then and made my way to the bathroom. Half an ablution later I heard Luke cough and then whisper my name.

"Unless you're hemorrhaging, wait a minute," I replied, and I dried myself off. "Need some water?" I asked while I was doing it.

"Yeah. Bring some."

I threw the towel over my shoulder and took him a drink.

"Is she still around?" he asked me.

"No."

"Give me a glass and go check the hall, will you? I'll manage."

I nodded and passed it to him. I kept it quiet as I eased the door open. I stepped out into the hall, walked up to the corner. There was no one in sight.

"All clear," I whispered as I came back into the room.

Luke was gone. A moment later I heard him in the bathroom.

"Damn! I'd have helped you!" I said.

"I can still take a leak by myself," he replied, staggering back into the room, his good hand on the wall. "Had to see whether I could negotiate," he added, lowering himself to the edge of the bed. He put his hand against his rib cage and panted. "Shit! that smarts!"

"Let me help you lie back."

"Okay. Listen, don't let her know I can do even that much."

"Okay," I said. "Take it easy now. Rest."

He shook his head. "I want to tell you as much as I can before she comes busting back in here," he said, "and she will, too—believe me."

"You know that for a fact?"

"Yes. She's not human, and she's more attuned to both of us than any blue stone ever was. I don't understand your style of magic, but I've got my own and I know what it tells me. It was your question about who she was that got me to working on the problem, though. Have you figured her out yet?"

"Not completely, no."

"Well, I know she can switch bodies like changing clothes—and she can travel through Shadow."

"Do the names Meg Devlin or George Hansen mean anything to you?" I asked.

"No. Should they?"

"Didn't think so. But she was both of them, I'm sure."

I'd left out Dan Martinez, not because he'd shot it out with Luke and telling Luke would raise his distrust of her even further, but because I didn't want him to know that I was aware of the New Mexico guerrilla operation—and I could see that it might lead in that direction.

"She was also Gail Lampron."

"Your old girlfriend, back in school?" I said.

"Yes. I thought there was something familiar about her immediately. But it didn't hit me till later. She has all of Gail's little mannerisms—the way she turns her head, the way she uses her hands and eyes when she's talking. Then she mentioned two events to which there had only been a single common witness—Gail."

"It sounds as if she wanted you to know."

"I believe she did," he agreed.

"Why didn't she just come out and say it then, I wonder?"

"I don't think she can. There's something could be a spell on her, only it's hard to judge, her not being human and all." He glanced furtively at the door as he said this. Then, "Check again," he added.

"Still clear," I said. "Now what about—"

"Another time," he said. "I've got to get out of here."

"I can see your wanting to get away from her—" I began.

He shook his head. "That's not it," he said. "I've got to hit the Keep of the Four Worlds—soon."

"The shape you're in—"

"That's it. That's what I mean. I've got to get out of here so I can be in shape soon. I think old Sharu Garrul's gotten loose. That's the only way I can figure what happened."

"What *did* happen?"

"I got a distress call from my mother. She'd gone back to the Keep after I'd gotten her away from you."

"Why?"

"Why, what?"

"Why'd she head for the Keep?"

"Well, the place is a power center. The way the four worlds come together there releases an awful lot of free power, which an adept can tap into—"

"Four worlds actually do come together there? You

mean you're in a different shadow depending on the direction you might take off in?"

He studied me for a moment. "Yes," he finally said, "but I'll never get this thing told if you want all the details."

"And I won't understand it if too much gets left out. So she went to the Keep to raise some power and got in trouble instead. She called you to come help her. What did she want that power for, anyway?"

"Mm. Well, I'd been having trouble with Ghostwheel. I thought I almost had him talked into coming over to our side, but she probably thought I wasn't making progress fast enough and apparently decided to try binding him with a massive spell after—"

"Wait a minute. You were talking to Ghost? How did you get in touch? Those Trumps you drew are no good."

"I know. I went in."

"How'd you manage it?"

"In scuba gear. I wore a wet suit and oxygen tanks."

"Son of a gun. That's an interesting approach."

"I wasn't Grand D's top salesman for nothing. I almost had him convinced, too. But she'd learned where I'd stashed you, and she decided to try expediting matters by putting you under control, then using you to clinch the deal—as if you'd come over to our side. Anyhow, when that plan fell through and I had to go and get her away from you, we split up again. I thought she was headed for Kashfa, but she went to the Keep instead. Like I said, I think it was to try a massive working against Ghostwheel. I believe something that she did there inadvertently freed Sharu, and he took the place over again and captured her. Anyhow, I got this frantic sending from her, so—"

"Uh, this old wizard," I said, "had been locked up there for—how long?"

Luke began to shrug, thought better of it. "Hell, I don't know. Who cares? He's been a cloak rack since I was a boy."

"A cloak rack?"

"Yeah. He lost a sorcerous duel. I don't really know

whether she beat him or whether it was Dad. Whoever it was, though, caught him in mid-invocation, arms outspread and all. Froze him like that, stiff as a board. He got moved to a place near an entranceway later. People would hang cloaks and hats on him. The servants would dust him occasionally. I even carved my name on his leg when I was little, like on a tree. I'd always thought of him as furniture. But I learned later that he'd been considered pretty good in his day."

"Did this guy ever wear a blue mask when he worked?"

"You've got me. I don't know anything about his style. Say, let's not get academic or she'll be here before I finish. In fact, maybe we ought to go now, and I can tell you the rest later."

"Uh-uh," I said. "You are, as you noted last night, my prisoner. I'd be nuts to let you go anywhere without knowing a hell of a lot more than I do. You're a threat to Amber. That bomb you tossed at the funeral was pretty damn real. You think I want to give you another shot at us?"

He smiled, then lost it. "Why'd you have to be born Corwin's son, anyway?" he said. Then, "Can I give you my parole on this?" he asked.

"I don't know. I'm going to be in a lot of trouble if they find out I had you and didn't bring you in. What terms are you talking? Will you swear off your war against Amber?"

He gnawed his lower lip. "There's no way I can do that, Merle."

"There are things you're not telling me, aren't there?"

He nodded. Then he grinned suddenly. "But I'll make you a deal you can't refuse."

"Luke, don't give me that hard-sell crap."

"Just give me a minute, okay? And you'll see why you can't afford to pass this one up."

"Luke, I'm not biting."

"Only one minute. Sixty seconds. You're free to say no when I'm done."

"All right," I said. "Tell me."

"Okay. I've got a piece of information vital to the security of Amber, and I'm certain nobody there has an inkling of it. I'll give it to you, after you've helped me."

"Why should you want to give us something like that? It sounds kind of self-defeating."

"I don't, and it is. But it's all I've got to offer. Help me get out of here to a place I have in mind where the time flow is so much faster that I'll be healed up in a day or so in terms of local time at the Keep."

"Or here, for that matter, I'd guess."

"True. Then—uh-oh!"

He sprawled on the bed, clutched at his chest with his good hand and began to moan.

"Luke!"

He raised his head, winked at me, glanced at the door and commenced moaning again.

Shortly, there came a knocking.

"Come in," I said.

Vinta entered and studied us both. For a moment, there seemed to be a look of genuine concern on her face as she regarded Luke. Then she advanced to the bed and placed her hands upon his shoulders. She stood there for about half a minute, then announced, "You're going to live."

"At the moment," Luke replied, "I don't know whether that's a blessing or a curse." Then he slipped his good arm around her, drew her to him suddenly and kissed her. "Hi, Gail," he said. "It's been a long time."

She drew away with less haste than she might have. "You seem improved already," she observed, "and I can see that Merle's worked something to help you along." She smiled faintly for an instant, then said, "Yes, it has been, you dumb jock. You still like your eggs sunny-side up?"

"Right," he acknowledged. "But not half a dozen. Maybe just two today. I'm out of sorts."

"All right," she said. "Come on, Merle. I'll need you to supervise."

Luke gave me a funny look, doubtless certain she wanted to talk with me about him. And for that matter, I wasn't certain I wanted to leave him alone even though I had all of his Trumps in my pocket. I was still uncertain as to the extent of his abilities, and I knew a lot less concerning his intentions. So I hung back.

"Maybe someone should stay with the invalid," I told her.

"He'll be all right," she said, "and I might need your help if I can't scare up a servant."

On the other hand, maybe she had something interesting to tell me. . . .

I found my shirt and drew it on. I ran a hand through my hair.

"Okay," I said. "See you in a bit, Luke."

"Hey," he responded, "see if you can turn up a walking stick for me, or cut me a staff or something."

"Isn't that rushing things a bit?" Vinta asked.

"Never can tell," Luke replied.

So I fetched my blade and took it along. As I followed Vinta out and down the stairs, it occurred to me that when any two of us got together we would probably have something to say about the third.

As soon as we were out of earshot, Vinta remarked, "He took a chance, coming to you."

"Yes, he did."

"So things must be going badly for him, if he felt you were the only one he could turn to."

"I'd say that's true."

"Also, I'm sure he wants something besides a place to recover."

"Probably so."

"'Probably,' hell! He must have asked by now."

"Perhaps."

"Either he did or he didn't."

"Vinta, obviously you've told me everything you intend to tell me," I said. "Well, vice versa. We're even. I don't owe you explanations. If I feel like trusting Luke, I will. Anyhow, I haven't decided yet."

"So he *has* made you a pitch. I might be able to help you decide if you'll let me know what it is."

"No, thanks. You're as bad as he is."

"It's your welfare I'm concerned with. Don't be so quick to spurn an ally."

"I'm not," I said. "But if you stop to think about it, I know a lot more about Luke than I do about you. I think I know the things on which I shouldn't trust him as well as I do the safe ones."

"I hope you're not betting your life on it."

I smiled. "That's a matter on which I tend to be conservative."

We entered the kitchen, where she spoke with a woman I hadn't met yet who seemed in charge there. She left our breakfast orders with her and led me out the side door and onto the patio. From there, she indicated a stand of trees off to the east.

"You ought to be able to find a good sapling in there," she said, "for Luke's staff."

"Probably so," I replied, and we began walking in that direction. "So you really were Gail Lampron," I said suddenly.

"Yes."

"I don't understand this body-changing bit at all."

"And I'm not about to tell you."

"Care to tell me why not?"

"Nope."

"Can't or won't?"

"Can't," she said.

"But if I already know something, would you be willing to add a bit?"

"Maybe. Try me."

"When you were Dan Martinez you took a shot at one of us. Which one was it?"

"Luke," she replied.

"Why?"

"I'd become convinced that he was not the one—that is, that he represented a threat to you—"

"—and you just wanted to protect me," I finished.

"Exactly."

"What did you mean 'that he was not the one'?"

"Slip of the tongue. That looks like a good tree over there."

I chuckled. "Too thick. Okay, be that way."

I headed on into the grove. There were a number of possibilities off to the right.

As I moved through the morning-lanced interstices, damp leaves and dew adhering to my boots, I became aware of some unusual scuffing along the way, a series of marks leading off farther to the right, where—

"What's that?" I said, kind of rhetorically, since I didn't think Vinta would know either, as I headed toward a dark mass at the shady foot of an old tree.

I reached it ahead of her. It was one of the Bayle dogs, a big brown fellow. Its throat had been torn open. The blood was dark and congealed. A few insects were crawling on it. Off farther to the right I saw the remains of a smaller dog. It had been disemboweled.

I studied the area about the remains. The marks of very large paws were imprinted in the damp earth. At least they were not the three-toed prints of the deadly doglike creatures I had encountered in the past. They seemed simply to be those of a very large dog.

"This must be what I heard last night," I remarked. "I thought it sounded like a dogfight."

"When was that?" she asked.

"Some time after you left. I was drowsing."

Then she did a strange thing. She knelt, leaned and sniffed the track. When she recovered there was a slightly puzzled expression on her face.

"What did you find?" I asked.

She shook her head, then stared off to the northeast. "I'm not sure," she finally said, "but it went that way."

I studied the ground further, rising and finally moving along the trail it had left. It did run off in that direction, though I lost it after several hundred feet when it departed the grove. Finally, I turned away.

"One of the dogs attacked the others, I guess," I observed. "We'd better find that stick and head back if we want our breakfasts warm."

Inside, I learned that Luke's breakfast had been sent up to him. I was torn. I wanted to take mine upstairs, to join him and continue our conversation. If I did, though, Vinta would accompany me and the conversation would not be continued. Nor could I talk further with her under those circumstances. So I would have to join her down here, which meant leaving Luke alone for longer than I liked.

So I went along with her when she said, "We will eat in here," and led me into a large hall. I guessed she had chosen it because my room with its open window was above the patio, and Luke could have heard us talking if we ate out there.

We sat at the end of a long darkwood table, where we were served. When we were alone again, she asked, "What are you going to do now?"

"What do you mean?" I asked, sipping some grape juice.

She glanced upward. "With him," she said. "Take him back to Amber?"

"It would seem the logical thing to do," I replied.

"Good," she said. "You should probably transport him soon. They have decent medical facilities at the palace."

I nodded. "Yes, they do."

We ate a few mouthfuls, then she asked, "That *is* what you intend doing, isn't it?"

"Why do you ask?"

"Because anything else would be absolutely foolish, and obviously he is not going to want to do it. Therefore, he will try to talk you into something else, something that will give him some measure of freedom while he recovers. You know what a line of shit he has. He'll make it sound like a great idea, whatever it is. You must remember that he is an enemy of Amber, and when he is ready to move again you will be in the way."

"It makes sense," I said.

"I'm not finished."

"Oh?"

She smiled and ate a few more bites, to keep me wondering. Finally, "He came to you for a reason," she continued. "He could have crawled off to any of a number of places to lick his wounds. But he came to you because he wants something. He's gambling, but it's a calculated thing. Don't go for it, Merle. You don't owe him anything."

"I don't know why you think me incapable of taking care of myself," I replied.

"I never said that," she responded. "But some decisions are finely balanced things. A little extra weight this way or that sometimes makes the difference. You know Luke, but so do I. This is not a time to be giving him any breaks."

"You have a point there," I said.

"So you *have* decided to give him what he wants!"

I smiled and drank some coffee. "Hell, he hasn't been conscious long enough to give me the pitch," I said. "I've thought of these things, and I want to know what he's got in mind too."

"I never said you shouldn't find out as much as you can. I just wanted to remind you that talking with Luke can sometimes be like conversing with a dragon."

"Yeah," I acknowledged. "I know."

"And the longer you wait the harder it's going to be," she added.

I took a gulp of coffee; then, "Did you like him?" I asked.

"Like?" she said. "Yes, I did. And I still do. That is not material at this point, though."

"I don't know about that," I said.

"What do you mean?"

"You wouldn't harm him without good reason."

"No, I wouldn't."

"He is no threat to me at the moment."

"He does not seem to be."

"Supposing I were to leave him here in your care while I went off to Amber to walk the Pattern and to prepare them for the news?"

She shook her head vigorously. "No," she stated. "I will not—I cannot—take that responsibility at this time."

"Why not?"

She hesitated.

"And please don't say again that you cannot tell me," I went on. "Find a way to tell me as much as you can."

She spoke slowly then, as if choosing her words very carefully. "Because it is more important for me to watch you than Luke. There is still danger for you which I do not understand, even though it no longer seems to be proceeding from him. Guarding you against this unknown peril is of higher priority than keeping an eye on him. Therefore, I cannot remain here. If you are returning to Amber, so am I."

"I appreciate your concern," I said, "but I will not have you dogging my footsteps."

"Neither of us has a choice."

"Supposing I simply trump out of here to some distant shadow?"

"I will be obliged to follow you."

"In this form, or another?"

She looked away. She poked at her food.

"You've already admitted that you can be other persons. You locate me in some arcane fashion, then you take possession of someone in my vicinity."

She took a drink of coffee.

"Perhaps something prevents you from saying it," I continued, "but that's the case. I know it."

She nodded once, curtly, and resumed eating.

"Supposing I did trump out right now," I said, "and you followed after in your peculiar fashion." I thought back to my telephone conversations with Meg Devlin and Mrs. Hansen. "Then the real Vinta Bayle would wake up in her own body with a gap in her memory, right?"

"Yes," she answered softly.

"And that would leave Luke here in the company of a woman who would be happy to destroy him if she had any inkling who he really is."

She smiled faintly. "Just so," she said.

We ate in silence for a time. She had attempted to fore-close all my choices, to force me a trump back to Amber and take Luke with me. I do not like being manipulated or coerced. My reflexive attempt to do something other than what is desired of me then feels forced also.

I refilled our coffee cups when I had finished eating. I regarded a collection of dog portraits that hung on the wall across from me. I sipped and savored. I did not speak because I could think of nothing further so say.

Finally, she did. "So what are you going to do?" she asked me.

I finished my coffee and rose. "I am going to take Luke his stick," I said.

I pushed my chair back into place and headed for the corner of the room where I had leaned the stick.

"And then?" she said. "What will you do?"

I glanced back at her as I hefted the staff. She sat very erect, her hands palms down on the table. The Nemesis look overlay her features once again, and I could almost feel electricity in the air.

"Whatever I must," I replied, and I headed for the door.

I increased my pace as soon as I was out of sight. When I hit the stairs and saw that she was not following, I took the steps two at a time. On the way up, I withdrew my cards and located the proper one.

When I entered the room I saw that Luke was resting, his back against the bed's pillows. His breakfast tray was on the smaller chair, beside the bed. I dropped the latch on the door.

"What's the matter, man? We under attack or something?" Luke asked.

"Start getting up," I said.

I picked up his weapon then and crossed to the bed. I gave him a hand sitting up, thrust the staff and the blade at him.

"My hand has been forced," I said, "and I'm not about to turn you over to Random."

"That's a comfort," he observed.

"But we have to clear out—now."

"That's all right by me."

He leaned on the staff, got slowly to his feet. I heard a

noise in the hall, but it was already too late. I'd raised the card and was concentrating.

There came a pounding on the door.

"You're up to something and I think it's the wrong thing," Vinta called out.

I did not reply. The vision was already coming clear.

The doorframe splintered from the force of a tremendous kick, and the latch was torn loose. There was a look of apprehension on Luke's face as I reached out and took hold of his arm.

"Come on," I said.

Vinta burst into the room as I led Luke forward, her eyes flashing, her hands extended, reaching. Her cry of "Fool!" seemed to change into a wail as she was washed by the spectrum, rippled and faded.

We stood in a patch of grass, and Luke let out a deep breath he had been holding.

"You believe in cutting things close, buddy-boy," he remarked, and then he looked around and recognized the place.

He smiled crookedly.

"What do you know," he said. "A crystal cave."

"From my own experience," I said, "the time flow here should be about what you were asking for."

He nodded and we began moving slowly toward the high blue hill.

"Still plenty of rations," I added, "and the sleeping bag should be where I left it."

"It will serve," he acknowledged.

He halted, panting, before we reached the foot. I saw his gaze drift toward a number of strewn bones off to our left. It would have been months since the pair who had removed the boulder had fallen there, long enough for scavengers to have done a thorough job. Luke shrugged, advanced a little, leaned against blue stone. He lowered himself slowly into a sitting position.

"Going to have to wait before I can climb," he said, "even with you helping."

"Sure," I said. "We can finish our conversation. As I

recall, you were going to make me an offer I couldn't refuse. I was to bring you to a place like this, where you could recover fast *vis-à-vis* the time flow at the Keep. You, in turn, had a piece of information vital to the security of Amber."

"Right," he agreed, "and you didn't hear the rest of my story either. They go together."

I hunkered across from him. "You told me that your mother had fled to the Keep, apparently gotten into trouble there and called to you for help."

"Yes," he acknowledged. "So I dropped the business with Ghostwheel and tried to help her. I got in touch with Dalt, and he agreed to come and attack the Keep."

"It's always good to know a band of mercenaries you can get hold of in a hurry," I said.

He gave me a quick, strange look but I was able to maintain an innocent expression.

"So we led them through Shadow and we attacked the place," he said then. "It had to be us that you saw when you were there."

I nodded slowly. "It looked as if you made it over the wall. What went wrong?"

"I still don't know," he said. "We were doing all right. Their defense was crumbling and we were pushing right along, when suddenly Dalt turned on me. We'd been separated for a time; then he appeared again and attacked me. At first I thought he'd made a mistake—we were all grimy and bloody—and I shouted to him that it was me. For a while I didn't want to strike back because I thought it was a misunderstanding and he'd realize his mistake in a few seconds."

"Do you think he sold you out? Or that it was something he'd been planning for a long time? Some grudge?"

"I don't like to think that."

"Magic, then?"

"Maybe. I don't know."

A peculiar thought occurred to me. "Did he know you'd killed Caine?" I asked.

"No, I make it a point never to tell anybody everything I'm about."

"You wouldn't kid me, would you?"

He laughed, moved as if to clap me on the shoulder, winced and thought better of it.

"Why do you ask?" he said then.

"I don't know. Just curious."

"Sure," he said. Then, "What say you give me a hand up and inside, so I can see what kind of supplies you've left me?"

"Okay."

I got to my feet and helped him to his. We moved around to the right to the slope of easiest ascent, and I guided him slowly to the top.

Once we'd achieved the summit he leaned on his staff and stared down into the opening.

"No really easy way down in," he said, "for me. At first I was thinking you could roll up a barrel from the larder, and I could get down to it and then down to the floor. But now I look at it, it's an even bigger drop than I remembered. I'd tear something open, sure."

"Mm-hm," I said. "Hang on. I've got an idea."

I turned away from him and climbed back down. Then I made my way along the base of the blue rise to my right until I had rounded two shiny shoulders and was completely out of Luke's line of sight.

I did not care to use the Logrus in his presence if I did not have to. I did not wish for him to see how I went about things, and I did not want to give him any idea as to what I could or could not do. I'm not that comfortable letting people know too much about me, either.

The Logrus appeared at my summons, and I reached into it, extended through it. My desire was framed, became the aim. My sending extending sought the thought. Far, far....

I kept extending for the damnedest long time. We really had to be out in the Shadow boonies....

Contact.

I did not jerk, but rather exerted a slow and steady pressure. I felt it move toward me across the shadows.

"Hey, Merle! Everything okay?" I heard Luke call.

"Yeah," I answered, and I did not elaborate.

Closer, closer. . . .

There!

I staggered when it arrived, because it came to me too near to one end. The far end bounced on the ground. So I moved to the middle and took a new grip. I hefted it and carried it back.

I set it against a steep area of the rise a bit in advance of Luke's position and I mounted quickly. I began drawing it up behind me then.

"Okay, where'd you get the ladder?" he asked.

"Found it," I said.

"Looks like wet paint on the side there."

"Maybe someone lost it just recently."

I began lowering it into the opening. Several feet protruded after it reached the bottom. I adjusted it for stability.

"I'll start down first," I said, "and stay right under you."

"Take my stick and my blade down first, will you?"

"Sure."

I did that thing. By the time I climbed back he had caught hold and gotten onto it, had begun his descent.

"You'll have to teach me that trick one of these days," he said, breathing heavily.

"Don't know what you're talking about," I answered.

He descended slowly, pausing to rest at each rung, and he was flushed and panting when he reached the bottom. He slumped to the floor immediately, pressing his right palm against his lower rib cage. After a time, he inched backward a bit and rested against the wall.

"You okay?" I asked.

He nodded. "Will be," he said, "in a few minutes. Being stabbed takes a lot out of you."

"Want a blanket?"

"No, thanks."

"Well, you rest here and I'll go check the larder and see

whether anything's gotten at the supplies. Want me to bring you anything?"

"Some water," he said.

The supplies proved to be in good order, and the sleeping bag was still where I'd left it. I returned with a drink for Luke and a few ironic memories of the occasion when he'd done the same for me.

"Looks as if you're in business," I told him. "There's still plenty of stuff."

"You didn't drink all the wine, did you?" he asked between sips.

"No."

"Good."

"Now, you said you have a piece of information vital to the interests of Amber," I said. "Care to tell me about it?"

He smiled. "Not yet," he said.

"I thought that was our deal."

"You didn't hear the whole thing. We were interrupted."

I shook my head. But, "All right, we were interrupted," I acknowledged. "Tell me the rest."

"I've got to get back on my feet, so I can take the Keep and free my mother. . . ."

I nodded.

"The information is yours after we rescue her."

"Hey! Wait a minute! You're asking a hell of a lot!"

"Not for what I'm paying."

"Sounds like I'm buying a pig in a poke."

"Yes, I guess you are. But believe me, it'll be worth knowing."

"What if it becomes worth knowing while I'm waiting?"

"No, I've figured the timing on this. My recovery is only going to take a couple of days, Amber time. I can't see the matter coming up that fast."

"Luke, this is starting to sound like some sort of trick."

"It is," he said, "but it will benefit Amber as well as myself."

"That's another thing. I can't see you giving something like this away to the enemy."

He sighed. "It might even be enough to get me off the hook," he added.

"You're thinking of calling off your feud?"

"I don't know. But I've been doing a lot of thinking, and if I did decide to go that route it would make for a real good opener."

"And if you decided not to, you'd be screwing yourself. Wouldn't you?"

"I could live with it, though. It might make my job harder, but not impossible."

"I don't know," I said. "If word of this gets out and I've got nothing to show for letting you get away like this, I'll be in real hot water."

"I won't tell anybody if you won't."

"There's Vinta."

"And she keeps insisting that her big aim in life is to protect you. Besides, she won't be there if you go back. Or rather, there will be the real Vinta, having awakened as from a troubled sleep."

"How can you be so sure?"

"Because you've left. She's probably already off seeking you."

"Do you know what she really is?"

"No, but I'll help you speculate sometime."

"Not now?"

"No, I've got to sleep some more. It's catching up with me again."

"Then let's go over this deal one more time. What are you going to do, how do you intend to do it and what are you promising me?"

He yawned. "I stay here till I'm back in shape," he said. "Then when I'm ready to attack the Keep I get in touch with you. Which reminds me, you still have my Trumps."

"I know. Keep talking. How do you intend taking the Keep?"

"I'm working on it. I'll let you know that too. Anyhow, you can help us or not at that point, as you see fit. I wouldn't mind having another sorcerer with me, though.

Once we're in and she's freed, I'll tell you what I promised and you can take it back to Amber."

"What if you lose?" I asked.

He looked away. "I guess there's always that possibility," he finally agreed. "Okay, how's this? I'll write the whole thing out and keep it with me. I'll give it to you — by Trump or in person — before we attack. Win or lose, I'll have paid my way with you."

He extended his good hand and I clasped it.

"Okay," I said.

"Then let me have my Trumps back, and I'll be talking to you as soon as I get moving again."

I hesitated. Finally, I drew out my pack, which was now grown quite thick. I shuffled out my own then — along with a number of his — and passed him what remained.

"What about the rest?"

"I want to study them, Luke. Okay?"

He shrugged weakly. "I can always make more. But give me back my mother's."

"Here."

He accepted it, then said, "I don't know what you've got in mind, but I'll give you a piece of advice: Don't screw around with Dalt. He's not the nicest of guys when he's normal, and I think there's something wrong with him right now. Keep away from him."

I nodded, then got to my feet.

"You're going now?" he asked.

"Right."

"Leave me the ladder."

"It's all yours."

"What are you going to tell them back in Amber?"

"Nothing — yet," I said. "Hey, you want me to bring some food up here before I go? Save you a trip."

"Yeah. Good idea. Bring me a bottle of wine, too."

I went back and got him a load of provisions. I dragged in the sleeping bag also.

I started up the ladder, then paused. "You don't know your own mind on this yet," I said, "do you?"

He smiled. "Don't be too sure of that."

When I got to the top I stared at the big boulder that had once sealed me in. Earlier, I'd thought of returning the favor. I could keep track of the time, come get him when he was back on his feet. That way, he couldn't pull a disappearing act on me. I had decided against it, though, not only because I was the only one who knew he was here and if something happened to me he'd be dead. Mainly, it was because he wouldn't be able to reach me with my Trump when he was ready to move, if I kept him fully confined. That's what I told myself, anyhow.

I stooped and caught hold of the boulder, anyway, and pushed it nearer the opening.

"Merle! What are you doing?"—from below.

"Looking for fishing bait," I answered.

"Hey, come on! Don't. . . ."

I laughed and pushed it a little nearer.

"Merle!"

"Thought you might want the door closed, in case it rains," I said. "But it's too damned heavy. Forget it. Take it easy."

I turned and jumped. I thought the extra adrenaline might do him some good.

CHAPTER 8

When I hit the ground I kept going, back to the place from which I had conjured the ladder, out of sight from several directions.

I withdrew one of the blank cards. Time was running. When I fished out the pencil, I discovered that its point had broken. I unsheathed my blade, which was about the length of my arm. I'd found another use for the thing.

A minute or so later I had the card before me on a flat rock, and I was sketching my room back at the Arbor House, the forces of the Logrus moving through my hands. I had to work deliberately, getting the proper feeling of the place into the drawing. Finally, when it was finished, I stood. It was right, it was ready. I opened my mind and regarded my work until it became reality. Then I walked forward into the room. Just as I did I thought of something I wanted to ask Luke, but it was too late.

Beyond the window, the shadows of the trees were stretching into the east. I had obviously been gone for most of the day.

When I turned I saw a sheet of paper upon the now made-up bed, secured against breezes by the edge of a pillow. I crossed to it and picked it up, removing the small blue button which lay atop it before I did so.

The writing was in English. It said: PUT THE BUTTON IN A SAFE PLACE TILL YOU NEED IT. I WOULDN'T CARRY IT AROUND TOO MUCH. I HOPE YOU DID THE RIGHT THING. I GUESS I'LL FIND OUT PRETTY SOON. SEE YOU AROUND.

It was unsigned.

Safe or not, I couldn't just leave it there. So I wrapped the button in the note and put it in my pocket Then I fetched my cloak from the closet and slung it over my arm.

I departed the room. The latch being broken, I left the door standing wide. I stopped in the hallway and listened, but I heard no voices, no sounds of movement.

I made my way to the stairs and headed down. I was almost to the bottom before I noticed her, so still did she sit, there beside the window to my right, a tray of bread and cheese, a bottle and a goblet on a small table at her side.

"Merlin!" she said suddenly, half rising. "The servants said you were here, but when I looked I couldn't find you."

"I was called away," I said, descending the final stair and advancing. "How are you feeling?"

"How do you—what do you know about me?" she asked.

"You probably don't remember anything that happened during the past couple of days," I replied.

"You are right," she said. "Won't you sit down?"

She gestured at the empty chair at the other side of the small table.

"Please join me." She indicated the tray. "And let me get you some wine."

"That's all right," I said, seeing that she was drinking the white.

She rose and crossed the room to a cabinet, opened it and took out another goblet. When she returned she poured a healthy slug of Bayle's Piss into it and set it near my hand. I guessed it was possible they kept the good stuff for themselves.

"What can you tell me about my blackout?" she asked.

"I'd been in Amber, and the next thing I knew I was back here and several days had gone by."

"Yes," I said, taking up a cracker and a bit of cheese. "About what time did you become yourself again?"

"This morning."

"It's nothing to worry about—now," I answered. "There shouldn't be a recurrence."

"But what was it?"

"Just something that's been going around," I said, trying the wine.

"It seems more like magic than the flu."

"Perhaps there was a touch of that too," I agreed. "You never know what might blow in out of Shadow. But almost everyone I know who's had it is okay now."

She furrowed her brow. "It was very strange."

I had a few more crackers and sips of the wine. They did keep the good stuff for themselves.

"There is absolutely nothing to worry about," I repeated.

She smiled and nodded. "I believe you. What are you doing here, anyhow?"

"Stopover. I'm on my way back to Amber," I said, "from elsewhere. Which reminds me—may I borrow a horse?"

"Certainly," she replied. "How soon will you be leaving?"

"As soon as I get the horse," I said.

She got to her feet. "I didn't realize you were in a hurry. I'll take you over to the stables now."

"Thanks."

I grabbed two more crackers and another piece of cheese on the way out and tossed off the rest of the wine. I wondered where the blue fog might be drifting now.

When I'd located a good horse, which she told me I could have delivered to their stable in Amber, I saddled him and fitted his bridle. He was a gray, named Smoke. I donned my cloak then and clasped Vinta's hands.

"Thanks for the hospitality," I said, "even if you don't recall it."

"Don't say good-bye yet," she told me. "Ride around to the kitchen door off the patio, and I'll give you a water bottle and some food for the road. We didn't have a mad affair that I don't remember, did we?"

"A gentleman never tells," I said.

She laughed and slapped my shoulder. "Come see me sometime when I'm in Amber," she told me, "and refresh my memory."

I grabbed a set of saddlebags, a bag of chow for Smoke and a longish tethering rope. I led him outside as Vinta headed back to the house. I mounted then and rode slowly after her, a few dogs capering about me. I circled the manor, taking the long way around, drew rein and dismounted near the kitchen. I considered the patio, wishing I had one just like it where I could sit and take coffee in the morning. Or had it just been the company?

After a time, the door opened and Vinta came out and passed me a bundle and a flask. As I was securing them, she said, "Let my father know that I'll be back in a few days, will you? Tell him that I came to the country because I wasn't feeling well, but that I'm all right now."

"Glad to," I said.

"I don't really know why you were here," she said. "But if it involves politics or intrigue I don't want to know."

"Okay," I said.

"If a servant took a meal to a big red-haired man who seemed to be pretty badly injured, this would be better forgotten?"

"I'd say."

"It will be, then. But one of these days I'd like the story."

"Me too," I said. "We'll see what we can do."

"So, have a good journey."

"Thanks. I'll try."

I clasped her hand, turned away and mounted.

"So long."

"See you in Amber," she said.

I mounted and continued my circuit of the house until I was back near the stables again. I headed past them then to a trail we had ridden that led off in the direction I wanted. Back toward the house, a dog began to howl and another joined it moments later. There was a breeze out of the south, and it carried a few leaves past me. I wanted to be on the road, far away and alone. I value my solitude because that is when I seem to do my best thinking, and right now I had many things to think over.

I rode to the northwest. About ten minutes later I came to a dirt road we had crossed the other day. This time I followed it westward, and it finally took me to the crossroads with the marker indicating that Amber lay straight ahead. I rode on.

It was a yellow dirt road that I traveled, showing the impress of many wagon wheels. It followed the contours of the land, passing between fallow fields bordered by low stone fences, a few trees at either hand. I could see the stark outlines of mountains far ahead, standing above the forested area I was soon to encounter. We moved along at an easy gait, and I let my mind drift over the events of the past few days.

That I had an enemy I did not doubt. Luke had assured me that it was no longer him, and I had found him to be more than a little persuasive. He need not have come to me to be patched up, as both he and Vinta had pointed out. And he could have found his own way to the crystal cave or some other sanctuary. And the business about my helping him to rescue Jasra could have waited. I was more than half convinced that he was trying to get back on better terms with me again quickly because I was his only contact with the Court of Amber, and his fortunes had taken a turn for the worse. I had a feeling that what he really wanted was an official determination as to his status with Amber, and that he had mentioned the piece of important information he would be willing to surrender both as a sign of good faith and as a bargaining chip. I was not at all certain that I, personally, would be very crucial to any plan he might have for rescuing Jasra. Not when he knew the Keep inside and out, was some kind of sorcerer himself and had a band of mercs he could transport from the shadow Earth. For all

I knew, that fancy ammo of his would work there as well as in Amber. And whether that was true or not, why couldn't he just trump his attack force into the place? He wouldn't even really have to win a battle—just get in, grab Jasra and get out. No, I did not feel that I was really necessary to whatever operation he finally decided upon. I'd a feeling he'd waved a red herring at me, hoping that when the air cleared we would simply consider what he had and what he wanted and make him an offer.

I'd a feeling, too, that he might be willing to call it quits on the vendetta now that Caine was out of the way and family honor satisfied. And I'd a notion that Jasra was the stumbling block on his side. While I'd no idea what hold she might have over him, it had occurred to me that the piece of information to which he'd referred might represent some means of neutralizing her. If he got it to us quietly and it seemed to come from our side, he could save face with her as well as buying peace with us. Tantalizing. My problem now was to find the best way to present this at court without looking like a traitor for having let him go. Which meant I had to show that the profit would be worth the investment.

There were more trees at the roadside now, and the forest itself was nearer. I crossed a wooden bridge above a clear stream, and the gentle splashing sounds followed me for a time. There were brown fields and distant barns to my left, a wagon with a broken axle off to my right. . . .

And if I had read Luke wrong? Was there some way I might be able to pressure him and make my interpretation come out right anyway? A small idea began to form. I was not overjoyed with it, but I considered it nevertheless. Risk and speed were what it involved. It had its merits, though. I pushed it as far as I could, then put it aside and returned to my original train of thought.

Somewhere, there was an enemy. And if it wasn't Luke, who was it? Jasra seemed the most obvious candidate. She had made her feelings toward me pretty clear on the occasions of our two meetings. She could well be the one who had dispatched the assassins I had encountered in Death

Alley. In that case, I was probably safe for a time—with her a prisoner back at the Keep—unless, of course, she had sent along a few more before she had been captured. That would have been redundant, though. Why waste all that manpower on me? I had only been a minor figure in the event she sought to avenge, and the men who came after me had been almost sufficient for the task.

And if it wasn't Jasra? Then I was still in jeopardy. The wizard in the blue mask, whom I assumed to be Sharu Garrul, had caused me to be pursued by a tornado, which seemed a far less friendly overture than the flowers that had followed. This latter, of course, identified him with the individual behind my peculiar experience at Flora's apartment back in San Francisco. In that instance, he had initiated the encounter, which meant that he had some designs on me. What was it he'd said? Something about the possibility of us being at cross-purposes at some future time. How interesting, in retrospect. For I could now see the possibility of such a situation's occurring.

But was it really Sharu Garrul who had sent the assassins? Despite his familiarity with the power of the blue stone that had guided them—as evidenced by the blue button in my pocket—it didn't seem to follow. For one thing, our purposes were not yet crossed. For another, it did not seem the proper style for a cryptic, flower-throwing master of elements. I could be dead wrong there, of course, but I expected something more in the nature of a sorcerous duel with that one.

The fields gave way to wilderness as I approached the verge of the forest. Something of twilight had already entered its brightleafed domain. It did not seem a dense, ancient wood like Arden, however; from the distance I had seen numerous gaps within its higher reaches. The road continued wide and well-kept. I drew my cloak more fully about me as I entered the shadowed coolness. It seemed an easy ride, if it were all to be like this. And I was in no hurry. I had too many thoughts that wanted thinking. . . .

If only I had been able to learn more from that strange, nameless entity who had, for a time, controlled Vinta.

What her true nature might be, I still had no idea. "Her," yes. I somehow felt the entity to be more feminine than masculine in nature, despite its having controlled George Hansen and Dan Martinez. Perhaps this was only because I had made love to her as Meg Devlin. Difficult to say. But I had known Gail for some time, and the Lady in the Lake had seemed a real lady...

Enough. I'd decided on my pronoun. Other matters of greater importance were involved. Like, whatever she was, why was she following me about insisting that she wanted to protect me? While I appreciated the sentiment, I still had no insight into her motivation.

But there was something far more important to me than her motivation. Why she saw fit to guard me could remain her own business. The big question was: Against *what* did she feel I needed protection? She must have had a definite threat in mind, and she had not given me the slightest hint as to what it was.

Was this, then, the enemy? The real enemy? Vinta's adversary?

I tried reviewing everything I knew or had guessed about her.

There is a strange creature who sometimes takes the form of a small blue mist. She is capable of finding her way to me through Shadow. She possesses the power to take control of a human body, completely suppressing its natural ego. She hung around in my vicinity for a number of years without my becoming aware of her. Her earliest incarnation that I know of was as Luke's former girlfriend, Gail.

Why Gail? If she were guarding me, why go around with Luke? Why not become one of the women I'd dated? Why not be Julia? But no. She had decided upon Gail. Was that because Luke was the threat, and she'd wanted to keep a close watch on him? But she'd actually let Luke get away with a few attempts on my life. And then Jasra. She'd admitted that she'd known Jasra was behind the later ones. Why hadn't she simply removed them? She could have taken over Luke's body, stepped in front of a speeding car, drifted away from the remains, then gone and done the same with Jasra. She wasn't afraid to die in a host body. I'd seen her do it twice.

Unless she'd somehow known that all their attempts on my life would fail. Could she have sabotaged the letter bomb? Could she, in some way, have been behind my premonition on the morning of the opened gas jets? And perhaps something else with each of the others? Still, it would seem a lot simpler to go to the source and remove the problem itself. I knew that she had no compunction about killing. She'd ordered the slaying of my final assailant in Death Alley.

What, then?

Two possibilities came to mind immediately. One was that she'd actually come to like Luke—and that she'd simply found ways to neutralize him without destroying him. But then I thought of her as Martinez, and it fell apart. She'd actually been shooting that night in Santa Fe. Okay. Then there was the other possibility: Luke was not the real threat, and she'd liked him enough to let him go on living once he'd quit the April 30 games and she saw that we'd gotten friendly. Something happened in New Mexico that made her change her mind. As to what it was, I had no idea. She had followed me to New York, then, and been George Hansen and Meg Devlin in quick succession. Luke was, by that time, out of the picture, following his disappearing act on the mountain. He no longer represented a threat, yet she was almost frantic in her efforts to get in touch with me. Was something else impending? The real threat?

I racked my brains, but I could not figure what that threat might have been. Was I following a completely false trail with this line of reasoning?

She certainly was not omniscient. Her reason for spiriting me to Arbor House was as much to pump me for information as it was to remove me from the scene of the attack. And some of the things she'd wanted to know were as interesting as some of the things she knew.

My mind did a backward flip. What was the first question she had asked me?

Landing adroitly on my mental feet, back at Bill Roth's place, I heard the question several times. As George Hansen she had asked it casually and I had lied; as a voice on the telephone she had asked it and been denied; as Meg Devlin, in bed, she had finally gotten me to answer it honestly: What was your mother's name?

When I'd told her that my mother was named Dara she had finally begun speaking freely. She had warned me against Luke. It seemed that she might have been willing to tell me more then, too, save that the arrival of the real Meg's husband had cut short our conversation.

To what was this the key? It placed my origin in the Courts of Chaos, to which she had at no time referred. Yet it had to be important, somehow.

I had a feeling that I already had the answer but that I would be unable to realize it until I had formulated the proper question.

Enough. I could go no further. Knowing that she was aware of my connection with the Courts still told me nothing. She was also obviously aware of my connection with Amber, and I could not see how that figured in the pattern of events either.

So I would leave it at that point and come back to it later. I had plenty of other things to think about. At least, I now had lots of new questions to ask her the next time we met, and I was certain that we would meet again.

Then something else occurred to me. If she'd done any real protecting of me at all, it had taken place offstage. She had given me a lot of information, which I thought was probably correct but which I had had no opportunity to verify. From her phoning and lurking back in New York to her killing of my one possible source of information in Death Alley, she had really been more a bother than a help. It was conceivable that she could actually show up and encumber me with aid again, at exactly the wrong moment.

So instead of working on my opening argument for Random, I spent the next hour or so considering the nature of a being capable of moving into a person and taking over the controls. There seemed only a certain number of ways it might be done, and I narrowed the field quickly, considering what I knew of her nature, by means of the technical exercises my uncle had taught me. When I thought I had it worked out I backtracked and mused over the forces that would have to be involved.

From the forces I worked my way through the tonic vibrations of their aspects. The use of raw power, while flashy, is wasteful and very fatiguing for the operator, not to mention aesthetically barbaric. Better to be prepared.

I lined up the spoken signatures and edited them into a spell. Suhuy would probably have gotten it down even shorter, but there is a point of diminishing returns on these things, and I had mine figured to where it should work if my main guesses were correct. So I collated it and assembled it. It was fairly long—too long to rattle off in its entirety if I were in the hurry I probably would be. Studying it, I saw that three linchpins would probably hold it, though four would be better.

I summoned the Logrus and extended my tongue into its moving pattern. Then I spoke the spell, slowly and clearly, leaving out the four key words I had chosen to omit. The woods grew absolutely still about me as the words rang out. The spell hung before me like a crippled butterfly of sound and color, trapped within the synesthetic web of my personal vision of the Logrus, to come again when I summoned it, to be released when I uttered the four omitted words.

I banished the vision and felt my tongue relax. Now she was not the only one capable of troublesome surprises.

I halted for a drink of water. The sky had grown darker and the small noises of the forest returned. I wondered whether Fiona or Bleys had been in touch, and how Bill was doing back in town. I listened to the rattling of branches. Suddenly, I had the feeling I was being watched —not the cold scrutiny of a Trump touch, but simply the sensation that there was a pair of eyes fixed upon me. I shivered. All those thoughts about enemies. . . .

I loosened my blade and rode on. The night was young, and there were more miles ahead than behind.

Riding through the evening I kept alert, but I neither heard nor saw anything untoward. Had I been wrong about Jasra, Sharu or even Luke? And was there a party of assassins at my back right now? Periodically, I drew rein and sat listening for a short while. But I heard nothing unusual on these occasions, nothing that could be taken as sounds of pursuit. I became acutely aware of the blue button in my pocket. Was it acting as a beacon for some sinister sending of the wizard's? I was loath to get rid of the thing because I could foresee a number of possible uses for it. Besides, if it had already attuned me—which it probably had—I could see no benefit in disposing of it now. I would secrete it someplace safe before I made my attempt to lose its vibes. Until such a time, I could see no percentage in doing anything else with it.

The sky continued to darken, and a number of stars had put in hesitant appearances. Smoke and I slowed even more in our course, but the road remained good and its pale surface stayed sufficiently visible to present no hazard. I heard the call of an owl from off to the right and moments later saw its dark shape rush at middle height among the trees. It would have been a pleasant night to be riding if I were not creating my own ghosts and haunting myself with them. I love the smells of autumn and the forest, and I resolved to burn a few leaves in my campfire later on for that pungency unlike any other I know.

The air was clean and cool. Hoof sounds, our breathing and the wind seemed to be the only noises in the neighborhood until we flushed a deer a bit later and heard the diminishing crashes of its treat for some time afterward. We crossed a small but sturdy wooden bridge a little later, but no trolls were taking tolls. The road took a turn upward, and we wound our way slowly but steadily to a higher elevation. Now there were numerous stars visible through the weave of the branches, but no clouds that I could see. The deciduous trees grew barer as we gained a bit of altitude, and more evergreens began to occur. I felt the breezes more strongly now.

I began pausing more frequently, to rest Smoke, to listen, to nibble at my supplies. I resolved to keep going at least until moonrise—which I tried to calculate from its occurrence the other night, following my departure from Amber. If I made it to that point before I camped, the rest of the ride into Amber tomorrow morning would be pretty easy.

Frakir pulsed once, lightly, upon my wrist. But hell, that had often happened in traffic when I'd cut someone off. A hungry fox could have just passed, regarded me and wished itself a bear. Still, I waited there longer than I had intended, prepared for an attack and trying not to appear so.

But nothing happened, the warning as not repeated and after a time I rode on. I returned to my idea for putting the screws to Luke—and, for that matter, Jasra. I couldn't call it a plan yet, because it was lacking in almost all particulars. The more I thought of it, the crazier it seemed. For one thing, it was extremely tempting, as it held the potential for resolving a lot of problems. I wondered then why I had never created a Trump for Bill Roth. I felt a sudden need to talk to a good attorney. I might well want someone to argue my case before this was done. Too dark now to do any drawing, though . . . and not really necessary yet. Actually, I just wanted to talk with him, bring him up to date, get the views of someone not directly involved.

Frakir issued no further warnings during the next hour. We commenced a slightly downward course then, soon passing into a somewhat more sheltered area where the smell of pines came heavy. I mused on—about wizards and flowers, Ghostwheel and his problems, and the name of the entity who had recently occupied Vinta. There were lots of other musings, too, some of which went a long way back. . . .

Many stops later, with a bit of moonlight trickling through the branches behind me, I decided to call it quits and look for a place to bed down. I gave Smoke a brief drink at the next stream. About a quarter hour afterward, I thought I glimpsed what might be a promising spot off to the right, so I left the road and headed that way.

It turned out not to be as good a place as I'd thought, and I continued farther into the wood until I came across a small clear area that seemed adequate. I dismounted, unsaddled Smoke and tethered him, rubbed him down with his blanket and gave him something to eat. Then I scraped clear a small area of ground with my blade, dug a pit at its center and built a fire there. I used a spell to ignite it because I was feeling lazy, and I threw on several clumps of leaves as I recalled my earlier reflections.

I seated myself on my cloak, my back against the bole of a middle-sized tree, and ate a cheese sandwich and sipped water while I worked up the ambition to pull my boots off. My blade lay upon the ground at my side. My muscles began to unkink. The smell of the fire was a nostalgic thing. I toasted my next sandwich over it.

I sat and thought of nothing for a long while. Gradually, in barely perceptible stages, I felt the gentle disengagements lassitude brings to the extremities. I had meant to gather firewood before I took my ease. But I didn't really need it. It wasn't all that cold. I'd wanted the fire mainly for company.

However. . . . I dragged myself to my feet and moved off into the woods. I did a long, slow reconnaissance about the area once I got moving. Though to be honest, my main reason for getting up had been to go and relieve myself. I halted in my circuit when I thought that I detected a small flicker of light far off to the northeast. Another campfire? Moonlight on water? A torch? There had been only a glimpse and I could not locate it again, though I moved my head about, retraced my most recent few paces and even struck off a small distance in that direction.

But I did not wish to chase after some will-o'-the-wisp and spend my night beating the bushes. I checked various lines of sight back to my camp. My small fire was barely visible even from this distance. I circled my camp, entered and sprawled again. The fire was already dying and I decided to let it burn out. I wrapped my cloak about me and listened to the soft sounds of the wind.

I fell asleep quickly. For how long I slept, I do not know. There were no dreams that I can recall.

I was awakened by Frakir's frantic pulsing. I opened my eyes the barest slits and tossed, as if in sleep, so that my right hand fell near the haft of my blade. I maintained my slow breathing pattern. I heard and felt that the wind had risen, and I saw that it had fanned the embers to the point where my fire flared once again. I saw no one before me, however. I strained my hearing after any sounds, but all I heard was the wind and the popping of the fire.

It seemed as foolish to spring to my feet into a guard position when I did not know from which direction the danger was approaching as it did to remain a target. On the other hand, I had intentionally cast my cloak so that I lay with a large, low-limbed pine at my back. It would have been very difficult for someone to have approached me from the rear, let alone to have done so quietly. So it did not seem I was in danger of an imminent attack from that direction.

I turned my head slightly and studied Smoke, who had begun to seem a little uneasy. Frakir continued her now distracting warning till I willed her to be still.

Smoke was twitching his ears and moving his head about, nostrils dilated. As I watched, I saw that his attention seemed directed toward my right. He began edging his way across the camp, his long tether snaking behind him.

I heard a sound then, beyond the noise of Smoke's retreat, as of something advancing from the right. It was not repeated for a time, and then I heard it again. It was not a footfall, but a sound as of a body brushing against a branch which suddenly issued a weak protest.

I visualized the disposition of trees and shrubs in that direction and decided to let the lurker draw nearer before I made my move. I dismissed the notion of summoning the Logrus and preparing a magical attack. It would take a bit more time than I thought I had remaining. Also, from Smoke's behavior and from what I had heard, it seemed

that there was only a single individual approaching. I resolved, though, to lay in a decent supply of spells the first
chance I got, both offensive and defensive, on the order of
the one I had primed against my guardian entity. The trouble is that it can take several days of solitude to work a
really decent array of them out properly, enact them and
rehearse their releases to the point where you can spring
them at a moment's notice—and then they have a tendency
to start decaying after a week or so. Sometimes they last
longer and sometimes less long, depending both on the
amount of energy you're willing to invest in them and on
the magical climate of the particular shadow in which
you're functioning. It's a lot of bother unless you're sure
you're going to need them within a certain period of time.
On the other hand, a good sorcerer should have one attack,
one defense and one escape spell hanging around at all
times. But I'm generally somewhat lazy, not to mention
pretty easygoing, and I didn't see any need for that sort of
setup until recently. And recently, I hadn't had much time
to be about it.

So any use I might make of the Logrus now, were I to
summon it and situate myself within its ambit, would
pretty much amount to blasting away with a raw power—
which is very draining on the operator.

Let him come a little nearer, that's all, and it would be
cold steel and a strangling cord that he would face.

I could feel the presence advancing now, hear the soft
stirring of pine needles. A few more feet, enemy. . . . Come
on. That's all I need. Come into range. . . .

He halted. I could hear a steady, soft breathing.

Then, "You must be aware of me by now, Magus,"
came a low whisper, "for we all have our little tricks, and I
know the source of yours."

"Who are you?" I asked, as I clasped the haft of my
blade and rolled into a crouch, facing the darkness, the
point of my weapon describing a small circle.

"I am the enemy," was the reply. "The one you thought
would never come."

CHAPTER 9

Power.

I remembered the day I had stood atop a rocky promi-
nence. Fiona—dressed in lavender, belted with silver—
stood in a higher place before me and somewhat to my
right. She held a silver mirror in her right hand, and she
looked downward through the haze to the place where the
great tree towered. There was a total stillness about us, and
even our own small sounds came muffled. The upper por-
tions of the tree disappeared into a low-hanging fog bank.
The light that filtered through limned it starkly against another pile of fog which hung at its back, rising to join with
the one overhead. A bright, seemingly self-illuminated line
was etched into the ground near the base of the tree, curving off to vanish within the fog. Far to my left, a brief arc
of a similar intensity was also visible, emerging from and
returning to the billowing white wall.

"What is it, Fiona?" I asked. "Why did you bring me to
this place?"

"You've heard of it," she replied. "I wanted you to see
it."

I shook my head. "I've never heard of it. I've no idea what I'm looking at."

"Come," she said, and she began to descend.

She disdained my hand, moving quickly and gracefully, and we came down from the rocks and moved nearer to the tree. There was something vaguely familiar there, but I could not place it.

"From your father," she said at last. "He spent a long time telling you his story. Surely he did not omit this part."

I halted as understanding presented itself, tentatively at first.

"That tree," I said.

"Corwin planted his staff when he commenced the creation of the new Pattern," she said. "It was fresh. It took root."

I seemed to feel a faint vibration in the ground.

Fiona turned her back on the prospect, raised the mirror she carried and angled it so that she regarded the scene over her right shoulder.

"Yes," she said, after several moments. Then she extended the mirror to me. "Take a look," she told me, "as I just did."

I accepted it, held it, adjusted it and stared.

The view in the mirror was not the same as that which had presented itself to my unaided scrutiny. I was able to see beyond the tree now, through the fog, to discern most of the strange Pattern which twisted its bright way about the ground, working its passages inward to its off-center terminus, the only spot still concealed by an unmoving tower of white, within which tiny lights like stars seemed to burn.

"It doesn't look like the Pattern back in Amber," I said.

"No," she answered. "Is it anything like the Logrus?"

"Not really. The Logrus actually alters itself somewhat, constantly. Still, it's more angular, whereas this is mostly curves and bends."

I studied it a little longer, then returned her looking glass.

"Interesting spell on the mirror," I commented, for I had been studying this also, while I held it.

"And much more difficult than you'd think," she responded, "for there's more than fog in there. Watch."

She advanced to the beginning of the Pattern, near the great tree, where she moved as if to set her foot upon the bright trail. Before it arrived, however, a small electrical discharge crackled upward and made contact with her shoe. She jerked her foot back quickly.

"It rejects me," she said. "I can't set foot on it. Try it."

There was something in her gaze I did not like, but I moved forward to where she had been standing.

"Why couldn't your mirror penetrate all the way to the center of the thing?" I asked suddenly.

"The resistance seems to go up the farther you go in. It is greatest there," she replied. "But as to why, I do not know."

I hesitated a moment longer. "Has anyone tried it other than yourself?"

"I brought Bleys here," she answered. "It rejected him too."

"And he's the only other one who's seen it?"

"No, I brought Random. But he declined to try. Said he didn't care to screw around with it right then."

"Prudent, perhaps. Was he wearing the Jewel at the time?"

"No. Why?"

"Just curious."

"See what it does for you."

"All right."

I raised my right foot and lowered it slowly toward the line. About a foot above it, I stopped.

"Something seems to be holding me back," I said.

"Strange. There is no electrical discharge for you."

"Small blessing," I responded, and I pushed my foot a couple of inches farther downward. Finally, I sighed. "Nope, Fi. I can't."

I read the disappointment in her features.

"I was hoping," she said as I drew back, "that someone

other than Corwin might be able to walk it. His son seemed the most likely choice."

"Why is it so important that someone walk it? Just because it's there?"

"I think it's a menace," she said. "It has to be explored and dealt with."

"A menace? Why?"

"Amber and Chaos are the two poles of existence, as we understand it," she said, "housing as they do the Pattern and the Logrus. For ages there has been something of an equilibrium between them. Now, I believe, this bastard Pattern of your father's is undermining their balance."

"In what fashion?'

"There have always been wavelike exchanges between Amber and Chaos. This seems to be setting up some interference."

"It sounds more like tossing an extra ice cube into a drink," I said. "It should settle down after a while."

She shook her head. "Things are not settling. There have been far more shadow-storms since this thing was created. They rend the fabric of Shadow. They affect the nature of reality itself."

"No good," I said. "Another event a lot more important along these lines occurred at the same time. The original Pattern in Amber was damaged and Oberon repaired it. The wave of Chaos which came out of that swept through all of Shadow. Everything was affected. But the Pattern held and things settled again. I'd be more inclined to think of all those extra shadow-storms as being in the nature of aftershocks."

"It's a good argument," she said. "But what if it's wrong?"

"I don't think it is."

"Merle, there's some kind of power here—an immense amount of power."

"I don't doubt it."

"It has always been our way to keep an eye on power, to try to understand it, to control it. Because one day it might become a threat. Did Corwin tell you anything, anything at all, as to exactly what this represents and how we might get a handle on it?"

"No," I said. "Nothing beyond the fact that he made it in a hurry to replace the old one, which he'd figured Oberon might not have succeeded in repairing."

"If only we could find him."

"There still hasn't been any word?"

"Droppa claims that he saw him at the Sands, back on the shadow Earth you both favor. He said he was in the company of an attractive woman, and they were both having a drink and listening to a music group. He waved and headed toward them through a crowd, and he thought that Corwin saw him. When he got to their table, though, they were gone."

"That's all?"

"That's all."

"That's not much."

"I know. If he's the only one who can walk this damned thing, though, and if it *is* a menace, we could be in big trouble one day."

"I think you're being an alarmist, Aunty."

"I hope you're right, Merle. Come on, I'll take you home."

I studied the place once more, for details as well as feeling, because I wanted to be able to construct a Trump for it. I never told anyone that there had been no resistance as I had lowered my foot, because once you set foot into the Pattern or the Logrus there is no turning back. You either proceed to the end or are destroyed by it. And as much as I love mysteries, my break was at its end and I had to get back to class.

Power.

We were together in a wood within the Black Zone, that area of Shadow with which Chaos holds commerce. We were hunting *zhind,* which are horned, short, black, fierce and carnivorous. I do not much like hunting because I do not much like killing things I don't really have to. However, it was Jurt's idea, and since it was possibly also my last chance to work some reconciliation with my brother before I departed, I had decided to take him up on the offer. Neither of us was that great an archer, and *zhind* are pretty fast. So with any luck at all nothing would get dead and we'd have some chance to talk and perhaps come away on better terms at the end of the hunt.

On one occasion when we'd lost the trail and were resting, we talked for a long time about archery, court politics, Shadow and the weather. He had been much more civil to me of late, which I took for a good sign. He'd let his hair grow in such a fashion as to cover the area of his missing left ear. Ears are hard to regenerate. We did not speak of our duel, or of the argument that had led up to it. Because I would soon be out of his life, I felt perhaps he wished to close this chapter of his existence in a relatively friendly fashion, with both of us going our ways with a memory we could feel good about. I was half right, anyway.

Later, when we had halted for a cold trail lunch, he asked me, "So, what does it feel like?"

"What?" I said.

"The power," he answered. "The Logrus power—to walk in Shadow, to work with a higher order of magic than the mundane."

I didn't really want to go into detail, because I knew he'd prepared himself to traverse the Logrus on three different occasions and had backed down at the last moment each time, when he'd looked into it. Perhaps the skeletons of failures that Suhuy keeps around had troubled him also. I don't think Jurt was aware that I knew about the last two times he'd changed his mind. So I decided to downplay my accomplishment.

"Oh, you don't really feel any different," I said, "until you're actually using it. Then it's hard to describe."

"I'm thinking of doing it soon myself," he said. "It would be good to see something of Shadow, maybe even find a kingdom for myself somewhere. Can you give me any advice?"

I nodded. "Don't look back," I said. "Don't stop to think. Just keep going."

He laughed. "Sounds like orders to an army," he said.

"I suppose there is a similarity."

He laughed again. "Let's go kill us a *zhind,*" he said.

That afternoon, we lost a trail in a thicket full of fallen branches. We'd heard the *zhind* crash through it, but it was not immediately apparent which way it had gone. I had my back to Jurt and was facing the forward edge of the place, searching for some sign, when Frakir constricted tightly about my wrist, then came loose and fell to the ground.

I bent over to retrieve her, wondering what had happened, when I heard a *thunk* from overhead. Glancing upward, I saw an arrow protruding from the bole of the tree before me. Its height above the ground was such that had I remained standing it would have entered my back.

I turned quickly toward Jurt, not even straightening from my crouch. He was fitting another arrow to his bow.

He said, "Don't look back. Don't stop to think. Just keep going," and he laughed.

I dove toward him as he raised the weapon. A better archer would probably have killed me. I think when I moved he panicked and released the arrow prematurely, though, because it caught in the side of my leather vest and I didn't feel any pain.

I clipped him above the knees, and he dropped the bow as he fell over backward. He drew his hunting knife, rolled to the side and swung the weapon toward my throat. I caught his wrist with my left hand and was cast onto my back by the force of his momentum. I struck at his face with my right fist while holding the blade away from me. He blocked the punch and kneed me in the balls.

The point of the blade dropped to within inches of my throat as this blow collapsed a big piece of my resistance. Still aching, I was able to turn my hip to prevent another ball-buster, simultaneous with casting my right forearm beneath his wrist and cutting my hand in the process. Then I pushed with my right, pulled with my left and rolled to the left with the force of the turn. His arm was jerked free from my still-weakened grasp, and he rolled off to the side and I tried to recover—and then I heard him scream.

Coming up onto my knees, I saw that he lay upon his left side where he had come to a stop and the knife was several feet beyond him, caught in a tangle of broken branches. Both hands were raised to his face, and his cries were wordless, animal-like bleats.

I made my way over to him to see what had happened, with Frakir held ready to wrap about his throat in case it were some sort of trick he was playing.

But it was not. When I reached him I saw that a sharp limb of a fallen branch had pierced his right eye. There was blood on his cheek and the side of his nose.

"Stop jerking around!" I said. "You'll make it worse. Let me get it out."

"Keep your damn hands off me!" he cried.

Then, clenching his teeth and grimacing horribly, he caught hold of the limb with his right hand and drew his head back. I had to look away. He made a whimpering noise several moments later and collapsed, unconscious. I ripped off my left shirt sleeve, tore a strip from it, folded it into a pad and placed it over his damaged eye. With another strip, I tied it into place there. Frakir found her way back about my wrist, as usual.

Then I dug out the Trump that would take us home and raised him in my arms. Mom wasn't going to like this.

Power.

It was a Saturday. Luke and I had been hang gliding all morning. Then we met Julia and Gail for lunch, and afterward we took the Starburst out and sailed all afternoon. Later, we'd hit the bar and grill at the marina where I bought the beers while we waited for steaks, because Luke had slammed my right arm flat against the tabletop when we'd wrist wrestled to see who paid for drinks.

Someone at the next table said, "If I had a million dollars, tax free, I'd..." and Julia had laughed as she listened.

"What's funny?" I asked her.

"His wish list," she said. "I'd want a closet full of designer dresses and some elegant jewelry to go with them.

Put the closet in a really nice house, and put the house someplace where I'd be important...."

Luke smiled. "I detect a shift from money to power," he said.

"Maybe so," she replied. "But what's the difference, really?"

"Money buys things," Luke said. "Power makes things happen. If you ever have a choice, take the power."

Gail's usual faint smile had faded, and she wore a very serious expression.

"I don't believe power should be an end in itself," she said. "One has it only to use it in certain ways."

Julia laughed. "What's wrong with a power trip?" she asked. "It sounds like fun to me."

"Only till you run into a greater power," Luke said.

"Then you have to think big," Julia answered.

"That's not right," Gail said. "One has duties and they come first."

Luke was studying her now, and he nodded.

"You can keep morality out of it," Julia said.

"No, you can't," Luke responded.

"I disagree," she said.

Luke shrugged.

"She's right," Gail said suddenly. "I don't see that duty and morality are the same thing."

"Well, if you've got a duty," Luke said, "something you absolutely must do—a matter of honor, say—then that becomes your morality."

Julia looked at Luke, looked at Gail. "Does that mean we just agreed on something?" she asked.

"No," Luke said, "I don't think so."

Gail took a drink. "You're talking about a personal code that need not have anything to do with conventional morality."

"Right," Luke said.

"Then it's not really morality. You're just talking duty," she said.

"You're right on the duty," Luke answered. "But it's still morality."

"Morality is the values of a civilization," she said.

"There is no such thing as civilization," Luke replied. "The word just means the art of living in cities."

"All right, then. Of a culture," she said.

"Cultural values are relative things," Luke said, smiling, "and mine say I'm right."

"Where do yours come from?" Gail asked, studying him carefully.

"Let's keep this pure and philosophical, huh?" he said.

"Then maybe we should drop the term entirely," Gail said, "And just stick with duty."

"What happened to power?" Julia asked.

"It's in there somewhere," I said.

Suddenly Gail looked perplexed, as if our discussion were not something which had been repeated a thousand times in different forms, as if it had actually given rise to some new turn of thought.

"If they are two different things," she said slowly, "which one is more important?"

"They're not," Luke said. "They're the same."

"I don't think so," Julia told him. "But duties tend to be clear-cut, and it sounds as if you can choose your own morality. So if I had to have one I'd go with the morality."

"I like things that are clear-cut," Gail said.

Luke chugged his beer, belched lightly. "Shit!" he said. "Philosophy class isn't till Tuesday. This is the weekend. Who gets the next round, Merle?"

I placed my left elbow on the tabletop and opened my hand.

While we pushed together, the tension building and building between us, he said through clenched teeth, "I was right, wasn't I?"

"You were right," I said, just before I forced his arm all the way down.

Power.

I removed my mail from the little locked box in the hallway and carried it upstairs to my apartment. There were two bills, some circulars and something thick and first class without a return address on it.

I closed the door behind me, pocketed my keys and dropped my briefcase onto a nearby chair. I had started toward the sofa when the telephone in the kitchen rang.

Tossing the mail toward the coffee table, I turned and started for the kitchen. The blast that occurred behind me might or might not have been strong enough to knock me over. I don't know, because I dove forward of my own volition as soon as it occurred. I hit my head on the leg of the kitchen table. It dazed me somewhat, but I was otherwise undamaged. All the damage was in the other room. By the time I got to my feet the phone had stopped ringing.

I already knew there were lots of easier ways to dispose of junk mail, but I wondered for a long time afterward who it was that had been on the telephone.

I sometimes remembered the first of the series, too, the truck that had come rushing toward me. I had only caught a glimpse of the driver's face before I'd moved—inert, he was completely expressionless, as if he were dead, hypnotized, drugged or somehow possessed. Choose any of the above, I decided, and maybe more than one.

And then there was the night of the muggers. They had attacked me without a word. When it was all over and I was heading away, I had glanced back once. I thought I'd glimpsed a shadowy figure draw back into a doorway up the street—a smart precaution, I'd say, in light of what had been going on. But of course it could have been someone connected with the attack, too. I was torn. The person was too far off to have been able to give a good description of me. If I went back and it turned out to be an innocent bystander, there would then be a witness capable of identifying me. Not that I didn't think it was an open-and-shut case of self-defense, but there'd be a lot of hassle. So I said the hell with it, and I walked on. Another interesting April 30.

The day of the rifle. There had been two shots as I'd hurried down the street. They'd both missed me before I'd realized what was going on, chipping brickbats from the side of the building to my left. There was no third shot, but there was a thud and a splintering sound from the building across the street. A third-floor window stood wide open.

I hurried over. It was an old apartment house and the front door was locked, but I didn't slow down for niceties. I located the stair and mounted it. When I came to what I thought was the proper room, I decided to try the door the old-fashioned way and it worked. It was unlocked.

I stood to the side and pushed it open and saw that the place was unfurnished and empty. Unoccupied, too, it seemed. Could I have been wrong? But then I saw that the window facing the street stood wide and I saw what lay upon the floor. I entered and closed the door behind me.

A broken rifle lay in the corner. From markings on the stock I guessed that it had been swung with great force against a nearby radiator before it had been cast aside. Then I saw something else on the floor, something wet and red. Not much. Just a few drops.

I searched the place quickly. It was small. The one window in its single bedroom also stood open and I went to it. There was a fire escape beyond it, and I decided that it might be a good way for me to make my exit, too. There were a few more drops of blood on the black metal, but that was it. No one was in sight below, or in either direction.

Power. To kill. To preserve. Luke, Jasra, Gail. Who was responsible for what?

The more I thought of it, the more it seemed possible that there might have been a telephone call on the morning of the open gas jets, too. Could that be what had roused me to an awareness of danger? Each time I thought of these matters there seemed to be a slight shifting of emphasis. Things stood in a different light. According to Luke and the pseudo-Vinta, I was not in great danger in the later episodes, but it seemed that any of those things could have taken me out. Who was I to blame? The perpetrator? Or the savior who barely saved? And who was which? I remembered how my father's story had been complicated by that damned auto accident which played like *Last Year at Mar-*

ienbad—though his had seemed simple compared to everything that was coming down on me. At least he knew what he had to do most of the time. Could I be the inheritor of a family curse involving complicated plotting?

Power.

I remembered Uncle Suhuy's final lesson. He had spent some time following my completion of the Logrus in teaching me things I could not have learned before then. There came a time when I thought I was finished. I had been confirmed in the Art and dismissed. It seemed I had covered all the basics and anything more would be mere elaboration. I began making preparations for my journey to the shadow Earth. Then one morning Suhuy sent for me. I assumed that he just wanted to say good-bye and give me a few friendly words of advice.

His hair is white, he is somewhat stooped and there are days when he carries a staff. This was one of them. He had on his yellow caftan, which I had always thought of as a working garment rather than a social one.

"Are you ready for a short trip?" he asked me.

"Actually, it's going to be a long one," I said. "But I'm almost ready."

"No," he said. "That was not the journey I meant."

"Oh. You mean you want to go somewhere right now?"

"Come," he said.

So I followed him, and the shadows parted before us. We moved through increasing bleakness, passing at last into places that bore no sign of life whatsoever. Dark, sterile rock lay all about us, stark in the brassy light of a dim and ancient sun. This final place was chill and dry, and when we halted and I looked about, I shivered.

I waited, to see what he had in mind. But it was a long while before he spoke. He seemed oblivious of my presence for a time, simply staring out across the bleak landscape.

Finally, "I have taught you the ways of Shadow," he said slowly, "and the composition of spells and their working."

I said nothing. His statement did not seem to require a reply.

"So you know something of the ways of power," he continued. "You draw it from the Sign of Chaos, the Logrus, and you invest it in various ways."

He glanced at me at last, and I nodded.

"I understand that those who bear the Pattern, the Sign of Order, may do similar things in ways that may or may not be similar," he went on. "I do not know for certain, for I am not an initiate of the Pattern. I doubt the spirit could stand the strain of knowing the ways of both. But you should understand that there is another way of power, antithetical to our own."

"I understand," I said, for he seemed to be expecting an answer.

"But you have a resource available to you," he said, "which those of Amber do not. Watch!"

His final word did not mean that I should simply observe as he leaned his staff against the side of a boulder and raised his hands before him. It meant that I should have the Logrus before me so I could see what he was doing at that level. So I summoned my vision and watched him through it.

Now the vision that hung before him seemed a continuation of my own, stretched and twisting. I saw and felt it as he joined his hands with it and extended a pair of its jagged limbs outward across the distance to touch upon a boulder that lay downhill of us.

"Enter the Logrus now yourself," he said, "remaining passive. Stay with me through what I am about to do. Do not, at any time, attempt to interfere."

"I understand," I said.

I moved my hands into my vision, shifting them about, feeling after congruity, until they became a part of it.

"Good," he said, when I had settled them into place. "Now all you need do is observe, on all levels."

Something pulsed along the limbs he controlled, passing down to the boulder. I was not prepared for what came after.

The image of the Logrus turned black before me, becoming a seething blot of inky turmoil. An awful feeling of disruptive power surged through me, an enormous destructive force that threatened to overwhelm me, to carry me into the blissful nothingness of ultimate disorder. A part of me seemed to desire this, while another part was screaming wordlessly for it to cease. But Suhuy maintained control of the phenomenon, and I could see how he was doing it, just as I had seen how he had brought it into being in the first place.

The boulder became one with the turmoil, joined it and was gone. There was no explosion, no implosion, only the sensation of great cold winds and cacophonous sounds. Then my uncle moved his hands slowly apart, and the lines of seething blackness followed them, flowing out in both directions from that area of chaos which had been the boulder, producing a long dark trench wherein I beheld the paradox of both nothingness and activity.

Then he stood still, arresting it at that point. Moments later, he spoke.

"I could simply release it," he stated, "letting it run wild. Or I could give it a direction and then release it."

As he did not continue, I asked, "What would happen then? Would it simply continue until it had devastated the entire shadow?"

"No," he replied. "There are limiting factors. The resistance of Order to Chaos would build as it extended itself. There would come a point of containment."

"And if you remained as you are, and kept summoning more?"

"One would do a great deal of damage."

"And if we combined our efforts?"

"More extensive damage. But that is not the lesson I had in mind. I will remain passive now while you control it."

So I took over the Sign of the Logrus and ran the line of disruption back upon itself in a great circle, like a dark moat surrounding us.

"Banish it now," he said, and I did.

Still, the winds and the sounds continued to rage, and I

could not see beyond the dark wall which seemed to be advancing sowly upon us from all sides.

"Obviously, the limiting factor has yet to be achieved," I observed.

He chuckled. "You're right. Even though you stopped, you exceeded a certain critical limit, so that it is now running wild."

"Oh," I said. "How long till those natural limitations you mentioned dampen it?"

"Sometime after it has completely annihilated the area on which we stand," he said.

"It is receding in all directions as well as heading this way?"

"Yes."

"Interesting. What *is* the critical mass?"

"I'll have to show you. But we'd better find a new place first. This one is going away. Take my hand."

I did, and he conducted me to another shadow. This time I summoned the Chaos and conducted the operations while he observed. This time I did not let it run wild.

When I had finished and I stood, shaken, staring into a small crater I had caused, he placed his hand on my shoulder and told me, "As you knew in theory, that is the ultimate power behind your spells. Chaos itself. To work with it directly is dangerous. But, as you have seen, it can be done. Now you know it, your training is complete."

It was more than impressive. It was awesome. And for most situations I could visualize it was rather like using nukes for skeet shooting. Offhand, I couldn't think of any circumstances under which I would care to employ the technique, until Victor Melman really pissed me off.

Power, in its many shapes, varieties, sizes and styles, continues to fascinate me. It has been so much a part of my life for so long that I feel very familiar with it, though I doubt that I will ever understand it fully.

CHAPTER 10

"It's about time," I said, to whatever lurked in the shadows.

The sound that followed was not human. It was a low snarl. I wondered what manner of beast I confronted. I was certain an attack was imminent, but it did not come. Instead the growl died down, and whatever it was spoke again.

"Feel your fear," came the whisper.

"Feel your own," I said, "while you still can."

The sounds of its breathing came heavy. The flames danced at my back. Smoke had drawn as far away across the campsite as his lengthy tether permitted.

"I could have killed you while you slept," it said slowly.

"Foolish of you not to," I said. "It will cost you."

"I want to look at you, Merlin," it stated. "I want to see you puzzled. I want to see your fear. I want to see your anguish before I see your blood."

"Then I take it this is a personal rather than a business matter?"

There came a strange noise which it took me several

moments to interpret as an inhuman throat trying to manage a chuckle.

Then, "Let us say that, magician," it responded. "Summon your Sign and your concentration will waver. I will know it and will rend you before you can employ it."

"Kind of you to warn me."

"I just wanted to foreclose that option in your thinking. The thing wound about your left wrist will not help you in time either."

"You have good vision."

"In these matters, yes."

"You wish perhaps to discuss the philosophy of revenge with me now?"

"I am waiting for you to break and do something foolish, to increase my pleasure. I have limited your actions to the physical, so you are doomed."

"Keep waiting, then," I said.

There was a sound of movement within the brush as something drew nearer. I still could not see it, though. I took a step to my left then, to allow firelight to reach that darkened area. At that, something shone, low. The light was reflected, yellow, from a single glaring eye.

I lowered the point of my weapon, directing it toward the eye. What the hell. Every creature I know of tries to protect its eyes.

"Banzai!" I cried, as I lunged. The conversation seemed to have stagnated, and I was anxious to get on to other matters.

It rose instantly and with great power and speed rushed toward me, avoiding my thrust. It was a large, black, lop-eared wolf, and it slipped past a frantic slash I managed and went straight for my throat.

My left forearm came up automatically and I thrust it forward into the open jaws. At the same time, I brought the hilt of my blade across and slammed it against the side of its head. At this, the clamping force of the bite loosened even as I was borne over backward, but the grip remained, penetrating shirt and flesh. And I was turning and pulling before I hit the ground, wanting to land on top, knowing I wouldn't.

I landed on my left side, attempting to continue the roll, and added another belt of the pommel to the side of the beast's skull. It was then that fortune favored me, for a change, when I realized that we lay near the lip of my fire pit and were still turning in that direction. I dropped my weapon and sought its throat with my right hand. It was heavily muscled, and there was no chance of crushing the windpipe in time. But that was not what I was after.

My hand went up high and back beneath the lower jaw, where I commenced squeezing with all my strength. I scrabbled with my feet until I found purchase and then pushed with my legs as well as my arms. Our movement continued the short distance necessary to push its snarling head back into the fire.

For a moment nothing happened save the steady trickle of blood from my forearm into its mouth and out again. The grip of its jaws was still strong and painful.

Seconds later, my arm was released as the fur of its neck and head caught fire and it struggled to draw away from the flames. I was thrust aside as it rose and pulled free, an ear-piercing howl rising from its throat. I rolled to my knees and raised my hands, but it did not come at me again. Instead, it rushed past me into the woods in the opposite direction from which it had come.

I snatched up my blade and took off after it. No time to pause and pull on my boots; I was able to shapeshift the soles of my feet a bit to toughen them against the litter and irregularity of the forest floor. My adversary was still in sight, for its head still smoldered; though I might have been able to follow just from the howling, which was almost continuous. And strangely, the tone and character of the howls was changing, sounding more and more like human cries and less like the complaint of a wolf. Strangely, too, the beast was fleeing with something less than the speed and guile I would have expected from one of its kind. I heard it crashing through the shrubbery and running into trees. On several of these latter occasions, it even emitted sounds that seemed to bear the pattern of human cursing. So I was able to stay closer to it than I had any reason to expect, even gaining on it somewhat after the first few minutes.

Then, suddenly, I realized its apparent destination. I saw again that pale light I had noted earlier—brighter now and its source larger, as we moved toward it. Roughly rectangular in shape, I judged it as being eight or nine feet in height, perhaps five in width. I forgot about tracking the wolf by ear and headed for the light. That had to be its goal, and I wanted to reach it first.

I ran on. The wolf was ahead of me and to my left. Its hair had ceased to blaze now, though it still snarled and yipped as it rushed along. Before us, the light grew brighter still, and I was able to see into it—through it— and distinguish some of its features for the first time. I saw a hillside with a low stone building upon it, approached by a flagged walkway and a series of stone steps—framed like a picture within the rectangle—hazy at first, but coming clearer with each step. It was a cloudy afternoon within the picture, and the thing stood about twenty meters away now, in the midst of a clearing.

I realized as I saw the beast burst into the clearing that I was not going to be able to reach the place in time to snatch up the thing I knew must lie nearby. Still, I thought I might have a chance of catching the creature and halting its passage.

But it put on additional speed once it was in the clear. I could see the scene toward which it was headed more clearly than anything else in the vicinity. I shouted to distract it, but that did not work. My final burst of speed was not good enough. Then, on the ground, near the threshold, I saw what I was looking for. Too late. Even as I watched, the beast lowered its head and caught up in its teeth a flat rectangular object, without even breaking stride.

I halted and turned away as it plunged ahead, dropping my blade as I dove, rolling, continuing to roll.

I felt the force of the silent explosion, followed by the implosion and the small series of shock waves. I lay there thinking nasty thoughts until the turmoil had ceased; then I rose and retrieved my weapon.

The night was normal about me once again. Starlight. The wind in the pines. There was no need for me to turn, though I did, to know that the thing toward which I had been racing but moments before was now gone, without leaving any sign that it had been there, bright doorway to another place.

I hiked back to my camp and spent a while talking to Smoke, calming him. I donned my boots and cloak then, kicked dirt over the embers in my pit, and led the horse back to the road.

I mounted there and we moved on up the road toward Amber for the better part of an hour, before I settled upon a new campsite under a bone-white piece of moon.

The rest of my night was untroubled. I was awakened by increased light and morning bird calls through the pines. I took care of Smoke, breakfasted quickly on the remains of my rations, put myself in the best order I could and was on my way within half an hour.

It was a cool morning, with banks of cumulus far off to my left, clear skies overhead. I did not hurry. My main reason for riding back rather than trumping home was to learn a little more of what this area near Amber was like, and the other was to gain a bit of solitude for thinking. With Jasra a prisoner, Luke in sick bay and Ghostwheel occupied it seemed that any major threats to Amber or myself were in abeyance, and a small breathing spell could be justified. I felt that I was actually near to a point where I could handle everything personally with regard to Luke and Jasra, as soon as I'd worked out a few more details. And I was certain I could deal with Ghost after that, as I'd found our most recent conversation somewhat encouraging.

That was the big stuff. I could worry about loose ends later. A two-bit wizard like Sharu Garrul was only a pain when considered in conjunction with everything else that was troubling me. Dueling with him would be no problem when I had a bit of leisure—though I had to admit I was puzzled as to why he should be interested in me at all.

Then there was the matter of the entity which had for a time been Vinta. While I saw no real threat in it, there was certainly a mystery which affected my peace of mind, and which seemed ultimately to have something to do with my security. This, too, was a matter to be dealt with when that bit of leisure finally came along.

And Luke's offer to reveal a piece of information vital to Amber's security, once Jasra was rescued, troubled me. Because I believed him, and I believed he'd keep his word. I had a hunch, though, that he wouldn't be giving it away unless it was too late to do much about it. Guesswork was, of course, futile; there was no way of knowing what preparations would be appropriate. Was the offer itself, no matter how authentic, also a bit of psychological warfare? Luke had always been more subtle than his bluff exterior seemed to indicate. It had taken me a long time to learn that, and I wasn't about to forget it now.

I felt I could discount the business of the blue stones for the moment, and I planned soon to be rid of all traces of their vibes. No problem there, other than a mental string around the finger for extra wariness, just in case—and I was already in that frame of mind, had been for some time.

That left the business of last night's wolf to be fitted into the bigger picture.

Obviously, it had been no normal beast, and its intent had been apparent enough. Other matters concerning its visit were less than clear, however. Who or what was it? Was it a principal or an agent? And, if the latter, who had sent it? And finally, finally, why?

Its clumsiness indicated to me—since I had tried that sort of business myself in the past—that it was a shape-shifted human rather than a true wolf magically gifted with speech. Most people who daydream of transforming themselves into some vicious beast and going about tearing people's throats out, dismembering them, disfiguring them and perhaps devouring them tend mainly to dwell upon how much fun it would be and generally neglect the practicalities of the situation. When you find yourself a quadruped, with a completely different center of gravity and a novel array of sensory input, it is not all that easy to get around for a time with any measure of grace. One is generally far more vulnerable than one's appearance would lead others to believe. And certainly one is nowhere near as lethal and efficient as the real thing with a lifetime of practice behind it. No. I've always tended to think of it more as a terrorist tactic than anything else.

Be that how it may, the manner of the beast's coming and going was actually the main cause of my trepidation concerning the entire affair. It had employed a Trump Gate, which is not a thing one does lightly—or at all, for that matter, if it can be avoided. It is a flashy and spectacular thing to make Trump contact with some distant place and then pour tons of power into the objectification of such a gateway as a form possessed for a time of an independent existence. It is exceedingly profligate of energy and effort—even a hellrun is much easier—to create one which will stand for even fifteen minutes. It can drain most of your resources for a long while. Yet this was what had occurred. The reason behind it did not trouble me, as much as the fact that it had happened at all. For the only people capable of the feat were genuine initiates of the Trumps. It couldn't be done by someone who just happened to come into possession of a card.

Which narrowed the field considerably.

I tried to picture the werebeast about its errand. First, it would have to locate me and—

Of course. I suddenly recalled the dead dogs in the grove near Arbor House and the large doglike tracks in the vicinity. The thing had spotted me sometime before, then, and had been watching, waiting. It had followed me when I set out yesterday evening, and when I made my camp it made its move. It set up—or was set up with—the Trump Gate, for a retreat that would brook no pursuit. Then it came to kill me. And I had no way of telling whether it involved Sharu Garrul, Luke's secret, the blue stones or the body-switching entity's mission. For now it would simply have to dangle as yet another loose end, while I concentrated on basics.

I overtook and passed a line of wagons headed for Amber. A few horsemen went by me headed in the other direction. No one I knew, though everyone waved. The clouds continued to mount to my left, but nothing resembling a storm took shape. The day remained cool and sunny. The road dipped and rose again, several times, though overall it rose more than it dipped. I stopped at a large, busy inn for lunch, had a quick, filling meal and did not linger. The road improved steadily after that, and it was not long before I caught distant glimpses of Amber atop Kolvir, sparkling in the noonday light.

Traffic grew heavier as the sun advanced through the heavens. I continued to make plans and indulge in whatever speculations came to mind as I rode on into afternoon. My uphill way took several turnings as the route passed through the heights, but Amber remained in sight most of the time.

I recognized no one along the way, and I reached the Eastern Gate—part of an ancient fortification—late in the afternoon. I made my way up East Vine and stopped at the Bayle town house, where I had once attended a party. I left Smoke with a groom at the stable in the rear, and they both seemed happy to see each other. I walked around to the front door then and knocked. A servant informed me that the Baron was out, so I identified myself and gave him Vinta's message, which he promised to deliver when his employer returned.

That duty out of the way, I proceeded up East Vine on foot. Near the top, but before the slope grew roughly level, I smelled food and discarded my plan of waiting to eat until I was back at the palace. I halted and cast about me for the source of the aromas. I located it up a side street to my right where the way widened into a large circle, a fountain at its center—in which a rearing copper dragon with a wonderful green patina pissed into a pink stone basin. The dragon faced a basement restaurant called the Pit, with ten outside tables enclosed by a low fence of copper pickets, potted plants along its inside perimeter. I crossed the circle. As I passed the fountain I saw a great number of exotic coins within its clear water, including a U.S. Bicentennial quarter. Crossing to the fenced area, I entered, made my way through and was about to descend the stair when I heard my name called.

"Merle! Over here!"

I looked about but did not see anyone I recognized at any of the four occupied tables. Then, as my eyes retraced their route, I realized that the older man at the corner table to my right was smiling.

"Bill!" I exclaimed.

Bill Roth rose to his feet—more a touch of display than any formality, I realized immediately. I hadn't recognized him at first because he now sported the beginnings of a grizzled beard and a mustache. Also, he had on brown trousers with a silver stripe running down their outside seams, vanishing into a pair of high brown boots. His shirt was silver with brown piping, and a black cloak lay folded upon the chair to his right. A wide black sword belt lay atop it and a sheathed blade of short-to-medium length was hung upon it.

"You've gone native. Also, you've lost some weight."

"True," he said, "and I'm thinking of retiring here. It agrees with me."

We seated ourselves.

"Did you order yet?" I asked him.

"Yes, but I see a waiter on the stair now," he said. "Let me catch him for you."

Which he did, and ordered for me too.

"Your Thari's much better," I said afterward.

"Lots of practice," he replied.

"What've you been doing?"

"I've sailed with Gérard. I've been to Deiga, and to one of Julian's camps in Arden. Visited Rebma, too. Fascinating place. I've been taking fencing lessons. And Droppa's been showing me around town."

"All the bars, most likely."

"Well, that's not all. In fact, that's why I'm here. He

owns a half interest in the Pit, and I had to promise him I'd eat here a lot. A good place, though. When did you get back?"

"Just now," I said, "and I've another long story for you."

"Good. Your stories tend to be bizarre and convoluted," he said. "Just the thing for a cool autumn's eve. Let's hear it."

I talked throughout dinner and for a long while afterward. The day's-end chill began making it uncomfortable then, so we headed for the palace. I finally wound up my narrative over hot cider in front of the fireplace in one of the smaller rooms in the eastern wing.

Bill shook his head. "You do manage to stay busy," he finally said. "I have one question."

"What?"

"Why didn't you bring Luke in?"

"I already told you."

"It wasn't much of a reason. For some nebulous piece of information he says is important to Amber? And you've got to catch him to get it?"

"It's not like that at all."

"He's a salesman, Merle, and he sold you a line of shit. That's what I think."

"You're wrong, Bill. I know him."

"For a long time," he agreed. "But how well? We've been all through this before. What you don't know about Luke far outweighs what you do know."

"He could have gone elsewhere, but he came to me."

"You're part of his plan, Merle. He intends to get at Amber through you."

"I don't think so," I said. "It's not his style."

"I think he'll use anything that comes to hand—or anyone."

I shrugged. "I believe him. You don't. That's all."

"I guess so," he said. "What are you going to do now, wait and see what happens?"

"I've a plan," I said. "Just because I believe him doesn't

mean I won't take out insurance. But I've a question for you."

"Yes?"

"If I brought him back here and Random decided the facts weren't clear enough and he wanted a hearing, would you represent Luke?"

His eyes widened, and then he smiled. "What kind of hearing?" he asked. "I don't know how such things are conducted here."

"As a grandson of Oberon," I explained, "he'd come under House Law. Random is head of the House now. It would be up to him whether to forget about a thing, render a summary judgment or call a hearing. As I understand it, such a hearing could be as formal or informal as Random wanted. There are books on the subject in the library. But a person has always had the right to be represented at one if he wanted."

"Of course I'd take the case," Bill said. "It doesn't sound like a legal experience that comes along too often.

"But it might look like a conflict of interest," he added, "since I have done work for the Crown."

I finished my cider and put the glass on the mantelpiece. I yawned.

"I have to go now, Bill."

He nodded; then, "This is all just hypothetical, isn't it?" he asked.

"Of course," I said. "It might turn out to be *my* hearing. G'night."

He studied me. "Uh—this insurance you were talking about," he said. "It probably involves something risky, doesn't it?"

I smiled.

"Nothing anyone could help you with, I suppose?"

"Nope."

"Well, good luck."

"Thanks."

"See you tomorrow?"

"Later in the day, maybe. . . ."

* * *

I went to my room and sacked out. I had to get some
rest before I went about the business I had in mind. I don't
recall any dreams, pro or con, on the matter.

It was still dark when I woke. Good to know that my
mental alarm was working.

It would have been very pleasant to turn over and go
back to sleep, but I couldn't allow myself the luxury. The
day that lay ahead was to be an exercise in timing. Ac-
cordingly, I got up, cleaned up and dressed myself in fresh
clothes.

I headed for the kitchen then, where I made myself
some tea and toast and scrambled a few eggs with chilis
and onions and a bit of pepper. I turned up some melka
fruit from the Snelters, too—something I hadn't had in a
long while.

Afterward, I went out through the rear and made my
way into the garden. Dark it was, moonless and damp,
with a few wisps of mist exploring invisible paths. I followed a path to the northwest. The world was a very quiet
place. I let my thoughts get that way, too. It was to be a
one-thing-at-a-time day, and I wanted to start it off with
that habit of mind in place.

I walked until I ran out of garden, passing through a
break in a hedge and continuing along the rough trail my
path had become. It mounted slowly for the first few minutes, took an abrupt turn and grew immediately steeper. I
paused at one jutting point and looked back, from where I
was afforded a view of the dark outline of the palace, a few
lighted windows within it. Some scatters of cirrus high
above looked like raked starlight in the celestial garden
over which Amber brooded. I turned away moments later.
There was still a good distance to travel.

When I reached the crest I was able to discern a faint
line of lightening to the east, beyond the forest I had tra-
versed so recently. I hurried past the three massive steps of
song and story and began my descent to the north. Slow at
first, the way I followed steepened abruptly after a time
and led off to the northeast, then into a gentler decline.

When it swung back to the northwest there was another steep area followed by another easy one, and I knew the going would be fine after that. The high shoulder of Kolvir at my back blocked all traces of the pre-dawn light I had witnessed earlier, and star-hung night lay before me and above, rubbing outlines to ambiguity on all but the nearest boulders. Still, I knew approximately where I was going, having been this way once before, though I'd only halted briefly at that time.

It was about two miles past the crest, and I slowed as I neared the area, searching. It was a large, somewhat horse-shoe-shaped declivity, and when I finally located it I entered slowly, a peculiar feeling rising within me. I had not consciously anticipated all my reactions in this matter; but at some level I must have, I was certain.

As I moved into it, canyonlike walls of stone rising at either hand, I came upon the trail and followed it. It led me slightly downhill, toward a shadowy pair of trees, and then between them to where a low stone building stood, various shrubs and grasses grown wild about it. I understand that the soil was actually transported there to support the foliage, but afterward it was forgotten and neglected.

I seated myself on one of the stone benches in front of the building and waited for the sky to lighten. This was my father's tomb—well, cenotaph—built long ago when he had been presumed dead. It had amused him considerably to be able to visit the place later on. Now, of course, its status might well have changed. It could be the real thing now. Would this cancel the irony or increase it? I couldn't quite decide. It bothered me, though, more than I'd thought it would. I had not come here on a pilgrimage. I had come here for the peace and quiet a sorcerer of my sort needs in order to hang some spells. I had come here—

Perhaps I was rationalizing. I had chosen this spot because, real tomb or fake, it had Corwin's name on it, so it raised a sense of his presence, for me. I had wanted to get to know him better, and this might be as close as I could ever come. I realized, suddenly, why I had trusted Luke. He had been right, back at the Arbor House. If I learned of

Corwin's death and saw that blame could be fixed for it, I knew that I would drop everything else, that I would go off to present the bill and collect it, that I would have to close the account, to write the receipt in blood. Even had I not known Luke as I did, it was easy to see myself in his actions and too uncomfortable a thing to judge him.

Damn. Why must we caricature each other, beyond laughter or insight, into the places of pain, frustration, conflicting loyalties?

I rose. There was enough light now to show me what I was doing.

I went inside and approached the niche where the empty stone sarcophagus stood. It seemed an ideal safe deposit box, but I hesitated when I stood before it because my hands were shaking. It was ridiculous. I knew that he wasn't in there, that it was just an empty box with a bit of carving on it. Yet it was several minutes before I could bring myself to take hold of the lid and raise it. . . .

Empty, of course, like so many dreams and fears. I tossed in the blue button and lowered the lid again. What the hell. If Sharu wanted it back and could find it here, let him have the message that he was walking close to the grave when he played his games.

I went back outside, leaving my feelings in the crypt. It was time to begin. I'd a mess of spells to work and hang, for I'd no intention of going gently to the place where the wild winds blew.

CHAPTER 11

I stood on the rise above the garden, admiring the autumn foliage below. The wind played games with my cloak. A mellow afternoon light bathed the palace. There was a chill in the air. A flock of dead leaves rushed, lemming-like, past me and blew off the edge of the trail, rattling, into the air.

I had not really stopped to admire the view, however. I had halted while I blocked an attempted Trump contact— the day's second. The first had occurred earlier, while I was hanging a spell like a rope of tinsel on the image of Chaos. I figured that it was either Random—irritated that I was back in Amber and had not seen fit to bring him up to date on my most recent doings and my plans—or Luke, recovered now and wanting to request my assistance in his move against the Keep. They both came to mind because they were the two individuals I wished most to avoid; neither of them would much like what I was about to do, though for different reasons.

The call faded, was gone, and I descended the trail, passed through the hedge and entered the garden. I did not want to waste a spell to mask my passage, so I took a trail to the left, which led through a series of arbors where I was less exposed to the gaze of anyone who happened to glance out of a window. I could have avoided this by trumping in, but that card always delivers one to the main hall, and I had no idea who might be there.

Of course, I was headed that way. . . .

I went back in the way I had come out, through the kitchen, helping myself to a sandwich and a glass of milk on the way. Then I took the back stairs up a flight, lurked a bit and made it to my rooms without being spotted. There, I buckled on the sword belt I had left hanging at the head of my bed, checked the blade, located a small dagger I had brought with me from Chaos—a gift from the Pit-diver Borquist, whom I'd once fixed up with an introduction that led to a patronage (he was a middling-good poet)—and hung it on the other side of my belt. I pinned a Trump to the inside of my left sleeve. I washed my hands and face and brushed my teeth, too. But then I couldn't think of any other ways to stall. I had to go and do something I feared. It was necessary to the rest of my plan. I was overwhelmed by a sudden desire to be off sailing. Just lying on the beach would do, actually. . . .

Instead, I departed my quarters and made my way back downstairs, returning the way I had come. I headed west along the back corridor, listening for footsteps and voices, retreating once into a closet to let some nameless parties pass. Anything to avoid official notice for just a little longer. Finally, I turned left, walked a few paces and waited the better part of a minute before entering the major corridor, which led past the large marble dining hall. No one in sight. Good. I sprinted to the nearest entrance and peered within. Great. The place was not in use. It wasn't normally used every day, but I'd no way of knowing whether today was some state occasion—though this was not a normal dining hour either.

I entered and passed through. There is a dark, narrow corridor to its rear, with a guard normally posted somewhere near the passage's mouth or the door at its end. All members of the family have access there, though the guard would log our passage. His superior wouldn't have that information until the guard reported when he went off duty, though. By then it shouldn't matter to me.

Tod was short, stocky, bearded. When he saw me coming he presented arms with an ax that had been leaning against the wall moments before.

"At ease. Busy?" I asked.

"To tell the truth, no, sir."

"I'll be heading down. I hope there are some lanterns up here. I don't know that stairway as well as most."

"I checked a number inside when I came on duty, sir. I'll light you one."

Might as well save the energy that would have gone into the first spell, I decided. Every little bit helps. . . .

"Thanks."

He opened the door, hefted, successively, three lanterns which stood inside to the right, selected the second one. He took it back outside, where he lit it from the massive candle in its stand partway up the corridor.

"I'll be awhile," I said as I accepted it from him. "You'll probably be off duty before I'm finished."

"Very good sir. Watch your step."

"Believe me, I will."

The long spiraling stair turned round and round with very little visible in any direction but below, where a few chimneyed candles, sconced torches or hung lanterns flared along the central shaft, doing more for acrophobia than absolute blackness might, I suppose. There were just those little dots of light below me. I couldn't see the distant floor, or any walls. I kept one hand on the railing and held the lantern out in front with the other. Damp down here. Musty, too. Not to mention chilly.

Again, I tried counting the steps. As usual, I lost count somewhere along the way. Next time. . . .

My thoughts went back to that distant day when I had come this route believing I was headed for death. The fact that I hadn't died was small comfort now. It had still been an ordeal. And it was still possible that I could screw up on it this time and get fried or go up in a puff of smoke.

Around, around. Down, down. Night thoughts in the
middle of the afternoon....

On the other hand, I'd heard Flora say that it was easier
the second time around. She'd been talking about the Pattern moments before, and I hoped that's what she was re-
ferring to.

The Grand Pattern of Amber, Emblem of Order. Matching in power the Great Logrus of the Courts, Sign of
Chaos. The tensions between the two seem to generate
everything that matters. Get involved with either, lose control—and you're done for. Just my luck to be involved
with both. I've no one with whom to compare notes as to
whether this makes things rougher, though it massages my
ego to think that the mark of the one makes the other more
difficult ... and they do mark you, both of them. At some
level you are torn apart and reassembled along the lines of
vast cosmic principles when you undergo such an experience—which sounds noble, important, metaphysical, spir-
itual and lovely, but is mainly a pain in the ass. It is the
price we pay for certain powers, but there is no cosmic
principle requiring me to say I enjoy it.

Both the Pattern and the Logrus give to their initiates the
ability to traverse Shadow unassisted—Shadow being the
generic term for the possibly infinite collection of reality
variations we play about in. And they also give us other
abilities....

Around and down. I slowed. I was feeling slightly
dizzy, just like before. At least I wasn't planning on coming back this way....

When the bottom finally came into sight I speeded up
again. There was a bench, a table, a few racks and cases, a
light to show them all. Normally, there was a guard on duty
there, but I didn't see one. Could be off making rounds,
though. There were cells somewhere to the left in which
particularly unfortunate political prisoners might sometimes be found scrabbling about and going slowly out of
their minds. I didn't know whether there were any such
individuals doing time at the moment. I kind of hoped not.

My father had once been one, and from his description of the experience it did not sound like easy time to do.

I halted when I reached the floor and called out a couple of times. I got back a suitably eerie echo, but no answer.

I moved to the rack and took up a filled lantern with my other hand. An extra one might come in handy. It was possible I would lose my way. I headed to the right then. The tunnel I wanted lay in that direction. After a long while, I stopped and raised a light, as it almost seemed I had come too far. There was still no tunnel mouth in sight. I looked back. The guard post was still in sight. I continued on, searching my memories of that last time.

Finally, there was a shifting of sounds—abrupt echoes of my footfalls. It would seem I was nearing a wall, an obstacle. I raised a lantern again.

Yes. Pure darkness ahead. Gray stone about it. I went that way.

Dark. Far. There was a continuous shadow-show as my light slid over rocky irregularities, as its beams glanced off specks of brightness in the stone walls. Then there was a side passage to my left. I passed it and kept going. It seemed there should be another fairly soon. Yes. Two....

The third was farther along. Then there was a fourth. I wondered idly where they all led. No one had ever said anything about them to me. Maybe they didn't know either. Bizarre grottoes of indescribable beauty? Other worlds? Dead ends? Storerooms? One day, perhaps, when time and inclination came together....

Five....

And then another.

It was the seventh one I wanted. I halted when I came to it. It didn't go back all that far. I thought of the others who'd passed this way, and then I strode ahead, to the big, heavy, metal-bound door. There was a great key hanging from a steel hook that had been driven into the wall to my right. I took it down, unlocked the door and hung it back up again, knowing that the downstairs guard would check it and re-lock it at some point in his rounds; and I wondered—not for the first time—why it should be locked that way in the first place if the key was kept right there. It made it seem as if there were danger from something that might emerge from within. I had asked about that, but no one I'd questioned seemed to know. Tradition, I'd been told. Gérard and Flora had suggested, respectively, that I ask Random or Fiona. And *they* had both thought Benedict might know, but I'd never remembered to ask him.

I pushed hard and nothing happened. I put down the lanterns and tried again, harder. The door creaked and moved slowly inward. I recovered the lanterns and entered.

The door closed itself behind me, and Frakir—child of Chaos—pulsed wildly. I recalled my last visit and remembered why no one had brought an extra lantern upon that occasion: The bluish glow of the Pattern within the smooth, black floor lit the grotto well enough for one to see one's way about.

I lit the other lantern. I set the first one down at the near end of the Pattern and carried the other one with me about the periphery of the thing, setting it down at a point on its farther side. I did not care that the Pattern provided sufficient illumination to take care of the business at hand. I found the damned thing spooky, cold and downright intimidating. Having an extra natural light near at hand made me feel a lot better in its presence.

I studied that intricate mass of curved lines as I moved to the corner where they began. I had quieted Frakir but I had not entirely subdued my own apprehensions. If it were a response of the Logrus within me, I wondered whether my reaction to the Logrus itself would be worse were I to go back and essay it again, now that I bore the Pattern as well. Fruitless speculation....

I tried to relax. I breathed deeply. I shut my eyes for a moment. I bent my knees. I lowered my shoulders. No use waiting any longer....

I opened my eyes and set my foot upon the Pattern. Immediately, sparks rose about my foot. I took another step. More sparks. A tiny crackling noise. Another step. A bit of resistance as I moved again....

It all came back to me—everything I had felt the first

time through: the chill, the small shocks, the easy areas and the difficult ones. There was a map of the Pattern somewhere inside me, and it was almost as if I read from it as I moved along that first curve, resistance rising, sparks flying, my hair stirring, the crackling, a kind of vibration....

I reached the First Veil, and it was like walking in a wind tunnel. Every movement involved heavy effort. Resolve, though; that was all that it really took. If I just kept pushing I would advance, albeit slowly. The trick was not to stop. Starting again could be horrible, and in some places impossible. Steady pressure was all that was required just now. A few moments more and I would be through. The going would be easier. It was the Second Veil that was the real killer....

Turn, turn....

I was through. I knew the way would be easy now for a time. I began to stride with a bit of confidence. Perhaps Flora had been right. This part seemed a little less difficult than it had the first time. I negotiated a long curve, then a sharp switchback. The sparks reached up to my boottops now. My mind was flooded with April thirtieths, with family politics in the Courts, where people dueled and died as the succession to the succession to the succession wound and shifted its intricate way through blood rituals of status and elevation. No more. I was done with all that. Push it away. They might be a lot politer about it, but more blood was spilled there than in Amber, and for the damnedest small advantages over one's fellows....

I gritted my teeth. It was hard to keep my mind focused on the task at hand. Part of the effect, of course. I remembered that too, now. Another step.... Tingling sensations all the way up my legs.... The crackling sounds as loud as a storm to me.... One foot in front of the other.... Pick them up, put them down.... Hair standing on end now.... turn.... Push.... Bringing the Starburst in before an autumn squall, Luke running the sails, wind like the breath of dragons at our back.... Three more steps and resistance rises....

I am upon the Second Veil, and it is suddenly as if I am trying to push a car out of a muddy ditch.... All my strength goes forward, and the return of it is infinitesimal. I move with glacial slowness and the sparks are about my waist. I am blue flame....

My mind is abruptly stripped of distraction. Even Time goes away and leaves me alone. There is only this pastless, nameless thing I am become, striving with its entire being against the inertia of all its days—an equation so finely balanced that I should be frozen here in mid-stride forever, save that this cancellation of masses and forces leaves the will unimpaired, purifies it in a way, so that the process of progress seems to transcend the physical striving....

Another step, and another, and I am through, and ages older and moving again, and I know that I am going to make it despite the fact that I am approaching the Grand Curve, which is tough and tricky and long. Not at all like the Logrus. The power here is synthetic, not analytic....

The universe seemed to wheel about me. Each step here made me feel as if I were fading and coming back into focus, being broken down and reassembled, scattered and gathered, dying and reviving....

Outward. Onward. Three more curves then, followed by a straight line. I pushed ahead. Dizzy, nauseated. Soaking wet. End of the line. A series of arcs. Turn. Turn. Turn again....

I knew that I was coming up to the Final Veil when the sparks rose to become a cage of lightnings and my feet began to drag again. The stillness and the terrible pushing....

But this time I felt somehow fortified, and I drove onward knowing that I would win through....

I made it, shaking, and only a single short arc remained. Those final three steps may well be the worst, however. It is as if, having gotten to know you this well, the Pattern is reluctant to release you. I fought it here, my ankles sore as at any race's end. Two steps.... Three—

Off. Standing still. Panting and shuddering. Peace.

Gone the static. Gone the sparks. If that didn't wash off the blue stones' vibes I didn't know what would.

Now—well, in a minute—I could go anywhere. From this point, in this moment of empowerment, I could command the Pattern to transport me anywhere and I would be there delivered. Hardly a thing to waste to, say, save myself a walk up the spiral staircase and back to my rooms. No. I had other plans. In a minute. . . .

I adjusted my apparel, ran my hand through my hair, checked my weapons and my hidden Trump, waited for the pounding of my pulse to subside.

Luke had sustained his injuries in a battle at the Keep of the Four Worlds, fighting with his former friend and ally Dalt, the mercenary, son of the Desacratrix. Dalt meant little to me save as a possible obstacle, in that he now seemed in the employ of the keeper of the Keep. But even allowing for any time differential—which was probably not that great—I had seen him fairly soon following his fight with Luke. Which seemed to indicate that he was at the Keep when I had reached him via his Trump.

Okay.

I tried to recall it, my memory of the room where I had reached Dalt. It was pretty sketchy. What was the minimum amount of data the Pattern required in order to operate? I recalled the texture of the stone wall, the shape of the small window, a bit of worn tapestry upon the wall, strewn rushes on the floor; a low bench and a stool had come into view to his rear when Dalt had moved, a crack in the wall above them—and a bit of cobweb. . . .

I formed the image as sharply as I could. I willed myself there. I wanted to be in that place. . . .

And I was.

I turned around quickly, my hand on the hilt of my blade, but I was alone in the chamber. I saw a bed and an armoire, a small writing table, a storage chest, none of which had been in my line of sight during my brief view of the place. Daylight shone through the small window.

I crossed the room to its single door and stood there for a long while, listening. There was only silence on the other side. I opened it a crack—it swung to the left—and looked upon a long, empty hallway. I eased the door farther open. There was a stairway directly across from me, leading down. To my left was a blank wall. I stepped outside and closed the door. Go down or go right? There were several windows on both sides of the hallway. I moved to the nearest one, which was to my right, and looked out.

I saw that I was near to the lower corner of a rectangular courtyard, more buildings across the way and to my right and left, all of them connected at the corners save for an opening to the upper right which seemed as if it led to another courtyard where a very large structure rose beyond the buildings directly across from me. There were perhaps a dozen troops in the courtyard below, disposed near various entranceways, though not giving the appearance of being formally on guard—that is, they were engaged in cleaning and repairing their gear. Two of them were heavily bandaged. Still, most seemed in such a state that they could leap to service fairly quickly.

At the yard's far end was a strange bit of flotsam, looking like a large broken kite, which seemed somehow familiar. I decided to head along the hallway, which paralleled the courtyard, for it seemed that this would take me into those buildings along the farther edge of the perimeter and probably give me a view into the next yard.

I moved along the hallway, alert to any sounds of activity. There was nothing but silence as I advanced to the corner. I waited there for a long while, listening.

In that I heard nothing, I rounded the corner then, and froze. So did the man seated on the windowsill to the right. He wore a chain mail shirt, a leather cap, leather leggings and boots. There was a heavy blade at his side, but it was a dagger that he held in his hand, apparently giving himself a manicure. He looked as surprised as I felt when his head jerked in my direction.

"Who are you?" he asked.

His shoulders straightened and he lowered his hands as if to push himself from his perch and into a standing position.

Embarrassing to both of us. He seemed to be a guard. Whereas alertness or attempted stealth might have betrayed him to Frakir or myself, sloth had provided him with excellent concealment and me with a small dilemma. I was sure I couldn't bluff him, or trust to the result if I seemed to. I did not wish to attack him and create a lot of noise. This narrowed my choices. I could kill him quickly and silently with a neat little cardiac-arrest spell I had hanging in front of me. But I value life too highly to waste it when there is no need. So, as much as I hated to spend another spell that I carried this soon, I spoke the word that caused my hand to move reflexively through an accompanying gesture, and I had a glimpse of the Logrus as its force pulsed through me. The man closed his eyes and slumped back against the casement. I adjusted his position against slippage and left him snoring peacefully, the dagger still in his hand. Besides, I might have a greater need for the cardiac-arrest spell later.

The corridor entered some sort of gallery ahead, which seemed to bulge in both directions. In that I could not see what lay at either hand beyond a certain point, I knew that I would have to expend another spell sooner than I might wish. I spoke the word for my invisibility spell, and the world grew several shades darker. I had been hoping to get a little farther before I had to use it, since it was only good for about twenty minutes and I had no idea where my prize might lie. But I couldn't afford to take chances. I hurried along and passed into the gallery, which proved empty.

I learned a little more geography in that place, though. I had a view from there into the next courtyard, and it was gigantic. It contained the massive structure I had glimpsed from the other side. It was a huge, solidly built fortress; it appeared to have only one entrance, and that well guarded. From the opposite side of the gallery, I saw that there was also an outer courtyard, leading up to high, well-fortified walls.

I departed the gallery and sought a flight of stairs, almost certain that that hulking gray-stone structure was the place I should be searching. It had an aura of magic about it that I could feel down to my toes.

I jogged along the hallway, took a turn and saw a guard at the head of a stairway. If he felt anything of my passage it was only the breeze stirred by my cloak. I rushed down the stairs. There was an adit at its foot, leading to another corridor—a dark one—off to the left; and there was a heavy ironbound door directly before me, in the wall facing the inner courtyard.

I pushed the door open, passed through and stepped aside quickly, for a guard had turned, stared and was beginning to approach. I avoided him and moved toward the citadel. A focus of powers, Luke had said. Yes. I could feel this more strongly the closer I got to the place. I did not have time to try to figure out how to deal with them, to channel them. Anyway, I'd brought along my private stock.

When I neared the wall I cut to the left. A quick circuit was in order, for informational purposes. Partway around it, I saw that my guess that there was only one apparent entrance was correct. Also, there were no windows in its walls lower than about thirty feet. There was a high, spiked metal fence about the place, and a pit on the inside of the fence. The thing that most surprised me was not a feature of the structure, however. On its far side, near the wall, were two more of the large broken kites and three relatively intact ones. The matter of context no longer clouded my perception—not with the unbroken ones before me. They were hang gliders. I was eager to take a closer look at them, but time was running on my invisibility and I couldn't afford the detour. I hurried the rest of the way around and studied the gate.

The gate to the fence was closed and flanked by two guards. Several paces beyond it was a removable wooden bridge, reinforced with metal strapping, in place across the ditch. There were large eye bolts at its corners, and there was a winch built into the wall above the gate; the winch bore four chains terminating in hooks. I wondered how heavy the bridge was. The door to the citadel was recessed

about three feet into the stone wall, and it was high, wide
and plated, looking as if it could withstand a battering
ram's pounding for a good long while.

I approached the gate to the fence and studied it. No
lock on it—just a simple hand-operated latching mecha-
nism. I could open it, run through, dash across the span
and be at the big door before the guards had any idea as to
what might be going on. On the other hand, considering
the nature of the place, they might well have had some
instruction as to the possibility of an unnatural attack. If
so, it would not be necessary for them to see me if they
responded quickly and cornered me in the alcove. And I'd
a feeling the heavy door inside was not unlocked.

I mused for several moments, sorting through my spells.
I also checked again on the position of the six or eight
other people in the yard. None were too near, none moving
in this direction. . . .

I advanced upon the guards quietly and placed Frakir on
the shoulder of the man to my left with an order for a quick
choke. Three rapid steps to the right, then, and I struck the
other guard on the left side of his neck with the edge of my
hand. I caught him beneath the armpits, to prevent the rattling a fall would produce, and lowered him to his rump,
back against the fence, to the right of the gate. Behind me,
though, I heard the clatter of the other man's scabbard
against the fence as he slumped, clutching at his throat. I
hurried to him, guided him the rest of the way to the
ground and removed Frakir. A quick glance about showed
me that two other men across the courtyard were not looking in this direction. Damn.

I unlatched the gate, slipped within, closed it and
latched it behind me. I hurried across the bridge then and
looked back. The two men I had noticed were now headed
in this direction. Therefore, I was immediately presented
with another choice. I decided to see how arduous the more
strategically sound one might be.

Squatting, I caught hold of the nearest corner of the
bridge—to my right. The ditch it spanned seemed some-

thing like twelve feet in depth, and it was almost twice that in width.

I began straightening my legs. Damned heavy, but the thing creaked and my corner rose several inches. I held it there for a moment, got control of my breathing and tried again. More creaking and a few more inches. Again.... My hands hurt where the edges pressed into them. My arms felt as if they were being slowly wrenched from their sockets. As I straightened my legs and strained upward with even greater exertion, I wondered how many people fail in robust undertakings because of sudden lower back problems. I guess they're the ones you don't hear about. I could feel my heart pounding as if it filled my entire chest. My corner was now about a foot above the ground, but the edge to my left was still touching. I strained again, feeling the perspiration appear as if by magic across my brow and under my arms. Breathe.... Up!

It went to knee level, then above. The corner to my left was finally raised. I heard the voices of the two approaching men—loud, excited—they were hurrying now. I began edging to my left, dragging the whole structure with me. The corner directly across from me moved outward as I did so. Good. I kept moving. The corner to my left was now a couple of feet out over the chasm. I felt fiery pains all the way up my arms and into my shoulders and neck. Farther....

The men were at the gate now, but they paused to examine the fallen guards. Good, again. I still wasn't certain that the bridge might not catch and hold if I were to drop it. It had to slip into the chasm, or I was making myself a candidate for disk surgery for nothing. Left....

It began swaying in my grip, tipping to the right. I could tell that it was going to slip from my control in a few moments. Left again, left... almost.... The men had turned their attention from the fallen guards to the moving bridge now and were fumbling at the latch. Two more were rushing to join them from across the way, and I heard a series of shouts. Another step. The thing was really slipping now. I wasn't going to be able to hold it.... One more step....

Let go and get back!

My corner crashed against the edge of the chasm, but the wood splintered and the edge gave way and I kept retreating. The span flopped over as it fell, struck against the far side twice and hit the bottom with a terrific crash. My arms hung at my sides, useless for the moment.

I turned and headed for the doorway. My spell was still holding, so at least I was not a target for any hurled missiles from the other side of the moat.

When I got to the door it took all that I had of effort to raise my arms to the big ring on the right-hand side and catch hold of it. But nothing happened when I pulled. The thing was secured. I had expected that, though, and was prepared. I'd had to try first, however. I do not spend my spells lightly.

I spoke the words, three of them this time—less elegant because it was a sloppy spell, though it possessed immense force.

My entire body shook as the door exploded inward as if kicked by a giant wearing a steel-toed boot. I entered immediately and was immediately confused as my eyes adjusted to the dimness. I was in a two-story-high hall. Stairways rose to the right and the left ahead of me, curving inward toward a railed landing, the terminus of a second-floor hallway. There was another hallway below it, directly across from me. Two stairways also headed downward, to the rear of the those which ascended. Decisions, decisions....

In the center of the room was a black stone fountain, spraying flames—not water—into the air; the fire descended into the font's basin, where it swirled and danced. The flames were red and orange in the air, white and yellow below, rippling. A feeling of power filled the chamber. Anyone who could control the forces loose in this place would be a formidable opponent indeed. With luck, I might not have to discover how formidable.

I almost wasted a special attack when I became aware of

the two figures in the corner, off to my right. But they hadn't stirred at all. They were unnaturally still. Statues, of course. . . .

I was trying to decide whether to go up, go down or move straight ahead, and I'd just about decided to descend, on the theory that there is some sort of instinct to imprison enemies in dank, below-ground quarters, when something about the two statues drew my attention again. My vision having adjusted somewhat, I could now make out that one was a white-haired man, the other a dark-haired woman. I rubbed my eyes, not realizing for several seconds that I had seen the outline of my hand. My invisibility spell was dissipating. . . .

I moved toward the figures. The fact that the old man was holding a couple of cloaks and hats should have been the tipoff. But I raised the skirt of his dark blue robe anyway. In the suddenly brighter light from the fountain I saw where the name RINALDO had been carved into his right leg. Nasty little kid, that.

The woman at his side was Jasra, saving me the problem of seeking her amid rodents below. Her arms were also outstretched, as in a warding gesture, and someone had hung a pale blue umbrella upon the left and a light gray London Fog raincoat upon the right; the matching rain hat was on her head, at a lopsided angle. Her face had been painted like a clown's and someone had pinned a pair of yellow tassels to the front of her green blouse.

The light behind me flared even more brightly, and I turned to see what was going on. The fountain, it turned out, was now spewing its liquid-like fires a full twenty feet into the air. They descended to overflow the basin and spread outward across the flagged floor. A major rivulet was headed in my direction. At that point, a soft chuckle caused me to look upward.

Wearing a dark robe, cowl and gauntlets, the wizard of the cobalt mask stood on the landing above me, one hand on the railing, the other pointed toward the fountain. In that I had anticipated our meeting on this expedition, I was not unprepared for the encounter. As the flames leaped even higher, forming a great bright tower that almost immediately began to bend and then topple toward me, I raised my arms in a wide gesture and spoke the word for the most appropriate of the three defensive spells I had hung earlier.

Air currents began to stir, powered by the Logrus, almost immediately achieving gale force and sending the flames back away from me. I adjusted my position then so that they were blown toward the wizard upstairs. Instantly, he gestured, and the flames fell back within the fountain, subsiding to the barest glowing trickle.

Okay. A draw. I had not come here to have it out with this guy. I had come to finesse Luke by rescuing Jasra on my own. Once she was my prisoner, Amber would sure as hell be safe from anything Luke had in mind. I found myself wondering, though, about this wizard, as my winds died down and the chuckle came again: Was he using spells, as I was? Or, living in the midst of a power source such as this, was he able to control the forces directly and shape them as he chose? If it were the latter, which I suspected, then he had a virtually inexhaustible source of tricks up his sleeve, so that in any full-scale competition on his turf I would eventually be reduced to flight or to calling in the nukes—that is, summoning Chaos itself to utterly reduce everything in the area—and this was a thing I was not about to do, destroying all the mysteries, including that of the wizard's identity, rather than solving them for answers that might be essential to Amber's well-being.

A shining metallic spear materialized in midair before the wizard, hung a moment, then flashed toward me. I used my second defensive spell, summoning a shield that turned it aside.

The only alternative I could see to my dueling with spells or blasting the place with Chaos would be for me to learn to control the forces here myself and try beating this guy at his own game. No time for practice now, though; I'd a job to do as soon as I could buy a few moments in which to get it done. Sooner or later, however, it seemed that we would have to have a full confrontation—since he seemed to have it in for me, and may well even have been the motive force behind the attack by the clumsy werewolf in the woods.

And I was not hot on taking chances to explore the power here further at this point—not if Jasra had been good enough to beat the original master of this place, Sharu Garrul, and then this guy had been good enough to beat Jasra. I'd give a lot, though, to know why he had it in for me. . . .

So, "What do you want, anyway?" I called out.

Immediately, that metallic voice replied, "Your blood, your soul, your mind and your body."

"What about my stamp collection?" I hollered back. "Do I get to keep the First Day Covers?"

I moved over beside Jasra and threw my right arm about her shoulders.

"What do you want with that one, funny man?" the wizard asked. "She is the most worthless property in this place."

"Then why should you object to my taking her off your hands?"

"You collect stamps. I collect presumptuous sorcerers. She's mine, and you're next."

I felt the power rising against me again even as I shouted, "What have you got against your brothers and sisters in the Art?"

There was no reply, but the air about me was suddenly filled with sharp, spinning shapes—knives, ax blades, throwing stars, broken bottles. I spoke the word for my final defense, the Curtain of Chaos, raising a chittering, smoky screen about us. The sharp items hurtling in our direction were instantly reduced to cosmic dust on coming into contact with it.

Above the din of this engagement I cried out, "By what name shall I call you?"

"Mask!" was the wizard's immediate reply—not very original, I thought. I'd half expected a John D. MacDonald appellation—Nightmare Mauve or Cobalt Casque, perhaps. Oh, well.

I had just used my last defensive spell. I had also just raised my left arm so that that portion of my sleeve bearing the Amber Trump now hung within my field of vision. I had cut things a bit fine, but I had not yet played my full hand. So far, I had run a completely defensive show, and I was rather proud of the spell I had kept in reserve.

"She'll do you no good, that one," Mask said, as both our spells subsided and he prepared to strike again.

"Have a nice day, anyway," I said, and I rotated my wrists, pointed my fingers to direct the flow and spoke the word that beat him to the punch.

"An eye for an eye!" I called out, as the contents of an entire florist shop fell upon Mask, completely burying him in the biggest damned bouquet I'd ever seen. Smelled nice, too.

There was silence and a subsidence of forces as I regarded the Trump, reached through it. Just as the contact was achieved there was a disturbance in the floral display and Mask rose through it, like the Allegory of Spring.

I was probably already fading from his view as he said, "I'll have you yet."

"And sweets to the sweet," I replied, then spoke the word that completed the spell, dropping a load of manure upon him.

I stepped through into the main hall of Amber, bearing Jasra with me. Martin stood near a sideboard, a glass of wine in his hand, talking with Bors, the falconer. He grew silent at Bors's wide-eyed stare in my direction, then turned and stared himself.

I set Jasra on her feet beside the doorway. I was not about to screw around with the spell on her right now— and I was not at all sure what I'd do with her if I released her from it. So I hung my cloak on her, went over to the sideboard and poured myself a glass of wine, nodding to Bors and Martin as I passed.

I drained the glass, put it down, then said to them,

"Whatever you do, don't carve your initials on her." Then I went and found a sofa in a room to the east, stretched out on it and closed my eyes. Like a bridge over troubled waters. Some days are diamonds. Where have all the flowers gone?

Something like that.

CHAPTER 12

There was a lot of smoke, a giant worm and many flashes of colored light. Every sound was born into form, blazed to its peak, faded as it waned. Lightninglike stabs of existence, these—called from, returning to, Shadow. The worm went on forever. The dog-headed flowers snapped at me but later wagged their leaves. The flowing smoke halted before a skyhooked traffic light. The worm—no, caterpillar—smiled. A slow, blinding rain began, and all the drifting drops were faceted. . . .

What is wrong with this picture? something within me asked.

I gave up, because I couldn't be sure. Though I'd a vague feeling the occasional landscape shouldn't be flowing the way that it did. . . .

"Oh, man! Merle. . . ."

What did Luke want now? Why wouldn't he get off my case? Always a new problem.

"Look at that, will you?"

I watched where a series of bright bounding balls—or maybe they were comets—wove a tapestry of light. It fell upon the forest of umbrellas.

"Luke—" I began, but one of the dog-headed flowers bit a hand I'd forgotten about, and everything nearby cracked as if it were painted on glass through which a shot had just passed. There was a rainbow beyond—

"Merle! Merle!"

It was Droppa shaking my shoulder, my suddenly opened eyes showed me. And there was a damp place on the sofa where my head was resting.

I propped myself on an elbow. I rubbed my eyes.

"Droppa. . . . What—?"

"I don't know," he told me.

"What don't you know? I mean. . . . Hell! What happened?"

"I was sitting in that chair," he said, with a gesture, "waiting for you to wake up. Martin had told me you were here. I was just going to tell you that Random wanted to see you when you got back."

I nodded, then noticed that my hand was oozing blood —from the place where the flower had bitten me.

"How long was I out?"

"Twenty minutes, maybe."

I swung my feet to the floor, sat up. "So why'd you decide to wake me?"

"You were trumping out," he said.

"Trumping out? While I was asleep? It doesn't work that way. Are you sure—"

"I am, unfortunately, sober at the moment," he said. "You got that rainbow glow and you started to soften around the edges and fade. Thought I'd better wake you then and ask if that's what you really had in mind. What've you been drinking, spot remover?"

"No," I said.

"I tried it on my dog once. . . ."

"Dreams," I said, massaging my temples, which had begun throbbing. "That's all. Dreams."

"The kind other people can see, too? Like DTs *à deux?*"

"That's not what I meant."

"We'd better go see Random." He started to turn toward the doorway.

I shook my head. "Not yet. I'm just going to sit here and collect myself. Something's wrong."

When I glanced at him I saw that his eyes were wide, and he was staring past me. I turned.

The wall at my back seemed to be melting, as if it were cast of wax and had been set too near a fire.

"It appears to be alarums and excursions time," Droppa remarked. "Help!"

And he was across the room and out of the door, screaming.

Three eyeblinks later the wall was normal again in every way, but I was trembling. What the hell was going on? Had Mask managed to lay a spell on me before I'd cut out? If so, where was it headed?

I rose to my feet and turned in a slow circle. Everything seemed to be in place now. I knew that it could not have been anything as simple as hallucination born of all my recent stresses, since Droppa had seen it too. So I was not cracking up. This was something else—and whatever it was, I felt that it was still lurking nearby. There was a certain unnatural clarity to the air now, and every object seemed unusually vivid within it.

I made a quick circuit of the room, not knowing what I was really seeking. Not surprisingly, therefore, I did not find it. I stepped outside then. Whatever the problem, could it spring from something I had brought back with me? Might Jasra, stiff and gaudy, have been a Trojan horse?

I headed for the main hall. A dozen steps along the way, a lopsided gridwork of light appeared before me. I forced myself to continue, and it receded as I advanced, changing shape as it did so.

"Merle, come on!" Luke's voice, Luke himself nowhere in sight.

"Where?" I called out, not slowing.

No answer, but the gridwork split down the middle and its two halves swung away from me like a pair of shutters. They opened onto a near-blinding light; within it, I thought I glimpsed a rabbit. Then, abruptly, the vision was gone, and the only thing that saved me from believing everything was normal again was several seconds' worth of Luke's sourceless laughter.

I ran. Was it really Luke who was the enemy, as I had been warned repeatedly? Had I somehow been manipulated through everything which had happened recently, solely for the purpose of freeing his mother from the Keep of the Four Worlds? And now that she was safe had he the temerity to invade Amber herself and summon me to a sorcerous duel the terms of which I did not even understand?

No, I could not believe it. I was certain he did not possess that sort of power. But even if he did, he wouldn't dare try it—not with Jasra my hostage.

As I rushed along I heard him again—from everywhere, from nowhere. This time he was singing. He had a powerful baritone voice, and the song was "Auld Lang Syne." What sort of irony did this represent?

I burst into the main hall. Martin and Bors had departed. I saw their empty glasses on the sideboard near which they had been standing. And near the other door—? Yes, near the other door Jasra remained, erect, unchanged, still holding my cloak.

"Okay, Luke! Let's have it out!" I cried. "Cut the crap and let's settle this business!"

"Huh?"

The singing stopped abruptly.

I crossed slowly to Jasra, studying her as I went. Completely unchanged, save for a hat someone had added to her other hand. From somewhere else in the palace, I heard a shout. Maybe it was Droppa still alaruming.

"Luke, wherever you are," I said, "if you can hear me, if you can see me, take a good look and listen: I've got her here. See? Whatever you're planning, bear that in mind."

The room rippled violently, as if I were standing in the midst of an unframed painting someone had just decided to give a shake, to crinkle and then draw taut.

"Well?"

Nothing.

Then, a chuckle.

"My mother the hat rack. . . . Well, well. Hey, thanks, buddy. Good show. Couldn't reach you earlier. Didn't know you'd gone in. They slaughtered us. Took some mercs in on hang gliders, rode the thermals. They were ready, though. Took us out. Don't remember exactly then. . . . Hurts!"

"You okay?"

There came something like a sob, just as Random and Droppa entered the hall, the lank form of Benedict silent as death at their back.

"Merle!" Random called to me. "What's going on?"

I shook my head. "Don't know," I said.

"Sure, I'll buy you a drink," Luke's voice came very faintly.

A fiery blizzard swept through the center of the hall. It lasted only a moment, and then a large rectangle appeared in its place.

"You're the sorcerer," Random said. "Do something!"

"I don't know what the hell it is," I replied. "I've never seen anything like it. It's like magic gone wild."

An outline began to appear within the rectangle, human. Its form settled and took on features, garments. . . . It was a Trump—a giant Trump—hanging in the middle of the air, solidifying. It was—

Me. I regarded my own features and they looked back at me. I noted that I was smiling.

"C'mon, Merle. Join the party," I heard Luke say, and the Trump began to rotate slowly upon its vertical axis.

Sounds, as of glass bells, filled the hall.

The huge card turned until I viewed it edge-on, a black slash. Then the dark line widened with a ripple, like parting curtains, and I saw colored patches of intense light sliding beyond it. I also saw the caterpillar, puffing on a hookah, and fat umbrellas and a bright, shiny rail—

A hand emerged from the slit. "Right this way."

I heard a sharp intake of breath from Random.

Benedict's blade was suddenly pointed at the tableau. But Random laid his hand on his shoulder and said, "No."

There was a strange, disconnected sort of music hanging in the air now; it seemed somehow appropriate.

"C'mon, Merle."

"You coming or going?" I asked.

"Both."

"You made me a promise, Luke: a piece of information for your mother's rescue," I said. "Well, I've got her here. What's the secret?"

"Something vital to your well-being?" he asked slowly.

"Vital to the safety of Amber is what you'd said."

"Oh, *that* secret."

"I'd be glad to have the other one too."

"Sorry. One secret is all I'm selling. Which will it be?"

"The safety of Amber," I answered.

"Dalt," he replied.

"What of him?"

"Deela the Desacratrix was his mother—"

"I already know that."

"—and she'd been Oberon's prisoner nine months before he was born. He raped her. That's why Dalt's got it in for you guys."

"Bullshit!" I said.

"That's what I told him when I'd heard the story one time too many. I dared him to walk the Pattern in the sky then."

"And?"

"He did."

"Oh."

"I just learned that story recently," Random said, "from an emissary I'd sent to Kashfa. I didn't know about his taking the Pattern, though."

"If you knew, I still owe you," Luke said slowly, almost distractedly. "Okay, here's more: Dalt visited me on the shadow Earth after that. He's the one who raided my warehouse, stole a stock of weapons and special ammo. Burnt the place after that to cover the theft. I found witnesses, though. He'll be along—any time. Who knows when?"

"Another relative coming to visit," Random said. "Why couldn't I have been an only child?"

"Make what you will of it," Luke added. "We're square now. Give me a hand!"

"You coming through?"

He laughed, and the whole hall seemed to lurch. The opening in the air hung before me and the hand clasped my own. Something felt very wrong.

I tried to draw him to me, but felt myself drawn toward him instead. There was a mad power I could not fight, and the universe seemed to twist as it took hold of me. Constellations parted before me and I saw the bright railing again. Luke's booted foot rested upon it.

From some distant point to the rear I heard Random shouting, "B-twelve! B-twelve! And out!"

. . . And then I couldn't recall what the problem had been. It seemed a wonderful place. Silly of me to have mistaken the mushrooms for umbrellas, though. . . .

I put my own foot up on the rail as the Hatter poured me a drink and topped off Luke's. Luke gestured to his left and the March Hare got a refill too. Humpty was fine, balanced there near the end of things. Tweedledum, Tweedledee, the Dodo and the Frog Footman kept the music moving. And the Caterpillar just kept puffing away.

Luke clapped me on the shoulder, and there was something I wanted to remember but it kept slipping out of sight.

"I'm okay now," Luke said. "Everything's okay."

"No, there's something. . . . I can't recall. . . ."

He raised his tankard, clanked it against my own. "Enjoy!" he said. "Life is a cabaret, old chum!"

The cat on the stool beside me just kept grinning.